NIKKI GEMMELL

Lovesong

PICADOR

First published 2001 by Picador

This edition published 2001 by Picador
an imprint of Macmillan Publishers Ltd
25 Eccleston Place, London SW1W 9NF
Oxford and Basingstoke
Associated companies throughout the world

www.macmillan.com

ISBN 0 330 37292 0

Typeset by Intype London Ltd
Printed and bound in Great Britain by
Mackays of Chatham plc, Chatham, Kent

The excerpt from 'Suburban Song' on p. 222 is from
Elizabeth Riddell's Selected Poems (ETT Imprint, Sydney 1992).

For Andrew

And in the world's sea do not, like cork, sleep
Upon the water's face; nor in the deep
Sink like a lead without a line; but as
Fishes glide, leaving no print where they pass,
Nor making sound, so closely thy course go,
Let men dispute whether thou breathe or no.

JOHN DONNE

– 1 –

A Lifetime Ago

I don't remember much about the day that my world was stolen from me. It was cold, yes that, so cold that a boulder behind the house was cracked clean down the centre. But not much else. Some things we choose to forget, others are taken for us. It was a lifetime ago and I was another person then; I had a different name and I lived under a different sky.

Laying him on a rug by the fire.

Covering him with a crochet blanket that doesn't quite reach to his toes and the nag of that still and of the pillow stained sullen with age. My skittery breath: what to do, what to do next, as I work my fingers together and worry each knuckle like a rosary bead. His hair curling in slick commas at his forehead and smoothing and smoothing it back and the greedy fire and the clock chiming its hours and the clustering dark.

And then, and then, unpeeling the blanket like a wedding veil from a trousseaued dress. His left fist is clenched as if he's grasping a secret, his right arm is kinked over his head and the curve of his upper arm is as bare and as beautiful as a Sahara dune and the skin is as smooth as the lies and love is there like breath.

What to do, what to do next, the panic is hardening now.

And I'm leaning down to him and floating my lips over his body, as lonely as a speculator with a metal detector on a winter beach and his eyes are flickering to mine and my fingers are scuttling to his and I'm gathering him in the wet cave of my mouth.

I

His left fist clenched, as if he's clasping a secret.

There are nail marks in my palm even now, three months on from that night, there are ragged moons unscuffed by time's fret. And my fingernails by habit curl into those marks, they try to worry them off.

But now it can be told. About what I did, and where I'm from. Your father wanted that.

You see I was once snugged up tight within a God-fearing community in a land where the light roared and the sea hurt. But here I am now, out from under the thumb of Him and in a land where the sky's so low it almost brushes the rooftops. Here I am with you, my little tummy-tucked astronaut, and with all these whisperings back in that community that I've killed a six foot two man. *Me.* Ridiculous, baroque, I know, but things aren't always as they seem and this is the truth of it. So I'm pounding this keyboard like I've got boxing gloves on, dragging out the truth from its stubborn little lair, hauling it kicking and screaming into the light. I'm tired of it now and I want it gone, for my sake, and his, and yours.

Collector. Of my food, my air, my story. I can feel your greed as you brew in your vat.

It's not looking good, I know: Girl from Fundamentalist Religious Community Comes to Blighty, Kills a Man. Cloistered-Lillie-Catch-A-Man-And-Make-It-All-Atrocious. God, the Red Tops would have a field day but I'm not going to give them that. And to make matters worse there are some people from home who stamped me with an evilness almost from day one and when they got wind of this latest instalment they had it all worked out. For you see I did something once when I was very young, in that land of shouting blue, and nothing would surprise them now. But there are no regrets for what I did then roped the lives of your father and myself. Life, you just have to go out and get it, he said that to me once. Everyone creates God for themselves, he said that to me once. And so I did.

And here I am. Stealing solitude from my days and nights, grabbing furtive lunchbreaks and the stretched hours of the early morning when the rest of the world is smugly asleep, shedding the story, shedding the weight. It's been like the smudge of a giant's thumb on my chest for too long and it'll take until you're born to have it wiped. Well, that's the plan. And always with me as I work are the crescent stares on my palm, the moons that tap-dance my fingers over this splitting, crashing laptop. I have writing and I have you, it's all I've got left. But it's enough.

My name in the community-time, in the sun-smeared place, was Lillie. Imagine that, such an old-fashioned, Depression-era, meek scrap of a name, from day one meant to pale me.

And there that Lillie is, on a heat-thumped Christmas morning, just six, swift days from turning twenty-one. There are several photographs, they're all ship-sinking tilted and blurred for they were taken by a child and no permission had been asked. She's dressed unobtrusively, of course. There's an ominous quiet to the white, high-buttoned cotton frock that has something of a mother's will about it.

The word for the day was *grace*. I collected words once, they were dated into an exercise book that became over the years all fragile and thin from use. The book's here now, it's come in from the freezer in the laundry that's the mad museum cabinet of my youth. The pages are brittle with cold, they softly plume steam from the house's heat and the loosening handwriting marks the haul into adulthood, the coming confidence, and then on the back cover, cramming a corner, are all the velvety words that I never spoke of to anyone, let alone understood – words like *catamite* and *sapphic* and *quim* – and I'm blushing even now at my intrusion and closing the book and tombing it back. God, never free of it.

*

That Lillie lived in a place where the land came up through the people's feet, they could feel it sing. A place where people were afraid of the grass because of bush fires and snakes, where they always looked ahead of their step. Hey, don't worry, she's striding through benign grasses now, with her face to new skies.

But there she is on a hymn-walloped Christmas morning long, long ago. She's on the rim of womanhood and thinking of that lovely, still *grace* and how it's never been used in connection with herself. She's smiling, soaring, for she's making her annual appearance in the local House of God, a white-painted, wooden building that aspires to nothing holier than simplicity. The severe lines of its interior are redeemed by a pale, lemony light and how she loved that light once, her yearly dose.

The place where I am from is called Sunshine, don't laugh, it was named carelessly by impatient explorers who didn't linger long enough to be dazzled by the fractiousness of its mountain clouds. When I left, the community had shrunk to just three thousand souls. The Shiners, as they were known, had come en masse from a wilfully unproductive island long ago, an island abandoned to keening winds and pushy ponies and feral cows. There are photos from the Leaving Time with men long bearded and women smile-scrubbed and all staring into the camera as if awaiting execution. Their new island was founded on the top of a mountain and stranded sometimes in a sea of cloud and at others rubbed raw by the sun and the old people brought with them this nuggety fist of an accent, all vowels and song, that outsiders found difficult to decipher. I can't quite do it now, it's gone, it's been too long.

The Shiners claimed a tract of sheep-farming country where desiccated trees screeched across fields like a battalion of ghostly windmills and the grass was bleached pale by the summer heat. But they held on for this, after all, was their chosen place. A land singed by the sky and with no will to show off its beauty and yet, crikey Moses, it sings through my blood still and won't let me go, even as I sit at this desk on the other side of the world. That light is in my bones: the way it's tinged an apocalyptic yellow, pre-storm,

4

or is bullet-hard with heat or sullen with rain, the way it drops from the clouds in great shafts at sunset like tent ropes from God.

Don't dream of this place, don't ever attempt to track it down, promise me that – I fear for what you might find. The unwitting outsider who stumbled upon us was often at first open-mouthed, for it seemed that we were perched on the very roof of the world. But outsiders were rare, and those that found us usually gathered within a two-minute drive down the main street that a shrill climate and one haggard access road had stilled us. There was to the mean-windowed houses an odd quiet, a stranger-distrust, for our settlement had helmeted itself over the generations, had become sour and defensive with its God. If day trippers dared to stop at the public houses then the Shiners, en masse, would rise up and walk out. Go away, was the silent shout, leave us in peace, we don't want your shrill TV or your panic or your fret. They shunned social fragmentation and difference and change and into such a community a little blonde bawl of a girl was one day born, to outsiders within the flock.

Your name is Disturbance, my father giggled at the time, blowing a raspberry on my tummy to shut me up.

And so here I am now, anchorless. My passport is now my adopted land's for there are too many secrets, too many whispers in the old place and it's time to move on. I have a new voice, new vowels and a new name. It's for the best that the stained days are wiped, it's taken me such a long time to see that.

A light-drenched church, a plain wooden chair, stern backed, with an unyielding rush-mat seat. Almost twenty-one. Wedged between the rigid shoulder of my mother, Rebecca, and the firm lock of Tiriel, my father, and reading the nervousness of Tiriel's hand on my own; the sweat sheafing his fingers and the flea-leap of a pulse I can't bear to touch. Reading Rebecca's tension in her first, voiceless amen and the correcting tripping too quick and too loud but as the service falls into its drone the brace of flesh softens, forgets. Seized. Hmm mm. A knee's tucked under a chin and a foot squirms

5

off a sandal and rests on the opposite knee and the other shoe is dropped with a clap-clatter to the floor and Rebecca snaps a turn but nothing's said and there's a too-loud *look* from a stick of freckle-crammed child and then the rash of their curiosity is out, the eyes are all at me like an accident in a Sunday-suburban street.

Tiriel's body is crotchety with tension and he excuses himself too loudly for the toilet, he apologizes stumbly over knees and then he's gone and I stretch back and languish my arms behind my neck and the movement's unruffled, wrong, thick with sex. I can smell the eyes and I close my own and bask in it – I don't belong in this place.

Suddenly I'm not standing when I should be and not caring. My mother's resolute: eyes ahead, spine stout, not willing to give them the gift of a scene. Yet there I am tipping back on the seat and almost falling, tipping back with one finger anchored and steadying on the rim of the empty seat next to me and the other arm extended as if I'm blind, I'm poised and holding the glide of the moment and cruising serenely in it and smiling at the soaring and then the front legs of the chair are crashing to the floor and there's a smart slap of sound.

The visiting reverend, a pinched young man called Brother Paina, stops mid-sentence and glides on, unseeing, for he knows nothing of me or why I'm the object of the congregation's eye-greed. He's been called in at the last minute to replace our pro-claimer, Brother Sleet, whose mother has pneumonia and who's haranguing her son's guilt and time. The hunger of the children is the most honest, it's all open stares and the audacity of cameras and a whispery-chattery hum and there's the smell of their excitement, a fevered, clammy scent, I close my eyes and I have it with me again.

Red is your colour, your father said to me once, after reading a myth about the ruby. He'd found it in an age-spotted, never-borrowed book on Hindu legend from our local library. He told me that when the ruby was submerged in water it would cause it to boil because legend had it that something inextinguishable was

6

trapped within its depths, and I'd slugged my tongue into his ear and flourished a flicked lighter under his nose.

But there I am, on the cusp of twenty-one, dressed in a puff-sleeved frock with sandals rigorously flat, dressed unobtrusively as perhaps all true rebels are and dreaming of a rescuer-man and knowing, with certainty, that he'll never come from this flinty place; I'd never want him to, ugh, not that. Outside is a vibrant clamour of cicadas, their intensity mocks the uncertain waver of the hymn that's been created for a different country and accent and organ and God. And the eyes are all at me, there's greed in the neck stretches and tongue tips.

For the past eight years a similar, farcical scene's been enacted, for throughout my teenage years and into adulthood I've been dressed unobtrusively each cicada-shrill Christmas and the people of Sunshine have bashed me with curiosity because it's the only day of the year I'm allowed beyond my parents' farm. But this year is different, as I glide on my chair and smartly slap it to the ground, for I'm gently taunting each Shiner with the delicious unpredictability of my future: in six days I'll be free, and gone.

During Brother Paina's second reading I'm turning and facing the congregation and settling my glasses and netting every eye. The tension's held and cracked with a dazzle of a smile and there's not a single one back. You see, there was the confidence then of someone who knew exactly who she was and was comfortable with it and the Shiners were needled by that, it got right under their skin, for ours was a community where every inhabitant was taught that goodness was rewarded not only in heaven but within, and that a serenity and a shine would come from that. Me, of all people, daring such a mock: I could see it in the thinness of their mouths. For I was known as a broken one back then, a lost soul among them, and God forbid that there should be any gloating.

As Brother Paina broke his bread the flicker of his eyes tried to pinpoint the stir in his flock. One camera clicked and another, the young children were emboldened, a little girl popped up and there

7

was the cough of the Brother's miff, his city-smooth face was livid in the heat, his fine, blond hair barely visible through his skin's perplexed red. The girl snapped again and passed the camera along her fidgety family line and her older brother rolled over the film with a grate of his thumb and winked his thanks and I didn't catch the bowed smile but my mother did and wanted it wiped, for there was something adult in it that she didn't like.

Four photos, four different angles. I have them with me now, they were acquired from a Shiner who got away but I scarcely see them any more for the images are bunkered into my memory. The shots are slightly crooked and the faces are cropped or too close: remember, a child's wobbly attempts. The first is a back view, there's the wilful hair cut shaggy-blunt and then she's caught turning, and full on.

I barely recognize her now, except for the eyes, the yellow, the arrest of that. The colour ringing the pupils is a light honey colour – I'm sure you'll have that, God, I hope, such a shout – and it's contained by a thin rim of darkness. But the face is mostly gone, and glancing up now at the reflection from the night window I know that with sunglasses not one Shiner would recognize it. Long ago it was a face that seemed incapable of cruelty, wide-open and vulnerable with curiosity and not quite of this world, like someone mentally disturbed, but for those open enough to see it there was a dynamism in it, a lovely, ludic child-joy. It was absolutely unknowing, absolutely innocent. In one photo there's a wide clash of a smile that looks as if it could light up New York and in another a sadness, a pensiveness, that looks as if it could never be scrubbed out.

And there's the left ear, stark in the frontal shot and I flinch even now at the sight of it, the protruding little shell I used to hate so much, that one day began it all.

Hitchcock said that blondes always make the best victims for they're like the virgin snow that can't hide the bloody footprints and I think of that with those photos before me like knuckly bones on the centre spine of the window. But I showed those Shiners, I showed them all, and the face all vulnerable with curiosity became barely recognizable over time, a knowing closed it up like a door slamming shut on the light and a good thing that was, I think, for it was a face that was once ill-equipped for the world.

Brother Paina's quiet, university-clipped voice seeped through the sun-balmed room and I alone was leaning forward, chin-cupped, absorbing the mellow thrum that was starkly non-Shiner for I rarely got the chance to hear new voices in the flesh and I stored them away as if I was stocking a larder for some future occasion when I'd step into the world and decide who I was. My fingers raked the hair from my face and the Brother's eyes flitted over the pews and caught the attention and flickered warmth, for he didn't know it had been a year since the girl with the spill of gold hair had been seen or of the rumours that she'd turned in the head, didn't know of the jumpiness in the community – particularly among its young womenfolk – about the release date so swiftly upon us all.

You see, that tight, little phalanx of arse-rodded community elders was beginning to stew with the panic of their indecision, for none of them knew quite what to do next with the prisoner they'd created eight years earlier when they'd taken the law, spectacularly, into their own hands. Each year more and more families had cancelled their Christmases on the coast to album something of the buzz about me before it was too late and I was gone and this year, my last, the church was packed. And I was fluttering my hands with glee at all of this, I was blowing my joy through soft finger wings at my mouth.

So there that Lillie is, on the cusp of an unimaginable womanhood, at a time when several of the faces of the girls she'd once attended school with were settling into a premature, middle-aged sourness with their eyebrows pruned and hair brittled with perms and one or two already, defiantly, ball-bellied.

To some of the community's young, particularly the boys, she'd been for many years a strange kind of siren locked away from them all, all crease and colour in a starched world. It was a mix of untouchability and courage and stupidity and innocence, an innocence to be conquered or rescued, whatever foxed its way through to her first. She was the mild-named girl obsessed by heat and light. Oh yes, red was her colour; the colour of magic, of love and sacrifice and spontaneity and sun. And yet to many of the town's elders she was nothing but a long thin streak of trouble who at the age of thirteen had committed the community's most evil crime. But few were clear on the details, for the facts were all grubbied by fury and incomprehension and time.

It, too, was on a night so cold it almost cleaved stone, but it was at the end of the night when the day was leaking into the dark. The chill of that winter felt as if it had nestled into my bones like mould and that morning I was glad, so glad, to have the cold lit.

I'm thirteen years old, I'm drawn into the lovely warmth, drawn into the light.

Knuckles of heat are pummelling my face and my voice is sapped into a rasp by the bulldozer fury of the flames and I'm staring, wondrous, on the edge of it, at the loops of heat like soft velvet billowing and the chandeliers of sparks and the greedy fire fingers snatching at the air and the curling ash moths floating their glow into the black and I'm laughing and clapping my hands until my legs are invaded by scratchy hot and I'm stepping back, and back.

One classroom is gone and then another and there goes the verandah and the roof is sucked down with an enormous whoosh and I'm glancing at my bare shins, they're covered in flecks and streaks of ash and I'm smearing the creamy softness across my legs and my hands and smiling so tight.

Other kids in pyjamas begin congregating, piper-drawn in the bed-hauled dark and scattering ahead of grim, dressing-gowned parents and whooping at the gulping bonfire that lights all the world. Tiriel and Rebecca aren't there yet, they're late as usual and I desperately want them to see this, the carnival atmosphere at that start of it and their daughter thick among it, belonging at last. Five fifty-two a.m. flashes the oblong on my *Star Wars* watch and I'm looking across to the far hills and imagining the view from afar: a pimple of a glow on the mountain's dark expanse, a ruby on a black-skinned breast. I'm creeping forward again, daring myself with how close I can get, closer, closer, and no one's pulling me back.

The smiles spread on the tight-hot young faces as the implications of the blaze sink in and parents shout for calm and for water and for everyone to stay back, for someone to call Emergency, for blankets, a bucket line. This is a community, you see, too small for a government-funded fire-fighting service, proudly self-sufficient and preferring its own way. And there my parents are, they've arrived, finally, with their frowns. Someone hurls a rock into the great mess of flame and it hits a beam and there's a crack and a splintering and the crowd steps back with a collective theatre gasp and kids run for the last of other kids and cameras and long-forgotten flashes and they squeal from thin-lipped mothers trying to grab wayward shoulders and keep slithery families in check and then in the distance, way too late, there's the wail of the country fire brigade engine manned completely by pyjamaed volunteers and we kids roar at that, our child-smiles spread, our joy plumes high into the sky and I'm laughing and clapping my hands for the community's young are in splendid revolt. Mum and Dad haven't spotted me yet, their frowns are deepening and I wave across to them and jump up and down and wave again and finally Dad's eyes are caught.

And on that cold, cold night all the children's smiles will not be wiped, for every one of us knows the deliciousness that our parents will not speak of: that the main block of classrooms, with its head-proclaimer's office and soldier-rows of waiting canes, cannot be saved, that our school has been transformed into blackened, blistered beams and ash. Then the fire fingers begin caressing the church, and the hubbub is sucked to a stop.

There I am, falling away into the shadowy black. I can feel my mother's soft suspicion now, her thinking, Surely not.

A stink of sodden flame and fearful young bodies and faces of ash-smeared raggedness, tired now and trembly quiet. Many children shivery in pyjamas, still, two hours after the fire and some even shoeless in the winter cold. The parents gloomed down and talk tight, for someone's devil-child among all the devil-children in assembly before them is to blame, incendiary devices have been found near the scene and someone's child has an almighty blot in them and every parent is thinking, Please God, *please*, let that child not be mine.

Under my feet the tarmac's still softly hot and I knuckle my heels into it and none of the adults knows of that heat and I smile at its secret, putty warmth. Every scattered child has been dragged by shoulder and hand and ear back to the school corpse and the fire-licked church. My mother is among the squadron of worry-browed mothers, her face foreign and still, her arms crossed and her eyes straight into me, searching for clues.

My father's there too, notebook in hand and camera over his shoulder: a man at work. He's the community's newspaperman and he's plumped with the importance of a good yarn, it has legs, it'll travel, he'll get a byline and maybe even a quid or two from the rights. He feels sorry already for the poor bugger whose kid it is for there'll have to be the gentling questions and the right hesitations and the shoulder squeeze in farewell and then the tallest slug letters he's never before used. He looks across to his little princess and winks a smile; he's safe.

Swirls of black ash pock the pale winter skin of the town and I'm catching a soft flutter on the back of my hand and balancing its frailness and swiping it to dust. There's the blackened, smoking whale carcass of beams and rafters and tin, the belly dancers of smoke and sudden wood-cracks and soft nubs of glow and the sour, beautiful wend of a smell that's nestled into the air and I'm digging my heels deeper into the asphalt, pillowing them in warmth, and the children around me are shivering and sniffling and daring finger cracks and soft bubble-gum pops. We're lined up on the netball courts and by coincidence I'm standing exactly where I always hold the position of Wing Defence in the under-fourteens' matches. Defending the wing, I love the sound of that, it's the only thing I love about the game. I've never gotten the hang of sport, any sport, could never gracefully throw or catch, hate groups and teams and gangs, have a deep-seated dread of lunch hours and bus-stop clusters of kids and church meets.

Brother Sleet whooshes through my thinking as he sweeps out of the church. Imagine a demonic Mormon, he's found a wooden ruler from somewhere, he's raising it high, a conductor's baton that's ready to crash.

Well, he says, and that first word flinches all the slumps straight. We will *not* be leaving here until I have the little demon by the scruff of his neck.

There's a tinfoil ball of anger tight in him, I'm fascinated by someone so clotted and struck afresh by the little, piggy eyes that look as if two fingers have been pronged at them and jabbed deep.

We will stay here until *Christmas* if we have to.

A child laughs and it's abruptly clipped shut and Brother Sleet wheels and asks, Who was that? Sullenly no answer. He paces the assembly lines, poking backs straight and seizing chins and scouring fingertips for any leakages of clues. A rope of a vein dissects his fore-head and his sweat flicks, thumbing the crisp morning cold.

If Brother Sleet had ever been secular he would've been a pisser on lemon trees, all sour with his life and his work, clenched, for he has the energy of the city in him, the vividness of someone who jiggles keys in queues and cuts smartly across lanes and briskly opens doors and expects people to hurry through. And yet that energy is devoted to this little, little place, and with a single-minded zeal he's chiselled into the mantelpiece of the church hall's fireplace, as a Christmas present to the community, *Obey Them That Rule Over You* and it's a beloved creed he can't bear to see stained. Especially, God forbid, by some scrap of a kid.

A man who deals only in absolutes, in right or wrong and good or bad. But there has to be something else besides that, surely, something skittery and dynamic and magnificent and loose. How would he cope with that?

He raps the ruler above his open hand like a nurse shaking a thermometer: every one of us will be working on Christmas Day and there'll be times tables until fingers bleed and no school dance and religious instruction until eight every day of the week *unless, unless* someone comes forward to confess. Silence like a blanket and eyes at nowhere or the ground and no shuffling now but Brother Sleet is not going to tire and the civic buildings of Sunshine stay mostly unopened as the stand-off on the school playground battens down for the long day.

Children, hungry now, begin fainting as the day firms and breaks into a fey heat, little bodies flop to the ground and skin's grated on peevish asphalt and Brother Sleet strides across to the fallen and prevents anyone from making a move and he nudges the bodies for clues but doesn't help them up and the parents, unmoving, still ring the assembly of standing pupils who are left, some are crying and whimpering before the still smouldering school and *no excursions, no sports days, no early marks* Brother Sleet is pecking, hoarse now, and then at midday on the dot according to my *Star Wars* watch I raise my hand, and speak out.

Unsure, for years afterwards, why.

A gasp, my mother, I don't look.

W-who was that? asks Brother Sleet.

It was me, I say again, and he's oddly lost, oddly voiceless for a fraction of a second as if I'm too small, too insignificant, too *female* for any of this and his hand hovers by a frown but then the bewilderment's wiped and the full flurry of him bears upon me, the ruler isn't good enough, oh no, he wants the sting of skin and there's the full force of his open palm and my head snaps back and then I ball and fold my arms over my head like two recalcitrant little wings; I remember the tuck of that, and the fierce tingling through my cheek.

Smelling the held breaths, and the eyes. But not shock.

I'm straightening and through smarting eyes I'm looking around at all the Shiner faces I've never liked and in that moment I'm feeling the first murmuring of a tonic that helps sustain me through the years ahead: the tonic that in sacrifice there is power. And that I've finally, finally, done something to belong and God what an irony is in that. I feel oddly serene, and floating, and content. And so bloody sore, but they're not seeing that.

There's Rebecca's unreadable half-smile and a creeping flush on her neck slowly claiming her face and there's Tiriel's dutiful scribbling, his eyes solidly to his notebook for if he looks up he'll weep, over what he doesn't know, he can't comprehend. There's Brother Sleet's yank dragging me from the stage of that staring and there's the terrier bite of his fingers, I can feel it now, still, on my shoulder. And I'm half led, half dragged, half lifted away, I'm swallowed by the rectory, gone.

On that cinder-flecked day the fascination of an entire community is cemented and there are many reasons why this is so but for me there's just one I hold close: because from the age of thirteen I become one of those people who does what we all dream of – I step into exactly the life that I want.

But how to sustain it, that's the rub.

Lily is the namesake and it's a flower that's thick, waxy sensuality clashes with its role in Christianity as a symbol of untainted goodness and I tell you, I was never, ever seen as good, never granted that.

Difference clung to me like fluff to felt. From a young age all the squeals of the children around me were of the Sunshine world and I, very pointedly, was not. I'm not even sure I was ever a little girl: a young person, yes, but not a girl. I just didn't have all creamy in me those charming, dependable qualities like giving and serving and flirting and quiet for I was much too selfish for that. I was spiky, prickly, defensive, shut. An obsessive collector, not of best-friend lists and pony names, but of leaves and bike chains and cicada shells, of spiders in ice-cream cartons and rocks. And I was perfectly happy with my own company, wilfully, dangerously so and no one in Sunshine trusted that. Perhaps it had something to do with the hated left ear that shot out from day one and just would not lie flat, it was as if I'd never moved in the womb, had been wedged, cheek down and the result was an ear like a folded rose that refused ever to lie demure and tidy and right.

I tried. When I was eight. Because the taunts of all those children, who were very much of the Shiner world when I was not, eventually became too much.

Spaso.

Mongoloid.

Smelly Lelly.

Witch.

The superglue was pinched from my mother's toolbox and carefully applied to both surfaces, as per instructions, and for ten minutes clamped tight. And I was so proud of what I'd done for it had worked, so proud that I secreted my mother's diamanté drop-earrings into school to show the results off, screwing them on at the school gate and walking into that playground so tall, and knowing, and sure – a new me, and no more mock. But three minutes into class time Brother Sleet had been summonsed and when he asked me to remove the whorish abominations from my ears I gave him a steely look, and did not.

His tinfoil ball of anger. His onioned breath as he leant forward and yelped those earrings from my lobes and the skin on the two glued surfaces was destroyed and the resulting grafts took a year to heal and I screamed so loud on that day that the whole of Sunshine would have heard it and then I didn't utter another sound for a bursting seven months. I hated that place so much, why talk to it, why give them my voice, I was made of stronger stuff.

So magnificently stubborn, even back then, such a controlled, uncrackable little nut.

I was belled by my oddity, it clanged about me and drove others away. I was fiercely lonely but I pretended the alone was my choice for I was too proud for anything else. It was spread throughout Tupperware parties and morning teas that I was too fiercely willed, too absorbed in my books, too curious, antisocial, sport-hating, creepy, smelly, proud. But not so my father – and that's where the knot of all this lay.

At the time of the school fire Tiriel Bird was a pillar of the community, his energetic *Shiner Courier* a glue that held it together. The stale weekly had been without a buyer for eighteen months before Bird from the Big Smoke had rescued it and he'd rewarded the community's faith in him with a single-minded zeal that saw him each Wednesday night, an hour before the presses rolled, still deciphering the daily specials from Tom Colston, the local meat man, that were scrawled on blood-smudged scraps of butcher's paper. There was a quiet warmth about Bird, he leant forward with purpose when asking his questions and the love of his work shone from him and the town folk didn't want him leaving and neither did he. But the most spectacular Sunshine story of all never made it into the local paper, because for a month after the school attack the *Courier's* presses were shut down.

With the smell of cinders still threading the air Tiriel was taken to the local contending ground in a bush clearing behind the church, the community's way for a forgotten number of years. All the leading men were at Tiriel's contending and there was a volley of heated talk, shouts of handcuffs and reform school and parental discipline and outsiders' corrupting ways – the latter swiftly hushed.

Almost choking with shock he begged to be allowed to keep his only child and his reputation and his business and for God's sake his family home, for he knew that if his daughter was driven away he'd have to go too and he could never compete with the bigger papers and their presses, the *Shiner Courier* had saturated his entire working life and had sucked up all his savings and God knew if he'd ever be able to sell it. He cradled his furrowed brow in the heels of his hands and could see no way out.

There was argument into lengthening shadows, the community didn't want to lose a good paper and yet it didn't want a demon-child wandering freely among it, a strange child with a fascination for fire in a town on a mountain peak. Tiriel was led away while a final deal was nutted out and he waited in the front seat of his car, radio loud and not listening and as coldness seeped into the day he was summonsed back and a settlement was put to him by Brother Sleet who could only, intermittently, meet his eyes.

Best to keep the oddness clamped among them rather than have it out loose in the world, that was the nub of the decision. For there was a fear that if I was sent away I'd spill the secrets of the community's close ways, and God knew what I'd tinder next.

Never to be seen among us, Tiriel repeated, almost voiceless with shock.

Brother Sleet slid his head and his eyes to one side.

Well, at Christmas mass perhaps, but no more. I can't allow it, the risk to the other children is too great.

So a punishment had been found, a newspaper saved, a community protected – if the parents agreed to it all. Tiriel and the good Rebecca would be assisted by the local librarian who'd be my only regular contact with the outside world and the insurance would pay for the school and the good constable among them would see to the police records, there'd be a clean slate for the world and a token of appreciation would be in order for that and Tiriel and Rebecca could cope if they wanted to, or they could not cope. The men of Sunshine would trust Bird's word for his grit was legendary: he'd had a knee that had given him pain for years and he couldn't get it fixed so he'd gone to a mate's house in the nearest hospital town and had rung Emergency and had told the operator he was going to shoot himself in the joint to force treatment upon it and had then shot himself over the phone and an ambulance had arrived after eleven excruciating minutes in which he'd not uttered a sound and an artificial knee had been installed and from that day the pain was gone. It didn't matter that Bird hadn't dazzled once, long ago, in his Big Smoke, he'd shot himself through the knee and that was the mark of the man.

With barely a sound Tiriel absorbed the demands of that winter afternoon – that he become master of a world scrubbed of lighters and matches and fire of any sort, that he be tyrannical with his discipline and blunt with his will. With barely a sound he pledged to create what was expected of him – the hardworking world of a fundamentalist, a world of certainty, devoid of any ambiguity or doubt. He would no longer advertise his city-different quirks, the transformation into a Shiner would be complete. And his oddball daughter would become the community secret, eave-tucked: a test he could pass, or not.

He could not look me in the eye on that day, he could barely speak, and only Rebecca and myself could read the guilt.

How do you feel now, eh? Brother Sleet asked, with eight years of imprisonment ahead of you?

It's all relative, I guess.

And the Brother lifted his chin, unnerved. He said later that the calm, yellow eyes staring at him were too old for a child's, and he'd sensed even then that the little brat thought she had won, and that the fight was not over yet. You see, I didn't want to escape my fate, oh no, I just wanted to make it work. For a life removed was exactly the life that I wanted.

To have been so sure, so young.

What will your womanhood be, I wonder, little girl? For I know you're a girl, the ultrasound has just told me that. What will you make of this strange tale? You'll not read it until you're eighteen at least, I'll be strict on that, you'll get the fairy tale before then. What new freedoms will you have, I wonder? Will you want to marry at sixteen, have a child at forty-six, or none of that? I'm not afraid of us being alone. My courage made people afraid, your father told me that. God, if only he knew it was the opposite of that but I was too good at masking myself once. Your father told me that I was too vivid for the nidderly, religion-soured little world I was from. Nidderly. I asked him what that meant and he took my word book and wrote it down and *cowardly* I read over the jut of his hip and his handwriting is still close, as neat as an architect's on a plan.

*

19

So there that Lillie is, at thirteen, with all her secret, bubbly glee at never having to go to school again, at never having to speak to those people again, at never having to conform to their ways. Can you imagine hating so much, so young? There she is exploding bubble gum softly over her lips and seeing with new eyes that house she's lived in all of her life. She's stepping across the threshold with her father's hands trembling and drained on her shoulders, both of them knowing that for the next eight years there'll be no other building besides a Christmas Day church. Her mother's pale and tight as she comes from the kitchen and does not touch her, just looks, as if she will never fathom this child from her blood and Lillie's ignoring her staring and walking the familiar rooms with her hands sifting and her heart thudding as she assesses the size of the windows, the shift of the light, the height of the ceilings, the heaviness of the curtains, the push of the breeze, the never-opened books, the ways out.

You love this place that much, my mother challenges. She's brittle, breakable on that day and I've never before seen that. I do now, I reply, and Rebecca nods and there's a beginning of some kind of knowing from her. It's all falling into place for you, isn't it? Well this punishes us too, you know, and my father says, Bec, honey, we've had enough for one day, and she turns back to the kitchen and she says, I just want to make this work for you, Lil, for all of us, God knows how, and her fingertips concertina her brow.

I know.

Do you want us to leave Sunshine, is that it?

I'm not looking at her and the question is hanging in the air and my father's life is entrenched in this place and my mother's beside him, she loves this land and this house that she's moulded into a home, loves it fiercely and romantically as only an exile can, I know that.

Mum, I want to stay here. Don't worry, I'm all right.

I didn't want to uproot their tightly spun lives, didn't want to leave Sunshine; I just wanted to be distanced from the community but I couldn't tell them that. I, too, loved this high pocket of land where the sky brushed the land like a cow's belly on grass, loved my old mountain dragster that flew over gullies and ruts, half horse and half bike and the trustiest of steeds and loved my spiders in their cartons and my books and my rocks. And our house.

Tiriel and Rebecca had discovered the wooden building at a time when a horse had found shelter in an empty room and when the wind licked the leaves that had gathered on the floor and danced them through a tunnel from the front doorway to the back. The family mythology was steeped in the sinking shock of arrival, the skull-hole gaps for windows and doors, the walls stiffly flaking with a sunburnt paint-skin and the lace scraps on the main bedroom window speaking of love and some enigmatic loss, industrious euphoria then hasty abandonment. Rubbled around the house were sticks and logs bleached to the colour of bones and inside were Depression-era blankets that were just scratchy chaff bags, newspaper-stuffed, and cow pats and animal remains and ghosts.

But Tiriel and Rebecca had seen beyond all that, to the fact that the building had good bones. The community talked, said the green city couple were mad to take on the mess of the old place but they'd made a pact never to get a flat, regular property with a new house, square fields, circular dams. They wanted hills and energy and surprise and their fields dipped and leered down slopes to the gurgle of mountain creeks and the ground was freckled with granite boulders and the soil in places was three inches deep but on the afternoon they'd first seen it there was dusk creeping in and it had washed over the bleached land and everything had softened and Rebecca had turned to Tiriel and smiled want in her eyes and that was that. The rain dripped through the light fittings in heavy weather and the water from the taps was the colour of weak tea but the couple had brewed a happiness in the place until one pale winter afternoon when it was decreed that a thirteen-year-old child was to be bound within it. And over the years her little fingers trailed so consistently down the staircase wall that eventually they permanently ribboned it, those marks just would not be wiped.

As was her knowing that when she was twenty-one she'd be free to walk away from the community and never live among it and she carried that knowing like a lantern before her for eight long years of her life.

The rules were set down on that winter afternoon that faded into the night like a sigh and they were never softened and I was initially comfortable with that for I knew how to make it work. I'd read about people who spent their entire childhood on remote farms, educated by radio and mail-order books and I'd often dreamed of that. The book-filled old attic at the top of the house became the eyrie and my mother the teacher and my father the boss, for he set me to work with his hobby-farm folly of a herd of sheep on his land. There was a rigid routine to those days: I worked farmer's hours, from first light to last, helping with the animals when the day was gentle at both ends and between those times sitting and dreaming at my desk. I didn't want to run, had nowhere to run to. Except books.

Every first Wednesday of the month Mrs Edith Jansun, the librarian, locked her library early and roared the bookmobile up our long driveway in a most unwomanly manner, fanning blonde dust in her wake. She was a woman of cool eggshell blue, predatorial in her wants. Few knew of this, although in her public life there was leakage: she slapped down her soles as if she was punishing the ground and signed her signature so savagely she sometimes tore paper and had a deep belly laugh under all the Shiner propriety that spoke of another woman entirely. She wasn't the best choice for me, and Hallelujah for that.

Ed Jansun was determined, very quietly, to plump out my days for our community shunned television and was too removed from city newspapers and visitors to the Bird home were rare. My parents rarely extended invitations, for no one quite trusted me back then, and so Ed's books and magazines and city newspapers and chat, and an inspired fourteenth birthday present of a shortwave radio, were the ways that I learned of the world. And by spinning endlessly an old globe under my fingers, and pausing it and dreaming of all the places at my tips.

Each month I filled my six–book quota and greedily read, over the years perfecting ways of gulping far worlds with minimal disturbance while I walked for the mail or hosed the lawn or compacted wool bales with my feet. I dwelt between those pages, and I remember even now that lovely, enveloping confidence and security that came from being alone with just my imagination and nothing else. When a good book wore out from too many readings I wanted to bury it like a person, to always have it close.

Waiting for Ed was always a ram of questions: What colour is Tiffany's blue? Do old people fall in love, do you think? What's a moor, a common, heath? Why would someone be called Major Major? What's it like in a plane, what happens to your ears? What's it like, a naked man, are they soft? It was as if I was seeking in books all the preparation I'd need for proper life, and sophisticated Ed with her Jackie-O shifts was to grout any gaps. I can still hear the young voice at her, spilling the past month and all the books in it like someone reading a children's story aloud, everything all exciting and wondrous and shiny-new. Can hear me racing through commas and running stop signs and leaping across dashes in my rush to get to the next sentence as if it was all dammed up during the weeks I hadn't seen her and spilling out in a tumble I couldn't control.

And at the desk I'd stare at the broadness of the sky and the arrowhead of birds across the wide blue, and occasionally, mysteriously, on sunny-breezy days when the light was so sharp it almost hurt a giant, white scribble would be licked from somewhere within Sunshine, would be pulled high into the air and would enchant me with its dance.

What is it, do you think, what do you reckon?

It's your knight in shining armour, Ed laughed, her pianist's fingers lightly tapping my shoulders.

God, yeah, it gives me hope, as I clasped my hands to my chest and raised my eyes to the heavens. Because I bet it's the only romance I'll ever get in this place!

And Ed was slapping me gently around the head and rubbishing the thought, she was telling me that she'd always envied my ability to do exactly what I wanted, envied my knack of making dreams work. And I'd stayed staring up at that scribble, perfecting a blue gum globe that was cracked smartly again and again over my lips and wondering who it was going to be who'd help me to climb out – I knew precisely what I wanted back then, for my interior life was consumed by men and I had the exact one picked.

So here I am now, sitting at my desk on the other side of the world with London all smugly asleep around us. Can you feel the winter chill? I hope not, for I'm slipping my palm under my red jumper, I'm slinging you in my hand's warmth.

No stars, no proper sky tonight, or any night.

It is the light pollution, my gentle Pakistani newsagent told me just this afternoon with a sideways dip of his head, all of the brightness has bled away the sky. And I had smiled at that for I wouldn't have stood for a bled-away sky once. Or even imagined it.

What I'm hearing towards the end of that Christmas sermon, on the cusp of getting out: Brother Paina quoting the words of a Saint someone and saying that at the end of our days the question should be not what we have done with our lives but *how well we have loved* and the words are falling onto me like soft rain, I'm determined to love well, I want to live by that, I'm tucking it away for my journal.

What I'm seeing towards the end of that Christmas sermon: the light behind the tall windows at the back of the church and the brisk wind dancing among the tall tree outside and creating a furnace of shifting, twinkling light, a white fire through the glass and the sun pushing through the windows in great highways of brightness and the dust motes spinning and the interior of the room alive with light. What I'm imagining: all the highways I can take on the cusp of being grown-up.

For in a gulp of six days I'll be walking down the main street of Sunshine, daring a bikini, swimming in a pool, relearning the stroke and memorizing the gears of a car and walking into Ed's library and visiting her much-imagined house. A gin and tonic perhaps, a candlelit bath, a first smoke, lipstick, learning men, learning skin, learning touch and those dust motes spin and dance.

I fly on the stern chair and hold out my hand and can't quash the beam, even when Tiriel returns from the toilet and clamps his hand on my knee and locks me to the ground, even when the slow brace of my parents shunts me into quiet, even when Brother Paina, to drag the frisky congregation back to attentiveness, raises his tone and says that life, if we haven't discovered it already, is difficult and always will be. For on that last Christmas morning I'm lifted high by a fluttery, jittery lightness, it's so intense and of such a brightness that it almost breaks into a scream.

Brother Paina strides purposely across to us after the service, the breeze tugging at his cassock and slapping it across his chest. He's absorbed with a glance the man's arm around my shoulder, the knuckles white in the flesh and he's struck by those steering, disciplining fingers. He makes Christmas cheer small talk and extracts names and then asks too quickly what I'm doing with my life and from Rebecca and Tiriel there are chest-tightenings and nervous foot shifts and eyes veering to the car.

I don't—

Butting my voice into the public domain for the first time in eight years and it's different to the casual tone I use with my parents or Ed, it's finding a right formality and it's not quite there yet.

I haven't decided yet, Brother, I'm not sure, I don't know.

Not used to talking publicly back then and not used to talking about myself and struck by the eyelashes too long for a man and the lone freckle on an ear lobe and the fingernails, woman-neat, and he asks me what I want to do but my mother's hand is curled into my arm and I know what's meant, for Rebecca's speaking fingers are her distinction, on many Shiners have they pressed their mark. I don't know, Brother, it's so hard, I'm crashing a smile into the talk and my voice is firming and I ask the priest what he thinks I should do. What a question! Something good, that your heart is in, and there's his smile, just to me, no one else. There's a grip in my belly like a fist has clutched at it and I laugh too loud and too old and there's a hush from the crowd ringing the distance for none of the congregation dares leave before my own family does, none of them wants to miss out, Ed there among them, I catch the keen watching in her powder-blue shift. Brother Paina invites us to join him for tea, he hands me his prayer books and propels my parents before him with arms outstretched and jollying too much and he asks Tiriel what he does in Sunshine and I've got the local paper is the curt reply meant to blunt all the talk but I'm having none of it for I'm enjoying it all too much and I turn ahead of them and say that the paper was known as the egg timer back when my father first bought it.

Why?

Because it took just three minutes to read!

The public voice locked, it's low and rich and there's velvet somewhere in it, it's as if I've listened over the years to too much left-on late-night radio and its tone has snuck under my sleeping skin. The accent is city-educated, not of my people and just as I'm getting into my stride Rebecca breaks from the priest's grasp and stumbles something about an oven to be preheated and a Christmas dinner to prepare and from Tiriel there's relief-soaked laughter, too much, Oh yes, the roast! Shame, says Brother Paina, another time perhaps? And he shakes my parents' hands at the rectory door with his arm still around me as if he wants to hold me back and there's the smell of him and the firm, owning grip and the clean nails and the gold ring too thick.

I've always liked people with a spark, he says, squeezing my shoulder and dropping his hand. I'm a firm believer that you must look for the life and vitality in people, Mr Bird, because you can redirect vitality but you can't give life to the lifeless and there's the soft, enquiring linger in the shake of his hand and I gulp his words as I read the panic flitting under my mother's skin, read her nerves, wire-taut. I'll have to find a mission for you, Lillie, something good. That my heart's in, Brother, and my grin's too loud for the ropes are loosening, I can feel them slipping, and I've found a public voice for the world.

Those ragged clumps of villagers watch all silent and suspicious as our high four-wheel drive pulls from the car park and several more cameras are held to eyes and among it is a toddler's lone wave that's snatched into stillness by a young mother. Brother Paina absorbs it, perplexed, from the rectory door. He doesn't extend his Christmas invitation to anyone else, he'll eat alone. He's not taken to this town.

Staring without talk as we drive past my old school, it's the same every Christmas, each weighted drive from the farm to the church and back. My eyes hungry as they snatch up the yearly changes, my face craning as Tiriel accelerates past.

That frightful man leaves in two weeks, thank God, says Rebecca, all held, wiping the day from her forehead and her voice and her movements betraying her other-country origins that are most pronounced in times of great stress. She's from England, that fairy-tale land of castles and queens and civilization and cold that's fiercely revered by our people and utterly unknown. Among the Shiners just to hear Rebecca's voice is to respect her, envy her, want a piece of her. Her skin shouts her birthplace, it's always rigorously shielded and so luminously pale that the whites of her eyes appear pale blue and there's much fascination at the blare of that. And at her aloofness. And her touch. And why she is here, in this place.

−2−

So, the Family

Who was your mysterious grandmother?

A woman with hands like pale rope, whose fingers had murmured and hummed across hundreds of bodies in her lifetime. A masseuse by trade and in her memory was a catalogue of flesh that her talk would only occasionally let out: strange whirls of hair like spirals of stars, deeply pitted navels where a finger could be lost, question mark moles, freckle-crams across stomachs, regretted tattoos. She collected all the journeys the bodies had been on, the stories their muscles and skin told − but no one had ever collected hers, she'd never allow that.

You can feel the anger in a pair of shoulders, you can feel it fighting you, she told me once but I'd never seen anger in my mother for she was a woman who wore a mask of unshakable calm. She reminds me, looking back, of a story I heard once about a newly married woman who lost her husband on a honeymoon beach, *I'm just off for a wander,* he'd said to her sun-fuddled sleepiness and it was never known if he'd drowned or been taken by a shark or had just walked away from his life and the woman got on with the terrible weight of her living because she had to, the legacy of it all just a strange serenity floating through her, a half-smile meaning nothing shielding her face. Rebecca taught me the secrets of massage and stoicism and bolting lives tight and knowing the true person was like trying to hold fog and I still don't, never will, I suspect. Her way was with touch, not talk, and I want you to know more about your own mother than I ever did about mine and it's another reason why I'm setting this down.

Your grandfather had seen something of the forest in the woman to be his wife, he let that slip once, a quality calm and strong-rooted and stable and sure. Tiriel had been a mess of a youth for he couldn't hook his journalism dream in the hungry city and he had a liking too much for its drugs. He was gangly-tall and hook-stooped in the shoulders, not wanting to abut the sky, but at the age of twenty-two, feebled by the success of others, he fell under the spell of the foreign-polished woman with red-setter hair and a wand of a body and thick-corded, tennis player arms and was hauled out. And they loved so enduringly that over the years their voices began to mirror cadences and sighs and there sprouted the same mispronunciations, *nothink, com-promise, the-ate-er*, that shouted two lives too closely lived. Even their toileting had synch-ronized, like two sisters with their monthly cycles moon-linked: get off, he'd laugh often, it's my turn now. God, what a pair. I felt left out from their tight little knot.

Our house had a kitchen kettle that was always warm and within its walls was the calm of a couple who'd been married many years and endured much and found a path. Sunny, gangly Tiriel had grown more like his partner of cool blues and deep forest greens for Rebecca dampened him down. But then I arrived, the cleat in all that calm. A square peg in a round hole and seemingly stork-sent, for the only obvious physical mark of either parent rests in two thumbs as ugly as big toes and a Chinese whisper of Rebecca's. I'm stubbornly left-handed and both parents are right and there's no history in either family of the devil's way: it was as if I'd been magic-sprung, it was declared once, and hushed.

It's been said that a child of two deeply bound lovers can feel an outsider, can feel orphan-bereft and I'd always thought that of my parents and me. Like an orphan I could veer from loving too much to not loving at all: opening out like an anemone that's softened in the tide's silky swirl and then jamming up tight if anything prodded, got too close. It was worse with Rebecca: her weighted

29

calm became the burr of those jagged young years, and Tiriel between us the salve.

On the cusp of twenty-one it was unknown if the pyrophitic addiction had been scraped from me: would the compulsion come dancing into me again when I glimpsed on release a match struck or a hearth stoked? No Shiner knew, not even my parents.

They fretted over the due date, I could tell. There were many reasons why Tiriel and Rebecca were reluctant to let me go but a fear of reoffending was only one of them. You see like a reformed smoker Tiriel had grown zealous with the wonder of his ascetic new way, for he'd lived the other side but had then found an anchoring in a world rarely invaded by the present, a community marooned by its choice. He had a vocation, at last, and a family, and a home, and he held on fiercely to all of them. The reformed junkie who'd once had a struggle of a beard growing light on his chin was now rigorously clean-shaven and determined to shield his brood from the worst: this distracted world, he was fond of saying, shaking his head. And so the man with the secret, city past sat high on his throne with the good Rebecca unwavering beside him. Her only known vice: the private tearing with her teeth of the cuticles around her nails, neatly so, and I only chanced upon that. She hid well. Even her yawns were stifled, quelled with a delicate flaring of the nose.

So how did a masseuse wheedle herself into such a strange community? By the gift of her hands. She worked wonders on the local football team, and from that drew in the sisters and the wives. It was a status symbol to be touched by her, and she was English to boot and there was nothing finer in the world than that. And why did Rebecca stay so faithfully within the community? Because she was deeply in love with her man and her house and the exotic, frontier land, deeply in love with the spirit of the sun-scorched place.

England is a cold, unreligious kind of country, she said to me once. Most of its churches are empty and its people are remote, I've always dreamed of somewhere else.

*

Dreaming of somewhere else, I knew all about that.

A recent medical article told of a young man who went to hospital seeking attention for stomach pains. Expecting to find some sort of cyst, the doctors opened him up. What they removed was a seven-inch long foetus with the teeth of a sixteen-year-old. The improbable entity was the man's twin, 'absorbed' long ago in the womb and still surviving off his brother's body.

The scrap had been excised by repeated pen gauges and glued into a journal and over many entries I'd referred to it, for like the man with stomach pains I'd felt long ago that I, too, had a restless twin inside me, a shadow-mate gnashing and tugging and nagging, nibbling at complacency and keeping away calm. Never content with the wait, or the tight fist that controlled my life.

On full-moon-flooded nights Tiriel and Rebecca allowed me to wander the farm, on clear summer evenings when the sky was saturated not with night but dark day and the air was vibrant with stillness. I walked with bare arms stretched into the caress of the air, breathing the hedged freedom and the sweetness of alone. I'd wear petticoats with hems that snared burrs and antique necklaces wrapped around my wrists and sometimes a tiara or a silken Chinois shawl, all raided from a dress-up box I'd never grown away from. They were Rebecca's clothes, salvaged from some never-spoken-of other-life and yet always on my feet were the two clumps of workboots, solid and steel capped and anchoring me to the land and with a rattle that was stilled by my father's thick socks. *Somewhere else* became more appealing the older I got.

The twenty-first birthday. Early. Washing and dressing with scurrying care.
I've never used make-up, don't own any but the radio's given me clues: I pinch colour into my cheeks like Scarlett O'Hara and prick a bead of blood from my thumb to stain my lips. Put on my mother's long silk skirt. Tiara. Party pumps. It's a good day, I can

feel it in the lightness of my movements, there are no spots and the hair's shiny and the chin's looking thin and I clatter down the stairs and pause on the threshold of the kitchen and take a deep breath and read, instantly, that something's wrong. My shock breaks the huddle of my parents, they're deep in head-hung talk and there's a sudden, tightening fear and a wobble of uncertainty in my good morning. Happy birthday, says my father, his eyes too bright with lying hope. My mother allows just a fading smile.

Well?

All my dreams are poised on the wings of that one word and I repeat it softer and take a deep breath and with my head lowered like a bull I hold out my arms with my palms to the ground as if pushing myself into a calm, and smile. Serene, floating. Lil, Tiriel says and stops, clogged. Rebecca takes over, all brisk at the kettle.

We've still got some things to work out.

Standing very still. Feeling as if a fist is slowly squeezing all the blood from my heart. I can taste panic in my throat, a ball of it, and then a wail pushing up. I'm twenty-one, I say in a very low voice that's never come from me before. It's the law, I'm twenty-one, and the voice gathers strength and finds the punch of a scream and I run up the stairs and ram myself onto the deeply familiar, deeply furrowed bed, pushing my face into the pillow and damming the tears, I'm twenty-one, it's the law, I'm twenty-one, I'm shouting it to my parents and then it stops and a tense quiet hovers in the waiting house.

Am I to die in this place, I've written in my journal on that blunted birthday, *before my life has even begun?* The words screech before me and I shut the book for the slice of it, even now, is still fresh.

Rebecca steps into that attic room and walks across to my bed and starts massaging my shoulders, finding the angry little whirls that always need to be found and working and working at them to soften them away. I shrug her off but the fingers trip and snake back – let me in, Lil, come on – but I tense my shoulders against the silky trickle of touch and tell her she can't just massage it all away and my voice is tight with hurt. There's the sudden weight of the pads of the still fingers as Rebecca tells me they don't know what to do, they're at a loss because there's a deep uneasiness about me coming back to the community and they're only just realizing its potency, still, after all these years, God help us and then my reluctance is dragged to her and I'm folded in her arms and it's all coming out and my hot, heaving head is cradled in her palm. I'm sorry, chick, we have to work something out, we're just not there yet, combing the hair-knots with the rake of her fingers, combing and combing them and soothing the heaving and combing the knots out.

You've had eight fucking years to work on it.

The hands still, I can taste the paling, I've never said aloud such a word and I savour the slap of it.

Fuck, Mum, *fuck*.

Ripping at the veneer of her infuriating stillness and revelling in the sweet, grubby power it gives me to have the word out. I want to hit her, wound her, but all I can do is rattle with words and she just bows her head and smiles as I tell her that I've dreamed of this day all my life, of my first ice-cream cone and a proper haircut and a bookshop and a restaurant steak and all the frustration and anger and want is spilling out at last and I know, she's saying, I know, not meeting my eyes, just nodding her half-smile. I've got her now, I'm crawling under her skin, I'm gnawing on the marrow of her guilt as I harangue about learning to drive and my own car and a car wash, God, even that and I'm walking across to the high window and staring out, a beach again and the Big Smoke and I'm shawling my arms across my shoulders.

A man.

Silence, the tension poised in the room.

A life.

We did it because we love you, chick.

Yeah.

We did it to protect you, we didn't want to see you hurt.

Yeah.

*

Rebecca leaves the room without any more talk and I don't turn and stare from my window and the landscape stretches ahead of me, resolutely empty and with no other people or houses in any direction as far as I can see and I hear the loneliness in the wind and the day yawns. My mind quarries the future, the bleakness of it. I'm used to planning and precision, used to *knowing* and I look at the teetering stacks of books that cram the room like rows of pillars all close to a crashing, the books that have plumped out my pruned little world with hundreds of other worlds but I can't bring myself to pick up anything that day even though I've spent so many years dwelling, resting, dreaming between their pages. I need my own story now.

I heel my palm on my cheek but the sound of my wristwatch, its frantic flutter, panics me too much. Jittery, searching for something to do that isn't endless thought, I slip my feet out of my mother's old party shoes and into the well-hollowed interior of the slippers whose soft dips and humps have been moulded through years of waiting but then stop, give up, don't leave the bedroom: there's nothing to leave it for.

Stare blankly at the shortwave radio by my bed, my eye to the planet, but don't switch it on. Its voices over the years have taught me the word *fuck* and late-night languidness and that bikinis are back and men prefer girls who like laughing in bed and God gave people the gift of suffering and Tirana is the lilt of a name for Albania's capital and London's weather is bleak. Deeply I love that plastic box with its topple-heavy tentacle of an antenna that nets sounds from all the world's air, it's been preparing me over the years for this patient day when I'm twenty-one, and decreed grown up, and free to walk out. And now I can't bear to hear the radio's boast.

My left hand teepees and absently whirls the globe, poises it abrupt, spins again, again. Thick quiet. No sounds from downstairs. I sit on the bed and stare into nothing for a very long time. Can't move, my whole body feels paralysed by heaviness. Topple slowly onto my side, my face nestling again into that too-bowed pillow. Stay there for a very long time and my voice becomes gutted of all crying and over the hours it shrivels to a voiceless husk, disappoint-ment-bloated and almost gone.

Tiriel yells several times – hollow, despondent, old – that there's a birthday cake to be cut and it seems like the loneliest voice I've ever heard and at the third calling I find the energy to say no thank you, I'm not up to it, my voice clogged. And you know, I feel utterly trapped for the first time in my life because for the first time there's no foreseeable way out. My spirit's now hobbled to the lounge-room clock that every day and night will chime its hours for God knows how many months and years of my life.

So the day softens into a full-mooned, light-flooded night and there that Lillie Bird is, striding into the midnight but there's no petticoat or shawl this time, no effort, just pyjamas that she should have grown away from long ago. She's lying on the driveway on her back with her arms behind her head and staring at the sky and softly keening in great gulps until her mouth aches from the stretch and there are no tears left. Then she's on her side, curling into a ball with her face to the hard grit and I can recall even now the press of it. For half an hour or more she lies like this, the warm January air her blanket and then Tiriel walks outside and lifts her up, his scratchy cheek a tissue to her tears until his own mingle there too as he carries her steadily back to the too-known house.

Over the years of confinement my journals have recorded the see-page of joy at what I'd managed so spectacularly at thirteen, the realization that perhaps, perhaps I'd made a mistake, for is anyone free to take no part in the world? They've recorded the gradual knowledge of every bump and crack and knot of that place that grew me in: the wood spiteful with splinters that was sucked dry by the years to a variegated grey, the walls nurturing the chill in winter and only reluctantly letting it go, the cold collecting in sheets and threading through hair and pooling in the pads of fingers, the wallpaper in the bedrooms that trapped a smell of stillness and surrender and, very faintly, stale beer, and when the sheets peel in far corners the house seems to be weeping, its crying leaks out in the early hours of the morning and panics me awake.

My room over the years becomes layered with stories and I talk aloud with the characters and in my journals scribble their lives down. There's an imaginary husband, Paul McGall, he's my dependable, dream-sharing mate who waits by my side for the release of disappearance, for the morning of that magic birthday when I'll be set loose to explore all the distractions of the world. And a real man. The night before my twenty-first I've written *I think I could be an erotic woman* even though I've never had sex, and God knows when, now, or how.

The nights hum with their stillness.

Days too.

The howl of the birthday grew fainter and one day the parents didn't talk of it any more and my incessant baiting gradually stopped for there was another swamp: Sunshine was bit by a drought and my want seemed puny in its midst. Talk was consumed by scorched dirt and grass stubble and flies worried at me as I walked the fields of the parched land, they fed off my sweat as the sun moved steadily like a bride up an aisle. I stared, all squint, at the high aeroplanes that winged their expectant cargo to every other place. And our beloved old creak of a bitch, Brown Dog, raised her head from her verandah retirement at the conclusion of every walk and her never-failing, sour grin would always spark a smile from me as the eternal optimist and the fresh pessimist came face to face. Sometimes I'd lean close and snap her jaw shut and Brown Dog would duck her head and snuffle and butt a lick that would crack from me a rare laugh.

The farm's dam had dried into petals of stiff cream, frail stepping stones that collapsed to powder underfoot and the water from the house's taps was brown and reluctant and viscous and thick and the lambs were skinny, way below optimum birth rate, for their mothers were a kilo underweight and they didn't stand much of a chance. I brought the newborn orphans home close to hand-feed but as the days wore on the deaths stacked up and my resolve wore out and I felt sucked under by it all for the first time in my life, my spirit snuffed.

The thirstlands, I snapped to Ed one Wednesday afternoon, that's what these are and what they'll always be, no one should live here and no one should've come in the first place, and I was startled at the ugliness in the tone, it was as if a bitter adult had finally pecked out and I could feel my spirit growing rank and penning me in, but couldn't stop.

Day after day there were fields of bleached grass as far as the horizon stretched and talk in the kitchen of cloud patterns and barometers and lows, of another sheep-batch being shot, of a scrap of a shower somewhere too far away, of native animals in the middle of the roads drinking from puddles that were sucked into bitumen too fast and I ranged the house and the farm with my hands crossed at my shoulders and at the sourness in my head. All I had for variety were grim sightings of eagles slamming into cars as they took off by the side of the road, their bodies pushed into metal by the oven-baked crosswinds.

Go out and help your father, said Rebecca, often, to scrape my listlessness from her head, for the situation had curdled between us and my mother felt keenly a blame as I shrugged away any touch.

Make yourself useful for once.

I would if I could, if I was ever allowed out.

All hurt and snap. Regressing, becoming the child I'd never really let out.

Above the farm thrust the peak of Bony Mountain, it had been christened Misery Mountain by the first white men that had crossed it but its early settlers had petitioned to soften the grimness of the name. Feeble change, I exploded to Rebecca and Ed in the kitchen one day, it's typical of this place, the whole community is a monument to feeble change, and Ed had smiled through her cool tut, had told me that to Brother Sleet those words would be deeply blasphemous, and too astute.

Ha!

Restlessly I walked and yet when I reached the farm's boundary fence I always turned back for the fences on our land weren't to be climbed. On two sides of the property there was a thick forest belt and I'd grown up with stories of ankle-loving snakes and belly-gouging boars and sudden gully-drops. And yet for the first time in my life, with the goal of release sunk, I felt that the farm was leeching all the spring from my years and that something, *soon*, had to be done. Or I'd go mad. I'd implode, I'd do something magnificently, irrevocably insane and from that there'd be no climbing back.

Day after day the sun beat down, the late summer heat like muslin stretched across the sky. The baked breeze sifted our topsoil onto other people's land and another eagle slammed and another lamb died and for the first time in twenty-four years Tiriel found a curse. And then another. I watched sheep feebly attempting to procreate in the sap of the heat as I idly bit juice from long stalks of grass, I was tetchy and irritable and frustrated about sex, about men, the great desire, the great unknown and the want was all nervy under my skin.

What's it like to touch them, Ed?

God, I dunno. Lovely, I guess. They smell the nicest in the little clearing just behind their ears, it's their true smell right there, and it's lovely to kiss. And under their arms, it's all soft.

What would it be like to be one? What do you think?

She looked at me helplessly and laughed.

God, we have to get you out of here, girl. You're ready to explode.

On several distant-memoried, golden days during my teens Tiriel and Rebecca had smuggled me out of Sunshine and driven six hours to a shiny city on the coast that was less than a century old. The reasons: to finally have the plastic surgery that would correct the wayward ear, and to fit me with glasses. But there was another agenda: to show me a glimpse of the world, to soften the future shock. My parents knew that the streets of a metropolis would give them their best chance at anonymity and the ritual never varied – I'd be hidden under a scratchy blanket on the floor of the car until the road widened at the foot of the mountain and when a fuel stop was got to I'd beg to put in the petrol, I'd pretend it was my penis and shake it a little just to try to understand the other side and Paul McGall would hysterically laugh.

And in that wondrous city with its canyon-runs and sun-sapped streets I'd stare at the young men and walk right up to them and smile and reach out and my parents, all embarrassed, would flurry me away. I trailed my fingers along any city-surfaces that I could, breathed deep the thick air, tasted its strangeness, gulped the bars on house windows and the cram of parked cars, the wild reach of the buildings, the confident glass, the stains in the pavements, the couples in scrappy parks, the shiny, chatty office girls and the men, all the men and tried, often, to brush a touch.

How would I slip into this wondrous world? I didn't know. What would it think of someone like me? I didn't know. But a mother's comment from long ago was etched deeply into me and it coloured a lot of my teenage life. The woman had visited Rebecca in a barely disguised gloat a week after the school fire and I'd hidden on a step and trapped scraps of their conversation in my journal.

If she were pretty, like that Cathie Cliffer, she'd never be so wilful.

The words faithfully written down through the barb of the hurt, as was Rebecca's misspelt reply.

Yeah, it's the gorgeous ones who are always the conservatives, isn't it? They've got no need to be rebels. I just wish she was sweet, and dependable, and quiet. Even her feet are ugly. And clumsy! She can't even open a bottle of milk without spilling it.

I'll never forget the sting of the words, I don't need them recorded in my journal for they're in my head too much.

Eight years later a quote was centre-stage on my bedroom wall, *My life is founded on the rock of change*, it came from an elderly, milky-skinned actress known for her character and not her looks who was interviewed in one of Ed's magazines. I ached for that life of change and yet all around me another eagle slammed and another lamb died and again my father cursed and I hated the very smell of it all now, felt tombed in that wide, empty space.

Bolted awake by a scuffle of sounds on the stairs and the blood booming in my ears and straining with the listening. Tiriel's *What the* – and a thud and a muffled melee of feet and it recedes and the front door slams and there's settling quiet and I leap from the bed and run to the window and catch, just, three figures running from the land and then one slows, and stops, and lingers a looking back. I crane my head, can't make the figure out, slam up the window for a better look. Tallness is all I can get. My thrumming heart. My arm lifting in salute, not knowing why and the figure raises a high hand in return, it hovers for a second or two and then the figure runs on, catching up with the others and then all three are claimed by the black, the night drinks their skin and they're gone. I lean on the window sill and cup my face in my palms and breathe in the still sky and no one comes to my room, no one explains. They aren't coming back and the familiar knot of sullenness seeps again into my chest but then lightning begins flickering in the rainless night, far away behind a cloud like a mosquito trapped in a net and there's God in that sky and I feel flooded with hope. For someone's got so far, three people, who care enough.

So there that Lillie is, slipping off her nightie and panties in the flush of that strange night and sleeping without any clothes on for the very first time, stretching luxuriously and wriggling with delight and there's the sweetness of bare limbs under the sheet, there's the flurry of softness between her legs, there's the sharp, flooding wet.

No mention in the kitchen the next morning of the sounds from the steps and I ask, I want to know. You must have dreamed it, silly billy Lillie, Tiriel says too quickly to Rebecca's calm smile. They wouldn't dare to, surely is all my mother says and then it's gone as the talk finds the drought. But I'd *felt* the person's wave, in the hairs on the back of my neck, and my mood tightens and I say nothing more that day. Or the next. Or the next.

Those stagnant days of wanting so much, I have them before me now in the spill of journals I've retrieved from the freezer. They're by a young woman I barely recognize, a woman not myself, for I never write or speak now with her voice or intensity or spark. I've unsprung, uncoiled, I guess. Even the handwriting's changed, it's become skittery and light and barely touching the page, whereas once it was wanting and urgent and bold.

Wanting to be large in a world that flicked her away, to be grand and spontaneous and disorderly and disturbing. Wanting to defy the film-extra status her life was assigned to, the silence of it and the meekness, the order, the obedience, the quiet. For at the age of twenty-one that Lillie was thoroughly sick of hands stained grey by waxy pelts and sheep the colour of the grass that they fed on, of endless sky and catalogue bras and a lone bed and remote hope. During the bulk of her youth she'd maintained her spark – Ed told her once she was a person who always gave the impression she was sitting in sunlight even if the room was in shadow.

Lil, it's as if you'd foreseen your punishment all that time ago and had calmly stepped into it, with your life all mapped out. You little bugger.

But after the shock of the twenty-first birthday her days had soured and her parents saw it and fretted for her. For by agreeing to a rescue plan all those years ago Tiriel and Rebecca had moulded a freak, and it was only after their daughter's coming of age that the sheer stubbornness of the knot was dawning upon them. They had, listless on their hands, a deeply curious young woman who was horrifically ill-equipped for the world, and stuck.

So days passed in bleached-yellow stares as I walked the land and counted the sheep and squinted at the sky for anything fresh. How can you draw stillness, how can you write it? I asked Ed one drought-sapped visit, not even bothering now with any life in my voice.

41

I'd given up, didn't sleep naked any more, didn't languish my arms behind my head or glide on a chair or chatter and laugh, it was as if all my senses had retracted deep into my body and were reluctant to ever come out again. I sat at my desk and just stared at my dreams, for so long, so still. Or I lay curled on my bed and listened endlessly to the radio, flicking the plastic knob through its bands of music and jingle and prayer and talk and more often than not settling on the BBC's World Service and letting the beautifully modulated tones wash over me, the calm, unflappable pace of the announcers and the correspondents scratchy from all corners of the globe, grimmed down with the importance of what they were witnessing and reminding me of the vice of my own place.

At night I slept restlessly and dreamed jagged rot, for all my vast want was contained in the weighted air of a little attic room and a house below me that nagged me with its stillness and I knew that almost anything was bearable if there was the hope of escape – but now this.

That Land

I can feel your greed for this now, little hoverer, little sucker, I can feel your wanting to know how, for I'd written that I could be an erotic woman but I'd never had the chance to find out. And so I push this story on as you feed from me, as you pull me inward, I can feel your tug as you float in your thrumming sac. I'm in your employ – I try to straighten my spine but the words pull me down.

That land where people are afraid of the grass has a stubborn petulance, it pushes away at the people that are on it and you won't believe it but following the drought that bit were the bush fires. It makes sense, I guess. Fires suddenly ringed the distance and at night their glow over the rims of far hills was like a beautiful, low eclipse and I monitored those hills, enchanted, for the world around me was tense with planning and packing and yet I was stabled tight. Flakes of ash were borne like royalty on the breeze and they shrouded our bathroom in a powdery grey and the air was soaked faintly by the smell of far flames and I breathed it in deep and held my head high for as the fires nudged closer I alone was beginning to thrill: rescued, again, by flames.

The worst since '79, Tiriel declared one breakfast. Sixty-eight, amended by dinner. The worst ever, late that night. How on earth would we set up again? Rebecca asked, her hands heavy in the bread dough with her thinking. A new town, God, the thought of it, and Tiriel slapped down his book.

I've got a business to run, we're not going anywhere.

I know, I know, it was only a thought.

Imagine a grubby white pick-up truck with flapping torn plastic as its window on one door, imagine it speeding up our driveway and barrelling with a stranger's confidence to the verandah's lip and stopping abruptly with a handbrake whinge and out of it stepping a new man. A volunteer returning from the fire's front, his home still three hours beyond the mountain but his woollen pants have shrunk in the heat and the itch is unbearable and he has to cut away the material, I'm as jumpy as a cut snake, ma'am, and I can't sit at the wheel a second longer, bejesus, oh quick.

Rebecca extends an arm over the broad shoulders and mobilizes the house: her husband's summonsed from his office garage to find a spare pair of trousers and a belt to snug them tight and her daughter's shunted to a chair in a kitchen corner and she hands over her cotton-clotted dressmaking shears and the man slices at the recalcitrant fabric right there in the room, hacking it away before Rebecca can usher him into the privacy of the bathroom and away from my greedy eyes.

The keg-thick thighs, the ropes of veins from the shoulders to the wrists, the bare heel on the chair rung, the sharp spread of bones in the foot, the water marks of grubbiness webbing the toes, the hip, Jesus-kinked, the soft bulge: my God, in such a short time I'm grabbing so much. The energy of his galloped fire talk booming into the room and the clatter of his teacup and the gobble of a biscuit in one crumb-spewing bite and the left thumbnail oddly ridged like a piece of card folded and the faded, two-striped scar across his right cheek, blunt, as if fingernails have been arrested in a drag through the skin but they couldn't do such permanence and I'm fidgety with almost-asking but all shyness-stunted and not trusting that my voice could ever come smoothly out.

His abrupt stand, the grate of his protesting chair, his suddenly shy thank you and kissing of Rebecca's hand. And then the turn, the assessing nod in farewell.

Are you free for the next fifty years?

The smile with dirt in it and his eyes telling me secrets and I feel wanted, sexually, for the first time, I can feel it deep in my belly, twisting it up, and in that moment I'm putty, lost. A deep flush is pluming under my skin and my voice is sapped when I want to say goodbye and see you again and could you tell me please how you got those scars. My mother notices the new shy-clam and laughs it aside, she playfully pushes the visitor out and hands him his shredded trousers which I want to keep and smell and touch and doesn't she know it, that I want them so much?

Give them to your mother, for her scrapbox, it's all they're good for now.

Why thank you, ma'am.

Or maybe I've just made that line up.

And there I am speeding to my room two steps at a time, lingering the sight of his going, watching his truck scattering its dust until it dips over the hilled horizon and is gone. I've dreamed for so long of someone who'll ride clean into my world knowing nothing of my past and yet I don't even have a proper name, just Bucky, a nickname, and some God knows, faraway town. Fuck.

Ed closes the library and no one complains for the imagined fate of her tinderbox flock is vivid in faces as books are hurried back. Her visits to our home increase for the town's shedding its people, many of the men have been called into fire service and her local's wilting with just the diehard dregs.

All my young boys have gone off.

Rebecca welcomes the increased coming, pleased to have a fresh pair of shoulders to work on and she uses the kneading times as an oil for her thoughts. I sit on the step just as I used to as a child and listen in secret to their talk: I've got to get her away, as she thumbs Ed's shoulders, I just don't know how to do it. She told me about the visitor. Mm, there's a fuse under her skin and it's ready to blow, God help us, and my mother's all newly tight.

Ow, Bec!

Sorry, love, sorry. I'm just not myself these days.

*

45

The paint-spattered trannie in the kitchen jabbers talkback and wind experts and extra news bulletins and prayer and then there's the flash that four volunteer fireman have been found huddled, charred, by the side of their blackened skeleton of a truck and the station sombres down and I stay close by the talk for a full nine hours until the details are announced – name, age, marital status, town – and sit back, smiling, it's not him.

It's all still possible.

The pips of the news mark our days and rain prayers increase as does the weight of Tiriel's stare at far hills and his cursing now slipping out quick.

Jesus Christ, Bec, I've got a business to run, we're not going any-where.

His mantraed phrase and yet every day now there's the startling sun, a fluorescent orange disc like an apocalyptic moon amid a dirty smudge of ash-cloud and then one morning the birds are all quiet and there's a black sky, death black, it's as if the day itself has shut down. Flames have claimed the Bony foothills and the scurrying intensifies and Sunshine's country fire brigade is put on alert.

God, I love the smell of smoke, I'm saying to Ed, pushing wide every window and holding my face to a sky all festive with ash. It's my favourite, I'm laughing, it's up there with the smell of cut grass and jasmine at sunset and horses and dirt after rain. Isn't it wonderful? Imagine this all burnt down, and everything gone and all of us somewhere else, and then something's shutting down in my face, I'm stopping abrupt for there's some code of behaviour I'm sensing has been transgressed. Ed is all stiff and arm-crossed at the table and I'm cottoning on to some way I'm meant to be, discreet, polite, demure, not a threat, like that meek flower name that was long ago meant to girl me down.

You've got to learn to fit in with the rest of us, Lil, you do it all wrong.

And I'm leaning on my elbows and thrusting a smile into her space.

*

Sure there's another deep-in-the-night visit for there's a stirring in my parents' bedroom and a door slams and I bolt to the window and catch the dark drinking pale skin, they're near the farm's gate, they haven't got close but they're there, they've come back. Another salute from my window, to what I don't know and one quiet, wolf-lonely howl to the night and then I flop back to the pillow, hating now this tunnelled life.

I've never thought seriously about running from it all, until now, I've never thought I could put my parents through it, until now. But how? I don't really know money or trains or the etiquette of hitching or smooth talk, I don't know any of that.

In a journal from that time is the story of an Englishman who ended up in a remote mountain village in Papua New Guinea in the 1930s, among people who'd never ventured from it. The Englishman had slashed an airstrip through the jungle and when it came time to leave a man from the village had cut vines from the trees and had lashed himself to the fuselage of the plane. Why? Because he had to see the place where the plane came from.

But I don't know where to begin.

The Shiners that are left wait jittery, eyes narrow to the sky and wet fingers to stained wind and finally, after four days of blazes skipping and roaring across the plains and exploding the trees and licking at the mountain foot there's the build-up of a storm in the air, there's a festering cloud all weighted with dirt and smoke.

Brown Dog is in the back of Tiriel's pickup when the first lightning strikes and she's spooked by it and leaps out and is hung by her collar. It's not a good sign, Tiriel says, weighed down, rushing her into his arms and bringing her inside and laying her gently on the kitchen table and stroking and stroking her flappy ear, his fingers searching the crevices for ticks just as he's always done, every Sunday night, for the past thirteen years.

It's not a good sign, it's not a good sign. Over and over.

*

I stop talk. It's all the protest I have left. Remembering the eight-year-old and the superglued skin, remembering the magnificent stew, the control, the discipline of it.

The storm cracks the back of the heat and the earth sighs, it rains for three days in great blustery wallops and I open my windows wide and come down to meals damp and voice-sucked and by the end of that raining Rebecca's resolved a way out.

Because I can't live like this any longer, she says to Tiriel, after another day of hedged daughter, her knuckles propping her temples and pressing them tight – it has to stop, it has to – and only then does he realize how nerve-frayed his wife has become. Rebecca's dared to imagine a solution she never has before, it's fallen over her suddenly and it will not be shaken loose by a husband who resolutely does not want a bar of it: it's too far and too odd and will never work. Rebecca's father has a house with a spare room in England. It'll only be for six months. It's a way out, yes a shaky one, but it's enough.

I've been driven into this, Til. There's no other way.

Digging in her heels like a horse with its hoofs firm and ears flat, no matter how hard the rope is tugged.

The relationship is remote. I hardly know anything about my grandfather, can barely imagine him. He detests flying and has only visited Sunshine once, before I was born, as the splendidly alone, sole paying passenger in the belly of a cargo ship. He'd vomited twenty-two times coming over and thirty-three going back and after the journey was completed he'd announced that he'd never subject himself to the ordeal again and his daughter, henceforth, was to come to him, sans scruffy husband and permanently, preferably. Rebecca never made it back. *I feel like I've lost a desire ever to come home, yes I'm homesick, of course, but I don't want to return.* The words were uncharacteristically blunt for a woman of Rebecca's tight upbringing for she'd changed since she arrived in the huge emptiness on the other side of the world, she'd found a voice with which to two-finger her past. Her father blamed the uncivilized land and the man with the funny wog name as he quoted King George the Sixth in return: *I don't like abroad. I've been there*, for he accepted without question the pronouncement of the great explorer, Cecil Rhodes, that to have been born in his own country was to have drawn first prize in the lottery of life, and what madness was there in ever wanting it left?

Rebecca, one rain-flogged afternoon, had made up her mind to give her daughter a chance at that lottery, to finally grow her up away from the blot of her past. Her father had a house with a spare room and it wasn't in Sunshine and her mind was made up, no ifs, no buts.

Wh-what about you two?

Talk knocked from me by the shock and I'm trying to corral scattering thoughts. My father looks knotted and my mother takes over with firm palms on my shoulders and says they'll be staying behind to keep a hand on the business and give me some breathing space. It's the best trial run that they can think of for they've racked their brains and it'll never work in Sunshine, there's too much past, but it might just work in that land I've read about all my life, whose God I've worshipped and whose history I've studied and whose books I've read to a much greater extent than any from my own land.

Why didn't you do it in the first place?

Well, I couldn't lump him with the responsibility of looking after a child, but you're an adult now, and there's a challenge in Rebecca's tone and her fingers are soothing, she's saying, Hey, it won't be such a jolt for it's the country that's done more than any other to shape me, the house that I live in and the food that I eat and the language that I speak.

I smile. There's no need for a soothing. I'm soaring.

The unknown factor is the grandfather.

Well, it's been a long time since he's had young people around him, says Rebecca, but there's my sister to shield you from the worst.

It's hard to get a firm picture and Ed doesn't think it's at all promising but I'm laughing away any doubt. There's just one photograph, it's tinted the colour of tea and curling at the corners, it's of a middle-aged man standing stiffly beside an old teapot of a car that's all rounded and cosy and meek and the man's unsmiling, he looks excessively neat and so does the car and Rebecca says his name is Cedric and it matches the shot.

I'll call him Ced.

I'm not sure he'll go for that, chick.

He can teach me to drive.

I'm not sure about that either.

The letter to England is composed over several nights and draft six is kissed at its sealing in cross-fingered hope, so achingly desperate am I for my life to begin. And then days laze into a week and then another and finally a flimsy oblong arrives with a stamp of a stern queen, perfectly set, and I'm running all the way home from the far letterbox and two-thirds of the way there I'm caught short by a stitch and then I'm hobbling the rest of the way and slapping the letter into Rebecca's hand, can't talk, no breath, open it, quick, *quick*.

Immaculate copperplate, museum-looped.

Cedric Henderson would be delighted to meet his only grand-child, he understands absolutely Rebecca's terms and will follow them to the letter of the law and there's nothing of the man in his two sentences and nothing in his sign off, *best*. We pass around the tissue-light sheet of paper and tears prick the eyes of all three of us, for different reasons.

A new purpose sings through my mother's days: she clears her scarred suitcase of silverfish and dust and writes off for a passport application and airs her one London coat and orders thermal under-wear and in the midst of it, absently, kneads the whirls from my shoulders and talks thought. Tries to tell me something of her past but it's rusted up too much and fragments are all I get. A loathed school, a lawyer of a sister and a garden-loving father determined to give them his best, who's excessively punctual, and neat.

Oh great.

He's a man who's never been known to say um. My sister and I always used to try to catch him out.

I laugh and backhand my mother on the shoulder, it tells me nothing and there must be more, the house perhaps, what's it like? It's very odd, Rebecca says, and very English, in the middle of a big estate and no gawping, miss. He's a humble man, with no money himself, and there's haste in her voice and a sudden clamp. I must warn you that he's always found people from here a little, ah, uncivilized, sort of clumsy and forceful and loud. He never took to your father's accent, or my moving here, or the sun.

Gosh, should I be terrified?

Just brave, chick, because fortune favours the brave.

A kiss on my crown and the massage is done.

So there that young Lillie was, all her days newly oiled as the departure drew close, all her joy geyser-high and the fireman as good as forgotten. The questions at Ed accelerated: can you see the stars from a plane? Are there Brown Dogs in England? Can I go to a car wash there, do you think? I wonder what it's like, seventy-two, being so old? But her mentor's Jackie-O shine was diminishing for she'd never left Sunshine despite all her talk, had never stepped onto a plane herself. She dwelt between the pages of gossip magazines and furnished an entire dream existence from mail-order catalogues and I could see, suddenly, the limitations of that, could feel a cooling off.

Daily my hands fevered the rich coffee colouring of Rebecca's leather suitcase, the creaky handle on its last legs, the patches snug on the corners relishing their anointed task, the crude stitching, the brass locks. I spoke my plans to the bewildered sheep, dived into the dress-up trunk and sifted out the best and talked of my dreams with a slightly pinched Paul McGall. My ambition was to live in a cigarette ad, to be as glamorous and carefree as that; never wanting home, a life lived in hotels and Paul McGall utterly disapproved, of course.

It's only provisional, Tiriel said one night, stroking my cheek, don't forget that a ticket home early is only a phone call away, and it was as if he was stamping my skin with the memory of his touch. I smiled, already broken from him, and said that my mother had told me I should be as brave as I could, stirring them both up. Rebecca raised her eyes to the heavens and crumpled a besieged grin.

God help us, my father sighed.

At the age of eight he'd mowed his suburban front lawn for the very first time after a letter from the council requested the Birds to do so, for there was a possibility that the young queen's cavalcade would pass down their street on the way to the opening of a university. She was on one of her royal tours to the far-flung colonies, it happened every decade or so. She never did pass that street but Tiriel never forgot and he was branded by the fervour of that time, from then on he'd collected England's stamps and watched its royal pageants and read his *Magnets* and *Gems* and dreamed of visiting it once. England *was* lottery's first prize, he knew that, the opportunity of a lifetime for any man's child, except his. For he'd never expected the Motherland on the edge of the world to one day swallow up his beloved hothouse daughter alone, and gnawed by worry he could hardly bear the thought.

What I knew then of my mother's past: a well-spoken young woman had one day come to her adopted land as the house-guest of farmers whose holdings stretched the length of a small European country, but she'd never seen it and never gone home for she'd fallen hurtlingly in love with the blare of the sun and a lope of a man who took dope in the evenings like another man would a whisky after a hard day's work, except he did no work. A man who lived in the peeling dampness of inner-city squats, who couldn't catch the right work, who was lost. Her family were horrified by the mire of the situation, they threatened and cajoled but she was heel-dug too deep.

Her vocation, she discovered, was reparation, she was fierce with the will to fix people up and her strong, speaking fingers became her tools. But Tiriel was driven ragged with the thought of his pale lover kneading and soothing other men's skin, day in and day out, in the line of her work.

I always imagine what it would be like, with every single man that I work on.

She'd let it slip once in a soft silliness coming over her during a sun-smeared picnic and a bottle of ragged wine and Tiriel didn't want others to get the chance. He feared that better, richer men would sniff his fairy-tale girl out and she would one day realize the diminished man he was, for he'd enchanted the traveller far from home and fed her the magic potion of experience and wonder and novelty and sex and he was terrified that one day she'd wake. His solution was to take her to a place so distracting, so ravishing, so unique, that she'd never want to go home.

He'd heard of a place, high up in granite country, a town so removed and insular that urban myth spoke of locals placing boulders in the middle of the approach road to warn visitors about getting too close. A community mysterious and bold with a moral code and as luck had it, needing a journalist to catalogue its days. All the locals wanted was a local product sustained and the last of his bride's stout English pounds would buoy the sagging business and a deal was swiftly done with few questions asked. It was obvious to the Contenders – the young newly-weds were searching for some ballast, they were lost, the city had become too noisy to work in, that was their explanation, they were looking for some quiet and the Shiners trusted that.

The last leg of the old Tanner Road into town was splintered and potholed and soft at its sides and the growl was explicit – leave us alone. The young Englishwoman had never climbed so dizzily high, the tarmac was a thin and reluctant ribbon through the density but then it all finally softened into a magical, cleared land gently brushed at its pate by low clouds. They got out of their car, breathed in air so thin it made them giddy with joy and Rebecca jumped onto the back of her sexy new husband and he spun her around and they looked across to the tops of other mountains and to the puffballs of clouds and to a village nestled in a fold of the crest and Tiriel said that he wanted to stay there for ever and never come out. They'd found a fugitive place on the top of the world and Rebecca, all flushed with the silky softness of just-married love, felt as if a great calm had bloomed over her and Tiriel felt a thrill of purpose for the first time in his life.

His mind was jumpy with dreams, for he'd dragged himself out of the unfocused, unemployed clot he'd got himself into in the city and he had a new addiction, Rebecca, that he had to hold on to. Sunshine was the perfect drying-out place, scrubbed of temptation and straight-backed. The flush of her love had made Rebecca willing to follow him to Bony Mountain, on one condition, that Tiriel came clean. And so she turned a large part of her professional attention to the knots and neglect in his body and it became her life-work. She was always looking for sick people to mend, she was a lay doctor, a hand healer, she needed the maimed to give a prop to her own life.

The only reminder of her husband's ragged former life was a battered silver wedding band worn stubbornly on his right thumb. A Shiner whisper: that the ceremony had never actually taken place for the ring placement was too strange. A Shiner whisper: that Rebecca was lapsed nobility, all because of the vowels in the voice. When I asked her once, willing it to be so, she ruffled my hair and laughed and said if I wanted it to be, then yes, chick, of course.

Ed visited on one of the last afternoons before I left, I remember sitting on the high 40s bed in my room of vivid oranges and reds and listening to her declaration that I lived differently from the rest of them, that if I was ever forced to live normally, or dully, or frugally I'd be somehow flattened, I wouldn't cope, remember that.

Oh rubbish! You're full of it, woman.

A pillow was thrown and my mother's suitcase between us was

a gutted fish on the wharf of the bed, spilling its petticoats and jumpers and dreams and in the room was the clean, child-aroma of graphite from all the pencils I wrote with and the smell of creativity, of books and paper and breeze and Ed leant back with her palms cradling her head, bemused and staring and cat-still.

What are you thinking, Edie-Ed? Huh?

But she wouldn't say. Because she couldn't, then, but she told me years later that I carried on that day, drum-tight under my skin, a buoyancy and an optimism that almost burst from me and there was something else too: the magical power of virginity, the strange elixir that could empower a young woman's weakness and make her unhindered and cheeky and boisterous and sure. She'd seen it also in some older women who've settled on celibacy and are comfortable with that choice but she couldn't speak of any of that yet, I was too innocent for it, she didn't want it pointed out.

At twenty-one I was this exceedingly odd young woman who absorbed the male gaze and stared straight back, my mother told me that, she'd seen it with the visiting fireman and with the men on the city streets and God knew what was ahead and the three adults in my life feared it so. I learned years later that Ed wanted to go with me on that trip, to shield me and to experience something of a life not caught by fear and a life not travelled along the highways of certainty, but the courage never came.

So there that young Lillie is, walking with Tiriel in companionable silence on her last morning on the farm and looking down as always and smiling at the memory of childhood instructions now ingrained: always look out for snakes, keep your eyes to the ground. She's staring at the wind-scorched land and breathing in deep the scent of dirt scraped off by the breeze and scrutinizing her father with new, leaving eyes, a man utterly without scorn and she's loving him for that, for the integrity that glows softly in him. But he's weakening, his stomach is becoming vulnerable and his face is falling into hollows and it's snagging at her joy. Come home in one piece, kiddo, he's saying, tweaking the warm lobe of her ear.

I'll be OK, you don't have to worry, you know.

Your mother says that too, she's really pushing this, God knows why.

The entire record of Lillie's captive years has been stored over the previous fortnight in an old lift-top freezer used for sheep bits in the shearing shed, all twelve of her journals, as well as scrapbooks and sketchpads, are stacked by the frozen ribs and shanks. For she's heard on the radio that fridges are the safest place to preserve things, that they withstand bush fires and cyclones and floods and atomic blasts and on that last afternoon she tells Tiriel of the stash. His face puckers, he sucks up the fold of his bottom lip and looks across his land.

Jesus, Lil, everything since the fire?

Yep.

They really mean that much to you?

Yep, and a pause. They're my fuel.

For what?

A book.

You want to write?

One day.

Oh, love, waste of time that.

And the dismissal burns in Lillie and something is hardened, there's a determination from that point and she knows in her heart that she will one day write of him. Who was it who said that every writer has in them a chip of ice? On that last morning it was just a question of when the betraying would begin, of when the story would be enough.

I'm bagsing the opening of the front gate for the car to pass through, it's the first time I've done it since I was thirteen and I hook the arch of my feet in the bottom rung and go to swing on it just as I used to as a child but the gate bogs under my weight, the swing holds stubbornly in the ground's grate and my parents clap their hands and roll their eyes and yell that I'm sacked. And the laughter-filled car drives from my past up a nave of whispering trees and there's a mosaic of moving shadow on the road's dusty floor and every few minutes I shudder with a bone-deep excitement, my arms crossed at my stomach and holding tight my glee. I scrutinize the next-door neighbour's yard, it's always cluttery with junk, the mess around the house is like a lily-pad skirting a bloom and the barking dog's gone that never wants to get out of its car but nothing else has changed except for a spray-painted sign above a crooked basketball hoop on the garage wall – *I bet you miss* – and I point to it and laugh.

I haven't noticed that for years.

Rebecca, returning to the plastic folder protecting the air ticket that's winging me into a glorious unknown. To my mother, the folder's newness smells of low skies and duty and endurance; to me, childhood Christmases and the plastic of fresh toys. Dust from the road hangs among the trees like smoke and the light through the branches dapples the lane in zebra shadows, flicking brightness across our vision. The dust has colonized the dashboard and windows of the car and I draw smiley faces in it and huge, mad flowers and graffiti my name, thumbing it at them all, can't resist.

The car passes lines of tin mailboxes, 44-gallon drums on their sides, some with suburban letter boxes perched jaunty in their hollowed insides and I promise to fill ours often as I look back to the farm and the rocks like sentinels on the hills, the huge grey boulders fiercely guarding the land. Ahead, a fallen tree is lying across the road and we get out and cup our arms under its bulk and lift the trunk out of the way and walk back to the car arm in arm in silence in the fading light, me in the middle and the quiet of my parents is settled and reflective and I try to trap the feel of their arms, want it vivid with me, that strong holding and concern and trust.

My fingers trail stiffly out the open car window, sifting the breeze, its rush and its scent. We drive over a knobbly wooden bridge whose wooden beams clank and shift under the car's weight and wind down the mountain until the road levels out and for half an hour follow the frolicking of the river that rushes headlong into the bash of the sea.

Gee, the run of the river's strong today.

Tiriel, from a deep thinking.

It's just on nightfall, there's the first star and I'm lying on my back along the length of the rear seat and watching its shadowing of the swift car and then others are coming, a few then so many all splashed across the Big Top of the sky and I'm dreamily smiling. For Brother Sleet and Ed have been told of my going and sworn to secrecy and they've been assured that in six months' time I'll return, changed, rehabilitated, even cured, my father has promised, but Ed has said to me that he doesn't believe it, his eye-fidget has told her and I'm holding that detail close.

On that last day I was given an envelope made of handmade paper and threaded to strength with fibre-slivers from the land. Inside was a spindly, silver-grey leaf and a short note of farewell. My mother had instructed me to crush the leaf and smell it if ever I got too homesick, she wrote that nestled in the paper's fibres were the threads of all that held me to my land. In the backward-slanting handwriting that twenty-five years later still bore the marks of a schoolgirl's obedience Rebecca had concluded with an Auden quote: *to be free is often to be lonely. Don't forget to come back to us,* she'd written, and you know, little one, I carried that letter and leaf close by me for years, until one day they were sent home and shut away in the sheep freezer, snap-frozen and bled of all smell.

After a night of frugal sleep in a motel on the capital's edge there we are, at last, driving through the early morning city with me all shuddery with excitement at the cars' nervy, agitated freeway-dance.
Here we are! Look!
As the lights of the airport are approached and I'm blowing through a flutter of soft finger wings at the sight of those tall planes close to the fence, those high, hungry birds with their beady eyes. I was the hungriest of travellers back then, it was whisky to me, cigarettes, coffee, speed, the only drug that I wanted.
And men.

−4−

Can You Imagine
My Parents Allowing Me
to Travel By Myself?

Me neither.

Every leg of the new alone had been meticulously plotted. The going was to coincide with a business trip of an old friend of my mother's, he'd met her sister years ago at a party and gradually befriended the whole family. It took months of preparation to cage the details and there was no room, anywhere, for slippage, oh no, my parents had seen to that.

His name was Richard Daunt. He was tall and thin within immaculately cut suits and he favoured slim, chocolate-brown cigarettes that jutted up jaunty at right angles between his second and third fingers. I was intrigued at that, would practise with a pencil in my room, cross my legs and lean back and grin secrets only I was aware of. For there was a twinkle in Richard's eye at some game he was always playing, a bemused upturn to his lips, he had a silvery glide to his walk and he leant backwards a little as if keeping the world at a distance and I loved the containment in that. He'd only sparsely sparkled into my growing up on weekend diversions from trips to the colonies, his tease of a voice filling our hallway as he stepped into the house – hello, wake up, party time – his arms cradling exotic tomatoes and squat pâté pots, and I would clatter to the kitchen and drink in his stories of a vivid other-world where butlers remembered ironing shoelaces and the class system even extended to the post. Faithfully I recorded all the talk: the premium gin, the timed local calls, the church bells on Sundays and the endless queues and I'd lean forward at the table, brimming with questions, but he'd barely see me for child-friendly he was not. His eyes and his chat were only for my mother, his dear, bonkers chum. Tiriel could hardly bear it, would always make himself busy with something pressing in his garage office. But nothing would tug me from that kitchen table, there was too much to be absorbed. The long hands, slivers of pale meat from the sharpness of his suits, and the stiff cuffs already nibbled by dirt and yet the nails clean, softly so, and it all seemed so wrong in our sky-drenched place. And when he left his presence clung to the kitchen, it didn't want to budge, for the smoke of his cigarettes would nestle into corners and even now just a whiff floats me back.

Richard Daunt was an institution boy made good, a slip of a kid who at thirteen had hauled himself out of a grim London orphanage and onto a cheap-passage scheme to the New World, had knuckled his way into university and then home and had been based silkily back in the city of his birth for three decades. He was greatly respected, newspaper-profiled, a much called upon public man. The headhunter's quarry who specialised in revitalizing tired but cherished national museums around the world, the genius at whittling businesses and prodding them into competitive life.

He doesn't know how to spell properly, or love, my mother told me once, in the sudden new silence after he'd gone. He never learned either as a child, bless.

The polished city ways had for a long time been a dreamed-of way out: *Richard Daunt, a heroine's match*, at fifteen I wrote, don't laugh. Oh, I had fantasies, they were extraordinarily vivid and startlingly pornographic if obscure on the details and that smooth London man was always at their heart. Tiriel, of course, would never have agreed to the chaperoning if he'd known. Rebecca had insisted and I'm still not sure what to make of that for her watching eyes never missed much.

All I could ever push into the banter between my mother and her guest were lame yeahs and soft wows for my questions were always snuffed by Rebecca's competitive glow. Back in my room I'd mimic Richard's vowels: I knew he'd bashed at his accent until it conformed, had cleansed it of any trace of its gnarly roots and I'd whisper to Paul McGall the strange, deformed words, the lengthened *year*, the shortened *room*, the curt *garage* and file them away for some future use, and dream a way out.

Richard is explaining to Tiriel that he's just finished with the national gallery of one of the world's biggest democracies and So a young lady from the bush is a piece of cake and all she'll need is a bit of sandpapering around the edges, eh, smiling at me like I'm all of six but for once in my life I'm not paying him rapt attention. There's competition, I'm galumphed into silence by the buzzy steel and glass airport that's soaring like a cathedral around me, I'm slowly spinning with my head thrown back to the far roof for in one daze of a morning I'm feeling as if all the stillness bottled up in me for so long is being wiped like a computer methodically deleting its files. This is urban energy, this is life, and the light of it is so wonderfully white! Tiriel reaches to my shoulder and Rebecca is smiling odd with the wrong muscles, and all I want is to slip off my shoes and feel the pale, cool marble under my feet, all I want is to run back to the tall windows and watch the planes tilting and climbing and dropping and queuing in their lovely synchronicity of landing and leaving. My father clutches his novel to his chest like a bibled preacher, subdued, disapproving, softly lost, and the flight flashes it's boarding and I squeal and clap my hands in delight.

Come on, young lady.

Richard holds out his arm and I forget to turn back to my parents and wave a final goodbye and when I remember I run to the gate but glimpse them too far and too gone and old suddenly, their arms tight around each other as if they're propping each other up and I smile for they're well and truly inland people now, it's deep in their walk.

He tells me that our paths will not cross on the flight. He tells me he has a deadline, he's in first class and I'm in economy and he has a lot of work to do and a lot of sleep to catch up on and the sting of my shaking-off is buried in a flung smile: so, my status is stumped from the start, a kid, hardly worth a look, and what a challenge is in that! I'm left in the snaking, slow boarding queue while Richard smoothes through his quickly and then he's gone and for the first time in my life I feel completely alone and look around and no one's looking back and I taste the personal space and begin to soar.

The magazine's densely worded, it's in a foreign language and rigorously unpictured and the hand that holds it is olive-smooth and marriage-ringed and I want to touch it, can hardly stop the reach. There's a stale, slightly nervous male smell as I squeeze across to my seat. On my other side is an elderly woman with a white cardigan and spun purple hair and heartbreaking pencil for eyebrows, someone who looks obviously married and for many years and yet there's no ring on her finger and I wonder at the story in that.

I follow the woman's buckling and there's a wide looking and rigorous checking of the seat pocket down to the vomit bag, I'm souveniring that, and I run my hands again and again along the seatbelt and armrest buttons and even the steward one but dammit, they never come. All the new lives, all the new stories ahead and beginning with new skin close, olive and crêped and aftershaved and powdered, for I haven't experienced much of any of that.

The plane judders like the inside of a washing machine and I grip the armrests, I'm sure that the engines can't get any louder without going bang but they do and I close my eyes and pray, knuckles white-capped, for I feel as if I've left my eardrums behind and my stomach somewhere in the tail and then the plane climbs high over the just-waking city in the soft morning air and I sense the cabin collectively relaxing from a clenching. Below us is the grey body of the metropolis with its veins of car lights as the workers scurry into their day, and as the plane leaves the land and climbs across the water there's just a faint outline of a toy jumbo, a shadow gliding across the sea and then it climbs higher and there is land again and the world becomes a satellite map and the shadow is lost.

We'll have to tidy you up a bit, says Richard, suddenly behind me on a transit stop and holding out a lank curl of hair as if it smells, I'm not sure that they'll let you into my country. I'm not sure about you either, mate, I bounce back, you're looking a bit creased, and my smile arrests his talk and there I am as startled as him, for scrubbed of my father's swaddling and my mother's keen watching I've found something resembling Rebecca's adult bantering. Over the years I've absorbed it and I can feel myself slipping into the shiny new shoes of a public way, shoes secretly boxed in my room for so long, for just such a day.

So on that very first flight there Lillie is, looking down at a desert of sand stretching as far as she can see but it's cloud, endless cloud, and she can barely imagine what she'll be stepping into. A crammed island nestling under cloud and continually spat at from a sweep of cold ocean, a continent where the dynamic is between people and architecture as opposed to people and the land. She knows it's wrong to expect trees and wide skies and the bush encroaching with any boldness upon her new cities, she's read that, for it's the creation of a new landscape, not of mountains or deserts or plains but of architecture, a forest of things. She's almost drunk with expectation.

The first London glimpse.
   A city sullen under the thumb of a low, bloated sky. The River Thames is a vein from an old man's temple and then a picture postcard shot of the Tower Bridge arcs into view and I shiver at the delight of being a foreigner in this place, can a local ever know the deliciousness of that? The plane flirts with England with a ragged tripping of bumps and solidly connects with my shiny new, God-knows life.
   The hit of a strange country, the smack of its smell pushes at me in the corridors of the airport. It's a feeling of being hemmed

in by low ceilings and the smell of dampness and, somewhere, unwashed towels and I can't wipe the shock of that first smell-assault of stale carpet and windows never opened, and in my lion of a new land! I wasn't expecting it, or the too few customs officials behind too few counters, bereft of country-pride. There's a multicoloured queue of people from all corners of the globe and a frustrated energy around me but I'm smiling and my eyes are greedy with the sights, all the craning waiting and shuffling and sighing because already I'm feeling intoxicated by London, fluid and confident and bright.

I'll see you out there, mouths Richard as he sweeps by in the lane for the continent's own people and a chuckle comes over me that will not go away: at being slingshotted so painlessly into a wondrous new life, at being left to my own devices at last.

So Lillie's lugging with gusto Rebecca's battered old case from the carousel with her dreamed-of man, her Richard stepping in front of her, a neat suit bag from his shoulder.

Let me, he's saying.

No it's fine, I can do it.

And for the second time there's his startled stopping as she takes the case from him, rejoicing in the sudden, bossy freedom that's come into her now that she's out from under home's weight, now that she can do exactly what she wants. Richard steps back and offers no more assistance, just appraises, nods, smiles. Her hands are full of traveller's cheques and suitcase and shoulder bag and a hair tendril flops in front of her face and she tries to fluff it away and as Richard tucks it behind her ear, fatherly firm, Lillie feels a tugging in her belly, a soft twist, and she knows that from now on whatever mistakes she makes will be hers and no one else's, for she's finally striding into a future that she owns. An adult grin to Richard, and she's not sure where it's come from.

Outside, the flinch of the cold. The light mealy, thin like gruel, and I can't read the sky for it hangs like the water-bowed ceiling of an old house. Richard lights a cigarette and becomes someone else, someone louche and almost feminine and I tell him this and he smiles like a teenager and hands the cigarette across: one hurting rasp and too much cough, too fast.

A car slides to us, shiny black and panther-low, and Richard opens a door and I puppy-scramble into the soft, moneyed creak of its leather. We pull away from the airport melee in a glide of heated quiet that's only broken by my squealing. The streets are reluctant from rain and clotted by traffic and there's greyness and flyovers and indifferent concrete blocks, there's stop-start tetchiness and cabbies waving to cabbies and shrill beeps and always the brooding sky, close, and from the stereo comes a voice with a moan like jagged tin cutting skin and I ask for it louder and who it is.

A woman called Nina Simone. Mad, but wonderful.

The name's jotted down, and somewhere in there he's telling me I'm like an empty canvas just waiting to be filled up and again, there's my adult grin.

We're driven straight to his office, there's no time for lingering and I despair at the flit of this London arrival, the brief snatch from the car window and that's it.

Oh please! Just a little tour, we'll be quick, it won't take long, *please!*

No. Don't blame me, blame the traffic. You'll just have to come back some time.

Oh *yes. Soon!*

The watermelon-split of my smiling.

Greedily I stare out at that new world with both palms pressed to the car window, stare at the sea of heads on footpaths and the people threading between stilled cars and gliding off the backs of buses like practised ballerinas and holding cupped palms for coins and thrusting umbrella sticks at taxis and deep in mobile talk and I imagine myself striding through it, long for that. Stare at streaks of grime and scrawls of graffiti and herdings of rubbish by old, tired doors and the smiling will not be wiped, for in twenty-four hours the whole tone of my living has been grubbied, gloriously so.

What do you think? Richard asks, bemused. Catching the blur of a phone-box row, the colour the scarlet of the energy of the place and telling him I adore it, why, because it's such a red city, the buses and those old phone boxes and the Great Fire and the mail boxes and what are those, poppies on lapels, yes those too and the bombs from the Blitz and even that woman, she's striding with her pregnancy before her like a galleon in full sail, robust and proud and complete and her hair's a fiery red and it's wonderful, all wonderful and oh my goodness I'm going to cry, just to be here at last, it's too much! Yes, he laughs, London has the whole of life in it, and I'm telling him I'd be happy to stay in it for ever and when can I come back, when does he think? He looks at me coolly, says I only have twenty minutes left and I spark, confident, that I'll see it all eventually and he says that he certainly hasn't and won't in his lifetime for it changes all the time but his motto is never relax and it should be mine too, he tries to live by it but a lot of the time fails. Then you're just being lazy, I laugh and he puts his head to one side and contemplates, as if he's a doctor scrutinizing me for service on the front, and he breaks into his trademark smile and tells me that I have the makings of a great character.

Why?

Because, Miss Bird, you have such an appetite for life.

Oh yes! I have to experience as much of it as I can.

Richard's smile gentles and he says that he has too much stimulation now and all that he longs for is some quiet. So what's *your* goal then? I ask.

To make as much money as I can.

But that's horrible, it's so lonely, you poor thing!

Momentary shock.

The first lesson you must learn, Miss Bird, is that in this country you must never, ever say what you think.

We'll see about that!

Laughing and laughing at that.

*

As I look out of the car window at the wonder of this land I'm thinking of a French king I read about once who'd wandered the cities of Europe wearing a mask and when he arrived in Venice he was so overwhelmed by its voluptuousness that he was never quite the same again and lived his life from then on in a daze. And as I look out at the wonder of this grubby, growly giant of a place I'm thinking of my own mask in it, a mask of utter anonymity for the very first time in my life and I'm thinking of how I, too, could be so overwhelmed by it that I'll never be the same again, dazzled so much by the new.

An air-kiss too soon on both cheeks in farewell and stiffly, like a pony, I jerk back. It's the way it's done here, hold still and Richard takes off my glasses and repeats the two kisses, slower and touching and teaching this time and holding down my skittery hands, clamming them tight. There's the whisper of skin and the grate of stubble and at his drawing back I'm blushing with both palms pressed to my cheeks, trying to stifle the heat.

You'll learn.

I hope so.

Ah, but I hope not.

My blooming heat once again and he loops another stray bit of hair behind my ear and tells me, matter-of-fact, that I'm really quite beautiful, as if he's only just noticed, and his words are as potent as a first kiss and I busy myself with my bags, all tongue-tied, hiding my face and my singing heart for no one has ever told me that.

I've hardly noticed you before under all that mountain dirt. I'd like to see you again, I know it's naughty but I would.

He puts my glasses back on and my fingers brush his at my ears and spring back.

Yeah, me too.

Inwardly wincing at the lameness of my too-young response but oh, such a day!

*

67

Thunder thumps across the city like a series of bombs being dropped and the sky is closing in as I turn to catch the last sights of London and Richard's personal assistant is telling me that I look too healthy to be from this part of the world and I'm trying to listen and respond and look, to grab as much as I can.

You're a great strapping Amazon, look, twice my height! Richard told me you were a wee little lass who'd barely stepped across your doorstep your whole life.

I smile, that's not far off, but I can't quite get it out, don't know the new person well enough yet. I still belong more to silence than to talk, I'm not quite ready for strangers but my eyes gulp the new woman up. The dyed red hair that ineffectually covers a recalcitrant grey and startlingly pruned vowels and a flap of clothes that are glaring against Richard's crispness. Her hands are rawly red as if they've been stained by years of scrubbing, bruising work and most of her fingers are heavily ringed, blurring her marital status. Her name is Constance Ledderman and she's to accompany me on the journey to my new home, my parents have insisted, and as the car slides from the curb I wave a furious farewell but Richard's already turned, his back's swallowed by the traffic, he's gone.

I slump in the seat and smile and hold my hands to my cheeks for God knows when I'll be kissed next and my palms hold that kiss in. It's a start, I'm off.

I heard the other day, Lillie, that I should be saying to foreigners I'm from Yorkshire rather than England. They'd like me then, they'd think I was cute.

But I-I like you wherever you're from.

A place called Little Broom, just out of London, and I take out my word book and jot down its loveliness and then as I wait for Constance to cram in a last cigarette I squat on my suitcase in a glass-roofed train terminal of pigeons and people and write out my exhilaration to be finally in the land that's been the subject of the world's collective envy for so long. And write that I have, perhaps,

68

a softly hooked man, my presence now like pollen gently on his skin and over time I'll make it grow.

The train hums away from the platform and gathers into speed and it doesn't sound train enough, it's not a clacket but a glide and I marvel at that, I've been cheated of trains from books, they must have all gone. This new train curves and crosses and weaves, it passes fat graffiti letters proclaiming their victory in difficult places and a fret of broken windowpanes and the eyelids of towering council blocks but then swiftly-soon the scumble of railway yards and flats has dropped away to houses, meek rows upon rows, Dickensian in their breadth and brick and it gives me a sense of this suburb-walled city but then green has its say. I watch the city workers getting off at their commuter-belt stations, the mothers being greeted by children, the husbands by wives, the girlfriends by boyfriends and then a lone businessman cutting unseeing through it all with his briefcase his shield and I wonder at his return to his house, no it must be a flat, and sparse, and still. The train pulls away and I gulp the sight of this new countryside, so soft and quiet and fragile and tamed, so removed from my wind-scorched home.

ALL tickets, please. THANK you very much.

The staccato self-importance of the conductor crashes into the staring and I love the rhythm of the new voice, it's a thickly regional one and I'm ghosting the crusty vowels of it as he moves up the aisle with his chant. The train slows at nowhere and there's an announcement about leaves on the track and a wait of half an hour and Constance rolls her eyes and says, It happens every year, Victorian madness, don't ask.

Finally the train hums back into its glide and we pass a sliver of a village cleaving to a mountainside, a lace tracery of branches in winter trees, a ruin of a castle tower half claimed by ivy, winter trunks cold with their whiteness and then a beautiful, seven-arched railway bridge with curls of wire at either end and grass claiming its tracks and the impression I have is of a countryside abandoned for the rush of another place, a city whose energy I, too, want a blanketing in and God knows when now, or how. I wasn't expecting such an abrupt start. Tiriel's insistence, perhaps.

In a field, thorns devour a huddle of abandoned minis like a posse of spiders spinning their webs and a huge fallen branch from an oak tree splays like a sunbaker on the green, but there's no sun. Clouds congregate. *This rain-soaked land*, I write, watching the migration of rainfall across the fields and in antidote jotting a remembered scrap from a poem: *my days burn with the sun*. For all the days of my life so far have been scoured by the wind and the sun and here I am now, ready for immersion in a land of soft days, a land saturated in green. My mother had said on the day I left that she couldn't remember England having proper weather, just a steady, damp gentleness and I slip out her camera and snap the journey for us both, reminding her back.

Just about all I can remember from my trip are messy telegraph wires and untidy country towns and barbed wire, says Constance. Oh and bikers, lots of them.

It's not all like that, I say, finding a voice and blurting my surprise. Out the window the land glooms down and I can taste the dropping light, can feel the mist-hugged fields.

But all you women are meant to be tough.

Not all of us.

The girls were all big and athletic, I remember that.

I laugh, unfazed, and Constance laughs too and the train zooms on and the gloom rolls in and I don't know if it's night or a storm. A mist's bringing in the dark and there I am, turning back to the journal and snapshotting in words all the wonder of the day.

Expectation blazing under my skin, for I'm feeling as if all the leaden textures that have dulled my life for so long have been combusted into light under a varnisher's hand, I'm feeling lit from within.

–5–

Confession

There was a photograph of a house, I carried it with me to England, its horizon line was tilted and the building was weighty, like nothing from my own land, for the dimensions were too substantial and the foundations clung too deep to the earth. None of our people would build with such vision, or arrogance, or splendour, or folly – it was a house so broad that its facade seemed to gulp the horizon. The sky around it was close, grim, a howl and a paper fold cracked it clean down the centre. The colours were bleached of vividness and the shot was blurred, as if taken surreptitiously or while fleeing. I still have the photo, it's odd and ill-fitting above my desk, but for years it was snug in the back of my journals, its origin a mystery and its promise soaking my days.

It had been pilfered long ago from your grandmother's Japanese jewellery box of her secret other-life crammed under her bed. I was always searching for any slippage of her past, she'd often scoffed at the village rumours – *I'm poor, my father was a working man, you'll soon find that out* – but there was something in me that refused to accept for I'd always believed that money and status could haul me out and around my mother were tantalizing leakings of another life. One Saturday she was detained at her massage clinic at the back of Sunshine's only hairdressing salon and Tiriel was bogged in a far field with a chattery vet and a sickly ewe and I seized the chance: my hands were flit-panicky as they scrabbled among a tangle of necklaces and old watches and business cards and cotton, searching for clues, and then the photo was found and I had no idea where the building was or who might own it but I was enchanted from that day.

On the back, just one word. *Evendon*. The ink luxuriously nudged each side of the card and the loops of the script were as sinuous and stately as the whispered syllables on my tongue and I imagined it all in the roll of that one word: a spindly-legged colt of a table, a pen resting in crystalled ink, a room of luxurious windows and piggybacking paintings and walls made noble by vast ladders of bookshelves climbing to their sky. Paul McGall was intrigued, and I was obsessed.

The subject was never raised for I didn't want the sneak of the taking found out. Ed was my one outlet and she puckered her mouth and concluded it was a souvenir and of little significance, a visited country house or some such thing and my mother would have said something, silly, if it had ever been anything more. Yes, you're probably right, I'd answered, but the snap had been taken by an amateur and there was some private intimacy to it and my dreaming wasn't blunted one bit by Ed's talk, oh no, worse luck.

The Bird family had stood on the verandah the day before I left Sunshine and looked out across the bleached land and Rebecca had said to me, with an arm around my shoulder, that in a certain light a great house back in England that she knew of seemed to float on the green sea of its meadows, so lush it was. She didn't explain what it was but I was sure I knew, for the house in the stolen photograph had been like a stilled ship for so long, its dividend resting snug under my skin for so many waiting years.

I can't wait to get there.

Rebecca had laughed.

It's, well, gosh, it's a shrunken country now, it's not what it used to be.

But—

England is all trapped by the weight of its past, chick, you'll learn that pretty quick.

A scowl: I wanted that past, I wanted to play in history.

But hey, you'll be surprised by where Cedric lives, I'm not saying anything but you'll love it, I just know.

I'd dammed so many questions on that day, not wanting to sour the farewell with a confession from long ago. I'd find out the house's story for myself and I was confident I knew something of it already, for I'd imagined for so long the sun slanting from tall windows and laughter floating to the ceiling and an unruffled quiet and the smell of pleasure and the absence of dust. *Evendon, a heroine's house,* there it is in my journal, written when I was seventeen. My mother had said that my grandfather was a humble man, who lived simply, with one abiding passion, a great garden, and it was all enough to fit.

Come on, dreamboat, said Constance, reaching up for her bag as the train slowed to a halt. We're here.

The thrill, even then, my heart-skip.

The taxi bullets along runnels of narrow, high-hedged green and there's the driver's knobbly growl and the weather's wily and slippery and changing too much and I try to grab it all with the camera but it's going too fast. There's a short flurry of snow and then pregnant grey and brief rain and snow again and it's all in a fading day and my face is craned to the piebald sky with its slate and white and every different consistency of cloud and I gape at the mongrel oddness and greedily snap shots for there's God in that sky and I want it caught. The different colour, light, cold.

My fingers return again and again to my pocket and brush the photo in it, for Constance has asked the driver for *Evendon*, dictating haltingly from her notes and it's all snuggling into place. The taxi rounds a corner and before us is the sea and my ribcage widens and my heart expands at the sight of the beautiful, restless width of it. France is just across the water tosses the driver, they used to hear the bombs from the battlefields during the First World War and wow I say, listening to the curl in his accent, the strange sing of it and the practised boom to cut across the weather. Ahead of us hail or snow falls from a cloud like an old man's beard and already I'm loving this land and saying my wows too much.

The sky's all over the place this week, ladies, it's throwing a party, it must be for your arrival.

We laugh and I whoosh down the window to a rush of cold and stare at the sea and blink tears in the wind's snap. Another land, another language just across the horizon and new accents and new stories and men, all the men, and have I ever been happier? A corner's turned and there's a row of cottages crammed close to the road and a sullen shoebox of an old church with moss cramming the seams of its stone. The car slows.

Here we are, then.

Sitting back, mute. A wall that gives nothing away except a curmudgeonly desire to be left alone. Above it, a competition of too-tall trees. The car pushes on and after a very long time there are matching gatehouses busily flanking a tall set of gates, the buildings as intricate and ludicrous as two tiny palaces.

Crikey Moses, I say.

Chiselled letters are fading from the stone of the right-hand post and I lean, strain, *Evendon* of course, just, the seven squat letters, the dreamed-of word, and my thumb hooks my teeth – my mother, my God, the secrets she tucks! The driver winds down his window and drums the car's roof and I run my fingers along the photo's edge, rutting the skin of my thumb and the driver nods to his fat meter and says he's happy to sit there all day and he just hopes that our wallets are well stocked.

I leap out, swing a gate wide, chuckle at that symmetry with home. My footfall sponges, it's different with another country's soil and I read the soft land, assess it with rural eyes: not often scraped by the gate, uncherished, sparely used, the grass wilfully too long and the undergrowth rampant and the gatehouses stained and their doors firmly jammed, for many years, surely not, and there's my hammering heart.

The taxi's swallowed by heavily bowered green and the road gently rises up a hill and it's protected by lichen-laden trunks and bowered branches and everything is burdened and pressing, too close, and then the road flattens into the relief of light and the ocean's wide and tame and cool-grey to one side of us and the trees thin to a stick-tangle of a hedge with branches stripped of greenery and dramatically slanted, almost horizontal, protesting at centuries of wind. The car crests a hill and ahead, there it is, the hover of the waiting house, the photograph's match. My breathing snags, I'm tall on the car seat, my posture child-obedient and anticipation-whipped.

So to my grandfather, his house, my new life. But as the taxi speeds to it, it's all wrong.

The house's facade like the open mouth of the newly dead. Vines spilling from the sills like a corpse's frail collar, grass lapping at the walls and window gaps and door blanks and lichen triumphant on the bare bones of the roof. Huge blocks of stone haphazard on the wide front steps, as if the chunks have been tossed from the windows by marauders who've plundered long ago and left. I can hear my mother's chuckle, *you'll love it, I just know*, but of course she has no idea I'm expecting anything else.

The taxi crawls along the sweep of a circular drive, ghoulishly slow and obviously not pulling up for there's nothing to pull up for and I want to prod the driver into a hurrying now, to get him out quick for I've seen enough and I'm sick of his voice and I want this to stop. The farm cottages are about a mile down the track, he booms, it must be that old snooper you're after, with a chuckle-grate and I don't know why he's laughing and I censor my face but my yes in reply is hardly voiced and disappointment-soaked.

There are fifty bedrooms in there, what on earth did they ever do with them, that's what I want to know. It'd only work if you had twenty wives. Ha, now there's an idea.

Not answering, not able to, husked.

Leaves and drink cans and plastic bags are banked up by the building's entrance like a litter of pups at a bitch's warmth. A tree's been split by lightning and heaved from the ground but never removed and all that's left is the frozen octopus-wave of it roots. Enthusiastic branches poke from the roof of a smashed greenhouse, giraffes from a too-small truck. Ovoid windows on their sides stare from a central pediment, eyes permanently awake and shocked of life. There's an avalanche of beams and columns and bricks on one side where an added-on wing has been weighted by neglect and given up and there's the monumental, ruined stillness of an old person's face. The place is gone, irreversibly so and God knows how long it's been like this.

We drive beyond the estate and through several farm gates that are sinkingly opened and humbler each time and the car with its new quiet crosses cow fields and bramble patches on ever rougher, muddier tracks and comes to rest at a little knuckle of land that's bashed on three sides by the wind and the sea. A cottage huddles upon it, tight and jammed shut against the sting of the sky.

Right, then, here we are.

My new home, and as simple as a graveyard's plain stone cross and my heart is contracting, it's pebbling with disappointment.

No right angle and no straight line and the roof and most of the windows lopsided, as if the structure's slowly slipping from the earth and the foundation fingers are clinging to the lip of the land. Constance clenches her handbag to her chest and surveys, her lips baby-pursed.

I think I'm going take up Ed's offer of that hotel by the station. I was warned that this place might be a little too, ah, basic for my liking.

We stare at the drunken perspective of the walls, the bowed roof, the sea-assaulted hedge hemming it in. Are you all right with that, Lil? A tight smile's holding the slide of my face and I'll see you back in London, I'm saying firm, even scraping a laugh. Constance scrawls her number on the back of a business card and hands it across.

If you ever need any help.

I tell the driver not to wait and no one comes out to greet me and it's bone-cold and my mother's coat isn't enough and the wind whooshes up my legs in a merry hello and curls into the gaps at the bottom of the sleeves and ruffles my skin into hurting bumps.

The taxi's rev is swallowed into the sea's roar and I stand very still and let the spirit of arrival wash over me: jilted, by moss-crammed stone and piggy-eye windows and a solidly shut, ridiculously short wooden door, jilted by the place that I've dreamed of for so long, the place that's to gild me and grow me up. And where had Rebecca's smooth accent come from? Surely not this.

The house is densely still amid the sea's restless chatter and then I realize it's hoodwinked me for it's two, it's Siamese-twinned by a central wall. Ivy claims one far window, triumphantly quenching any interior light and I head for the other end with my eyes all the time assessing the scale of the mean building under the thumb of the weather, my launching pad to the world and with nothing of the life's rush and no prospect of a man or a way out, I can tell. And glorious London only a few hours ago, and gone.

The colours around me spring into vividness in the steel-grey, post-storm sky and the sun paints a pathway of sprightly shine across the water and then it's snuffed and again an iron coldness falls over the day. I feel as if a hand has punched through my back and reached in and grabbed at my heart and I ask God to give me the gift of serenity, I even my breathing, and with a smile freshly glued I knock at the low door.

Miss Bird?

The shock of his face, no welcome in it. Unhealthily pale, almost yellow, the pallor of someone who's lived in a cupboard for most of their life. No neck, just a fall of skin from the chin and talk's jolted from me and I'm tired, so tired, and there's a betraying tremble I can't stop in my top lip.

You're late. The dinner is burnt. Obviously it's not two of you. Do hurry.

Some sort of triumph in the words, as if tardiness is exactly what he expects. Eye contact slips and he attempts my suitcase and the crown of his head is vulnerable with age and I've seen few elderly people in my life and have had little experience of their ways but they're meant to be helped, I know that, and I step in front of him, all limbs, and grab the suitcase handle with too-quick talk, filling up gaps with fluster: I'm fine and the bag's light and isn't it cold?

That suitcase was mine, once.

As if it had been stolen, and all I want in arrival is some gift of warmth, some give, it's all too defensive and tight and I do not need that, I'm deeply tired, I need to sit. A green vein curls under the tissue-paper-thin skin of his temple and his right foot scrapes across the ground, stroke-dead, as if gravity's defeated it, and I notice then that he's propped by a stick. I follow him inside, my foot snagging on the uneven stone floor but he doesn't look back and I feel loud, and clumsy, and young, and alone.

My first proper old person, and all hardened into his faults, and six months of it.

A foreign place closing in around me. A cottage all cluttery with faded floral print and smoke-licked from centuries of fire, a smell that's accumulated in the walls and soaked into the fabric and it faintly lays ownership to the air and will never be wiped. The ceiling's too low for a Tiriel, there are tight spaces and a sliver of a hall and the aroma somewhere of fading fruit and of too many meals the same as if the air's been salvaged from somewhere else. Nowhere that I can see is there the sprightliness of a woman's touch and a TV jangles too loudly an early evening game show, the room's raucous with punched fists and flashing buzzers and lights and I set down my suitcase and gulp the glow close, I haven't seen a TV since my teenage city-trips and I never much liked the push of it and from memory it hasn't changed much but it's there, it's something, a time-filler if nothing else. God, ahead.

He taps the suitcase with his stick, Yes mine, and then stops as if he's used up all his talk. A jagged silence. I can't think of a thing to say because all I'm thinking of is a life ahead so becalmed, so ported, and after all the lovely promise of the day. I steady myself against a chair. I'm sorry I missed dinner, the train was late and there were leaves, it's all I can get out and I sink into the cushion and there's another stretched pause and a tear threatens to tip and I flick roughly at it and smile tight with no teeth.

Ah yes, leaves, he says, and pauses. I'm not very good with people, Lillie.

As if the sound of the name has all rusted over and there's a sudden smile from him with a deep shyness buried in it and I see something else in that moment: he's afraid, could that be it, he doesn't have a clue what to expect. God, what to say, what comes next, I'm not sure.

I'm, ah, not the best with people either. I haven't had much practice, you know.

I don't know if it will work but there's a weak laugh and his face brightens into a youngness and then he slides the dead weight of his foot to me and I see now something else, a man uncomfortable in his body and there's a chink of a softening and nervously, my heart thudding, I stand and place my hands in the spidery wispiness of my grandfather's and his touch is as light as a sigh and I squeeze and I search for something of my own blood and recognize only my mother's high forehead, nothing else. He doesn't want me here, he's dreading it, his stance is telling me that. I've never been so close to someone so old and his eyes are faded as if from too much seeing, too much light and his temples are spotted and his skin is troughed in places like the ridges on my globe. His smell is of an old house whose windows have never opened and of central heating and stillness and routine, it's not a dirty smell but preserved and I break from him and skitter about the room, all movement and frittery talk, touching objects and assessing curtain fabrics and swiping surfaces, absorbing all the while the modesty of the place as I garble questions, how long has he been here and what's wrong with the big house and how is he connected to it but I'm battling now with a violent jet-lag tired that's pulling me into sleep, it's calling me away from this little room that's so barren of prospects, it's calling me into my dreams, my nightly movies, my escape.

But Cedric Henderson has not found what he was expecting and so he finds talk. The TV's turned down with a practised flourish of the remote control. Oh God, energy, not right now, I've had enough.

He'd been employed to work in Evendon at the age of eleven as a cobweb sweeper, as had his father. His father had progressed to becoming, daily, the winder of the clocks but Cedric had a liking for a world beyond all that and he'd wormed his way out of the destiny of cobwebs and into the garden and at the height of his days he was the head gardener of a thriving estate with a knack for exotic fruits for the house's desserts. Yet his life's so resolutely interior now and I can't work it out. He's allowed the use of the old place in gratitude for a lifetime of service and he completed his schooling at the age of fifty-two when the house's family had gone from the estate and he was the only one left. He peers at me, I seem very alive he says, he wonders what's to be done with me and I laugh weakly and say, I want to see the world, but I'm losing confidence, my sentences are soaked with tiredness, they're drifting apart.

From here?

Um yeah . . . I guess, yeah, and another half-hearted laugh.

My fight's all snuffed in such a will-wilted state but my grandfather won't be stopped and he says suddenly, flippantly, that from childhood women are taught that love is the adventure in their lives whereas men are taught that work is and what will it be for me? I want to say love, more than anything, want to ask about Richard and how often he visits but I say work, curt, there's no energy for anything else. Good, he says, slapping the arm of his chair, for he's heard that my countrymen have a liking for hard work and it'll come in handy for he's no longer a gardener, he's a country-house snooper and he needs a hard worker for that.

A *what?*

He's writing a book about snooping around England's great abandoned houses, it's a habit picked up as a child and it's grown into an obsession, he cares for the old relics too much, he tells me that England's lost a third of its great houses over the past fifty years and he was employed to care as a child of eight and he's never stopped doing it. He's cataloguing the dead, so to speak, and my mother's letter, bless, came at an opportune time, for he has a publisher's commission, a modest sum after five years of rejection letters: Never take no for an answer, Lillie.

And amid all the talk he waves something alcoholic under my exhaustion like a rescuer waking the daze of a shipwreck survivor and I tell him, I never drink, I've never had the chance and he says there's always a first time and I smile, beginning a sparking, as I breathe in the vapours from the beautiful balloon of a glass and swish the soft red.

It's called a sherry. Don't tell your mother.

I pull a face at the sour urine taste and Cedric says he'll have to teach me manners because my father obviously never did and it'll be interesting to see if I ever take to this place. Mum never talks about it, I say and Cedric asks too quickly how she is and I see in his gently crumbling face all the pain of the love that a parent can feel for a child and I suspect that there's nothing quite like it, that flinch of a parent's hurt.

She's fine.

The last time I visited her I discovered a phobia about shadows. I'm afraid I'm much better suited to a cloudy country like this one.

He leans close as if he's searching for something of his lost daughter in my face and tells me that he's very strong-willed and I say I am too, slipping into calling him Grandpa and he humphs for me not to, it ages him too much, his name's Cedric and I must call him that.

When will I see London, Cedric? When do you think?

Another humph.

He hates cities, for he's rigorous about tidiness and coherence and calm and every day of his life a battle's waged against mess and confusion and panic and clatter and he's deeply frustrated with all the blundering of the world. London exemplifies that, especially its Underground, which is always stopping when he's on it and making him late and leaving him in the dark.

He doesn't know how to relax, Rebecca had warned once, it eventually drove me out of the house, and the country. So why am

I being sent? I had asked. A shoulder shrug and a sigh: there's no one else.

The ground rules were etched on that night of diminished arrival. The sinners were distinguished by those who shunned a bookmark and creased the corner of a page and an eyebrow was raised in inquisition. Serial dog-earing was admitted, the gauntlet immediately thrown and from Cedric there was a quickening and I was asked if I finished a whole top row of chocolates in a box or went rummaging prematurely among the second layer, if I cut small bunches from grapes or pulled them off willy-nilly and left those repellent, damp plumes – as he spat the ragged syllables from his lips – and to every challenge I answered with the word he did not want to hear. Cedric Henderson sat back at the end of it and tented his fingers under his chin.

The disorderly, I know, are generally much more appealing characters. It's just that I cannot stand them.

Evendon was forbidden, for it was a house of supreme mess and soon the roof would collapse and its family had been faced with the accumulated neglect of fifty years and they'd held on grimly with little plumbing or heating and a kitchen so far from the living area they'd used bicycles to reach it until it all, quite simply, became too much. The grounds were banned too, the garden had run wild and it wasn't his responsibility now.

Is it anyone's?

The question was dismissed with a back-handed wave.

As a race you people can be extremely irritating. I've been warned, you know, and his pale hands trembled around his Diet Coke.

I must get to bed. I'm very tired, the flight, the travel, all that. Yes.

His face fell, bereft, and I had a softening then for this tight, trying man and kissed him on the cheek, afraid I might bruise him with the force of it, his skin was so thin, but he just smoothed the hair from my forehead with a sudden tenderness and I smiled at that, the swiftness of his claiming.

I'll see you to your room, Lillie.

Soaking up the weariness of my new home: the knobbly white walls, the corduroy curtains sapped long ago of brightness, the books on bowed bookshelves stripped of their jackets. I slipped out *Tess of the D'Urbervilles* and on the age-spotted first page was an admonition in stern ink, Never Read This Again, and I showed it to Cedric and he shrugged, God knows, and it was wedged under my arm to find out. I hope you're someone who shuts all their drawers? Nope, and a cackle from us both. A book creaser and a chocolate rummager, just as I feared, and he turned, smiling, and I caught in that moment some of the complication he'd embraced with taking me on, all the responsibility it entailed and the fear but the want in it too to have a daughter freshly hooked. *It's the first time I've asked my father for anything*, Rebecca had told me the day I left, *I hope it works. I have no idea. Don't tell your dad that, chick.*

How's that mad father of yours? Does he still have the beard?
No.

I've always been bare of ornamentation myself, save a wristwatch.

Cedric apologized for the smell of staleness as we climbed the narrow stairs to the eave-tucked guest room, he rarely came up to it and the salt had jammed all the windows shut. Great. The wooden floor creaked and bowed like a saddle beneath my feet and I stopped and symphonied it with my heels.

They're old coffin lids. They're held in place by thatchers' ladders, it was a way of building a house back then. My father helped put them in, you know.

He told me that the house would always be locked and I'd be called each morning, promptly at eight, and I'd be staying close to home, no straying, and my eyes felt suddenly bruised with emotion and exhaustion and shock. I've always believed that hardships and challenges are like a tree being pruned, he said, to make it grow, as he closed the door behind me with no goodnight. Not good with people, yes.

A sea-licked corner room facing water on two sides and there I am on that first day of my new life, ramming the windows with all the strength in my fists and letting in the sky and the restlessness of the ocean and leaning out and breathing in deep the water's beautiful, ceaseless bash and it's like living within the curve of a shell for there's the swish of the water, the faint, hollow moan of it mixed with the wind's breath and I'm closing my eyes and absorbing the newness of it, the loveliness of that sound at least.

Finally I turn. Assess the room's bareness. Gorgeousness will take a lot of work. Newspaper's stuffed up the chimney like food from a mouth, the bed dips with a tired sag, smell-laden blankets are topped by a faded quilt that reaches over a hill of stale pillows, dead flies are upturned in the far corners of bare shelves and a large wooden cupboard threatens to topple onto me and prints on the wall are rippled and watermarked like they've been dipped in water some long time ago, and forgotten. Not a lived room, not a loved room, and with a steep, hopeless drop to the ground outside.

I lean out the window again and sudden snow is dancing earthwards like dust in a stream of light back home and I smile at its play and feel refreshed, at least, by that wildness below me. The sound outside my far-flung windows is a swirl of wind and water and I know that on clear nights I'll be able to sit on the deep window ledge close to the sky, with the sea and the stars perhaps all the gorgeousness I'll need. God, I hope.

I open my journal, flicking exhaustion to one side and write of the taste of the air and the smell of the sea and the chink of Cedric's smile and his sudden touch. And Evendon, the first shock of it, the heartbreaking carcass clothed in the criminality of neglect. I write of my panic over a newly met grandfather who demands complete control of his universe and of my hankering now for the opposite of that, for all the spill and vividness and mess of life. I don't want my mother's strange ballast, I don't want my grandfather's tight fist, I want emotional freefall, spark, risk, and yet I'm in a remote cottage that's clamped by an iron will, hemmed in by meekness and order and quiet. I can't imagine the future and I wonder if Richard will ever feature strongly in it, or indeed any man and there's scant hope, that first, fettered night.

Richard Daunt wasn't my only prospect, but of course I didn't know that yet. This story must be told and time is running out, for you are yawing and pummelling now too much.

The snow turns to rain at the fag end of that first night and there that young Lillie is, all ready to gulp sleep, the sheets smooth with cold and the chill icy on her face and she's huddling deep into the blankets and listening to the lovely patter of the sky kissing the water and the land, a sound so different to home, and she's soon asleep.

A luxurious eleven a.m. is the princessy waking time – did I miss his knock? – and with a blanket around me I shiver to the windows and open them wide to feel that new day. Oh joy! The snow's raggedy and undisciplined, there are big, blowsy drops and they change from floating to being flung down and I know that my grandfather wants to make a crisp start but he can wait for the weather's so awake and there's too much novelty in it for work.

A bathroom's next door, proud in its centre is an old bath on a dragon's clawed feet, it's steep and as long as a coffin and I've never had a bath in my life and can't quite relax with it, I don't feel clean enough as I step from water to carpet that feels as if a lifetime of nail and skin has been ground into it, I feel as if I'm still wallowing in grime and maybe there's a trick to it all but there's no one to ask, not Cedric certainly, he wouldn't cope. Out the window are the great stumpy toes of the coastline and a sea crowded with sunken ships, I've read about them in Ed's books, some had been encouraged to founder long ago because of the greed of the villagers and yet it all looks so benign at that moment with its snow-dampened swell and gentle slap.

And I'm feeling suddenly refreshed for the day and the sleep has scrubbed my doubt and I'm sure it'll work: London will be visited, and a man found, and a life begun. I open my journal and over the weeks and months of my new existence I rush it all in for me, one day, to spin out.

So it's the story of a woman called Lillie Bird who did something once when she was very young, and at the age of thirteen was shut away in a high room that her parents had lovingly and misguidedly prepared for her.

Look under the pillow, don't forget, Rebecca had said on that first climb to the renovated attic. And I'd picked up the exercise book covered with its silver paper and *My Journal*, and name, neatly on it and I'd smelt the fresh paper inside and haltingly begun to write, discovering for the first time a new page's balm. There was the oblong of a newly installed skylight above me and just before I slept I'd stood on a chair and lifted up the heavy window and poked my head out into the slap of the cold, imagining I was Amelia Earhart in a soaring across the world, and as I climbed into womanhood it was Isabelle Eberhardt, Katherine Mansfield, Martha Gellhorn, Oriana Fallaci, travellers all, struggling, blazen women who'd seized their own future and not had it shaped for them. Just like me, once, when I was thirteen years old. And all of them perhaps, just like me, saddled sometimes with an accursed loneliness because of that choice.

And for so many years the blur of this photo of the waiting house has always been close. But now I've arrived, to a tiny cottage where the silence collects in corners and ponds its ennui, confident it'll never be disturbed. I speed the questions to my mother on that first full day in it: why has she never returned to England and why did she leave in the first place and in a scribbled over, much-changed reply Rebecca is more revealing than her talk ever is.

Because, I guess, a part of me couldn't bear to be in a place so weighted by class, where it's so difficult to reinvent yourself. I could never crack the code, I wasn't allowed. Maybe it's changed now, I don't know, and perhaps that's for you to find out. I like being somewhere else because you can be anonymous, you can change your life.

I reread the letter and think of the inarticulate woman whose speciality is touch coming long ago from this land, and how uncomfortably in it she must have sat. And how spectacularly she transformed her life.

−6−

Enter a Man, At Last

Just.

A sighting, but it's inauspicious: behind a tripod on the side of the road, taking photographs of Evendon's gates, God knows why. A red jumper, the only vividness in my head.

We get them all the time.

Cedric, as the car accelerates past.

But there's a new distraction: work. It spines my days and my muscles now know the deep, bone-tiredness of a hard day's labour. Hours sweep by and swiftly weeks, they're all gulped by fresh purpose for I've become my grandfather's legs and eyes and he's determined to extract as much juice as he can from my precious six months.

Most mornings, precisely at nine, we climb into Cedric's Morris that smells of old vinyl and care and hasn't changed by one scratch since the photo my mother showed me once. We potter along the country lanes and motorways of England, stopping for Cedric's neatly packed cheese sandwiches, stopping at tea rooms harbouring elderly people alone with their meat and three veg, stopping at blank houses and wild gardens and over those days falling into a deep, unacknowledged affection.

I'm my grandfather's faithful shadow, jotting his dictating and sitting by him as he reminisces with other milky-eyed gardeners about flower shows and handkerchief trees and expeditions to China for new stock; I collect all their memories in my notebook for few people are left to bother with them now and the old men want it all down. And as brightness bleeds from swiftly shutting winter skies we drive back to the cottage and deep into the nights I transcribe the narratives, typing two-fingered into a tall Underwood typewriter that lives in a stout black box. I love the strained slap of the keys in the close dark, the thudding of their weight into the paper. Cedric had demonstrated the typewriter on my first full day in the house, tapping rhythmically and lightly, a conductor not of music but of words.

In my day it was never expected that a labourer could be a dab hand at this, Lillie.

Reinventing himself, yes, and he's waited all his life.

I'm enchanted by all the beautiful new words like *architrave* and *arboretum* and *dovecote* and *frieze*, I'm pouring them into my word book and long letters home and whispering words like *orangery* and *topiary*, my tongue and lips feeling the contours of the strange syllables, their stately slide and I'm practising them for God knows what. In my journal I'm cataloguing all the stories of the houses we snoop, stories of great fires that have left them as ghosts, reckless sons staunching dynasties, shrewd mistresses, mad maids, female skeletons found locked in cupboards, fathers who've burnt down estates so hated sons will not inherit, family portraits collandered by darts, careless troops, divorce, madness, drugs. And I'm dreaming of reinventing myself.

My scrawl across the width of flimsy envelopes arrives in Sunshine at least once a week and Ed sits with Rebecca over cups of tea and reads them aloud. Ed writes to me that she loves the smell of our kitchen over that time, with its aroma of just-cooked bread and industry and warmth, loves it so much that she experiments with an aerosol bottle from a homewares catalogue to get her close.

I'm utterly mad, Lil, and only you know that.

She never writes of her husband, I accept that, never expect it. He's called Mike, he's an insurance salesman, he has a moustache, he allows her to do her own thing and that's as much as I know. Ed's letters are filled mostly with her library, that's her life. I write in return of giant topiaries that are overgrown and trembling like surreal floats waiting for a pageant to begin and of gardens with eighty-one varieties of daffodils and ponds used for witch drowning once and falcons with thread through their eyelids to tame them down. And I write of Evendon – *finally, Ed, I have the story, and it is, and isn't, what I ever imagined* – that the land was given to the original Duke by Henry VIII to guarantee loyalty to the Tudor succession, and in the Duke's journeys outriders would go ahead to clear peasants from his path so that he would not be defiled by their sticky gaze, *imagine that*, and I feel far from home but not homesick, anything but.

The second sighting.

No talk, no touch. But my curiosity snared.

A crisp day's leaking light and the sky is all softening into a spill of gold across the land. Cedric turns the car into the Evendon gates as a young couple is crossing the road up ahead of us and the woman's being piggybacked, she's wrapped in joy and oblivious but the man halts, he stares straight at me, into me, as the jean-limbed girl on his back laughs and laughs. The jumper again, I remember that.

Gypsies.

Cedric's tut-tut. But I look at them close for I want more than anything to be that woman, to have that glow of completeness, that certainty. The bowed man stares as I get out of the car and open the tall gate and shut it and am driven off, my cheeks patched with heat, and I look back at the couple until a turn in the road snatches the scene and I'm longing for it somewhere in the quietness of my own life, I'll never forget that, the want.

I can *feel* him in the grounds and I'm not afraid, just curious, consumingly so.

Why don't we take a look at the garden, Ced? Take some photos, for the book?

There's nothing left of it. It's not worth it.

Oh come on.

The two wars took all the men and I haven't been near it for twenty years. I can't bear to see it like it is. There's nothing left of it.

But something is for there I am, often now, kicking at the soft, pitted apples at the edge of the formal grounds that are like old people's faces with gums for teeth. The apples are the only indication that there's ever been something productive within the mess for nature's stolen back and claimed its place and the obedience of the show garden is utterly wiped, it's immoral, rampant, gone. And almost every day I'm kicking those apples and baiting Cedric and hoping for another sight of my red-jumpered man but he hasn't come back.

Please, Ced, *please.*

Lillie, that garden is like a young man's first love that he never wants to see old, all right?

I don't dare mention to Cedric the beacon of the forbidden house, that daily it saturates my gaze from my bedroom window, daily it calls me across.

The third sighting.

Held.

The tripod again, set up by the entrance, and as I swing the gate I can feel his lens upon me, can feel it in the hairs on the back of my neck, can feel his close looking in the heat of my cheeks.

What the devil does he want to do it all over again for?

Cedric, as we accelerate past.

Maybe the light? Maybe he got it wrong the first time? I dunno.

The photographer raises his head from the camera and lifts a hand and grins, one side up, one side down. I stare back, blank.

Ah yes, Daunt day, I'd forgotten, Cedric says, his finger firm on the diary's date and my heart tightens, tightens and What do you mean? I'm too-casually asking. We've been invited to examine Richard's newly acquired crematorium, it belongs to a house he's just bought, it's a calendar house because it has a room for every day of the year and it'll become a conference centre one day, of course. Will the owner be there? I ask, turning and hiding the neck-heat. Oh I hardly think so, the Architectural Society is checking it for soundness and two of their people will be attending and that will be it, I suspect. It'll probably end up as a cheese shop or something, but we have permission from young Daunt to tag along.

Dressing my best. A bead of blood to stain my lips. Feeling brinked. Tipped into what, though? I don't know.

Cedric accelerates past Evendon unseeing, it's the same every sweep of that drive.

I'd *love* to have a look inside, before I go.

It's all wonderclout now and nothing else.

All what?

Wonderclout. It's an old English word that means something showy but worthless.

Scribbling the word repeatedly on the edge of my hand, grinding the pen into a working, with Cedric bristling beside me at the grubby mess.

Sometimes I think that all you love me for, my dear, is my vocabulary.

But of course.

Our grins filling the car.

A white-coated official waits outside the small church, he's a family man as crisp and round as a well-fed sparrow, thickly banded and wife-neat. The other, the archaeologist, walks from the building and drops his eyes to my chest as if there are weights in his lids and his posture's pale and stooped by a life of too many low ceilings and walls too close and there's a wet look about him and I step pointedly from his gaze. Walk swiftly to the graves that are huddled in a squadron of close rows, it's as if a zealous housewife has tidied them up for the bodies could never be that short. I bend down to the tilting headstones and stare at writing smeared by centuries of wind and rain and the archaeologist's still looking and I can't concentrate, the stone is green-tinged and flaking like cardboard peeling and there's no sign of their new protector but he'll come, I'm sure, and there'll be a stopping, thank goodness, of that lidded man's look.

Protective white overalls are handed out and Cedric firms the fastenings of his paper mask and practises containing his body so that it never brushes a surface and slides on plastic gloves and the archaeologist persists with his looking, it's as if his eyelids are attached to his forehead by two slackening strings and I want to curtly tug them up. I strain for the sound of a car.

Above the church's only tomb a knight lies on his back under the canopy of a four-poster bed, he's peacefully asleep and too delicate for a man, smaller than me and with his right hand ungloved and resting on his heart in a gesture that's tender and tugging. There's a slit at the back of a raised flagstone in the floor and we peer down one by one into a torch-swept vault that seems bereft of death: a wine cellar of neat bundles and bones. The archaeologist's close, he brushes his damp body into mine, I flinch aside, savvy a glare.

A bank of cold hits as we descend and it's like the breath of a benign ghost – a wily vent is keeping the room well-aired. Five centuries of a glorious family await us and a sudden reverence quietens us down and yet not a single living descendent is left to care. Cedric whispers that the strange, mummy-like shapes are swaddled in the velvets and silks of their Sunday best and then sealed in lead to hold off the rot.

There's none of that mixing with all us dirty commoners outside.

The room's as scrubbed of horror as a grandmother's sunroom and I brush aside my mask and shake out my hair and Cedric frowns and the archaeologist sniggers and I sharpen my stare, I've momentarily forgotten him. In a far corner there's a neat mess of bones jumbled together, the skulls are a rich amber colour and the teeth are loose: The servants, whispers Cedric, they're the only ones left to look after them now.

*

One by one we ascend to the body of the church and I stretch my spine and breathe in deep but then hurriedly drop my arms for the lidded eyes are back. Ivy snuffs the light from most of the windows and around the walls are filth-obscured crests and there's a sense, still, of a family weighty and potent and eternally watching: this is their place. But the little church seems scrubbed of its God for the dark and the damp have done their stubborn work and it's just a building now and a crumbling one at that. The exterior stone carvings are scuffed by the elements and I think of such magnificence, now so heartbreakingly ignored and how their hungry, city owner has stamped not one sign of himself, how he's content to leave it to its slide. He won't be buried here, it's too decrepit for that.

And there he is as Cedric reverses the car, he's strolling breezily up the churchyard path with a mobile phone in his hand and he hasn't seen me yet.

Hey, Ced, lucky I caught you. What do you think of my instant family? Haven't *I* had a glorious past?

Then he stops and blushes like a youth and our eyes catch and I smile a quickly collected warmth for in his face's flooding there's a new vulnerability and Well hello, he says, I didn't see you there, and there's a nod in greeting and an awkward pause that tells me he's caught. You weren't alarmed by all those bodies, were you? Gosh no, they reminded me of eggs in a carton all snugly side by side, and he laughs and says that Cedric will have to bring his granddaughter up to London, he's sure there'll be something there to scare her with and he'd appreciate the challenge and she would too, no doubt. Cedric taps his pen on my notebook, shutting the banter down, there's no time for London for I've become too valuable and time's running out and he has to get home before he loses the light because his eyes don't take too kindly to driving in the dark. Disappointment drops over me. Richard darts across to my side of the car and flicks his eyes back to the archaeologist and whispers *axe murderer* and gets me into laughing and a smile is soft through my frustration as we drive from him, for there's a blush, I have that.

Please can I have a look at Evendon?

No. You'd bring it all down, it's not stable enough.

Well, what about London?

No, Lillie, I wasn't told to be your tour guide, I was told to keep you busy with work.

What about learning to drive?

What?

Ugh, this is so unfair! I want to get out, I want to *see* things.

My fingers are fanned and frozen by my head and Cedric stops the car and he's very still, very wounded, very quiet, and we sit side by side in a dip of a country lane and I'm brimming with fume and nothing is said. The car ticks. Finally I apologize, it's easier that way and the car pushes on in thick silence until it comes to a Roman spa town and all the seething's distracted by the vibrancy of a medieval abbey – a skeleton of stone and its flesh, light. I can understand your frustration, Cedric's saying, but this has all come from your parents and my hands are tied and there's a tight nod, head hung, nothing else.

Go have a look inside. I'll wait for you here.

A college choir's rehearsing and just three people dot the chairs and I sit and close my eyes and listen to the notes gather and rise to the ceiling, it's as if they're borne on the thrum of a thousand tiny wings and I float in the plume of song and calm and then as the sound softens into a silence I open my eyes and think of this strange new country of half-hearted toilets and plastic tubs in sinks that I can't get a proper grip on and perhaps never will now, for I've just been informed that the cottage is it on this trip, that no other cities or people are meant. And soon I'll be back.

I shiver in the abbey's chilly air and imagine being laid to rest in my own soil, close to the sun and the warm, loose dirt of my land and suddenly I want it no matter where I am at my death or how long I've been gone. For on that cold afternoon I feel for the first time the loneliness of the exile who has no firm footholding with home. I write to my parents and Ed of this but I don't write of Richard, and his blush, only my journals know that.

A faraway coated figure. A flash of red. I lean out of the bedroom window so as not to lose him: he's walking across fields and down to the estate's beach and there are cows in a few rented fields but the figure's moving with too much pause to be a farmer and the light calls me outside but it's not only that, it's the hunger for a fresh life and another male one at that and I'm not losing a single chance. I pause, feel like I'm stalking him and chuckle and wonder what on earth I'll do with him when he's got but I put on my gloves and boots and by the time it's all done and I'm ready, he's gone. Damn.

The beach is not a seductive strip. A huge ribbon of seaweed stretches the sand's length and there's a flurry of mites and I step gingerly across the slippery stink to the water, to the kelp-heavy waves that are heaving their load. There's no sign of anyone, it's desolately lonely and so different to my own country's beaches that are cherished and public and thronged. I don't linger, I walk back over firm, dark sand that's strewn with bullish plants and drink bottles and crisp packets and he's definitely nowhere, gone. And in the softening day I look back to the ocean from the bluff above the beach, to the sea bleeding into the sky and then I turn to the mist-shrouded land so differently snug to my own wild home. A pink fog has settled over the villages and the fields and bunkered them down, shutting in the people and shutting in my own jumpy want.

For someone to kiss awake. For a visit from Richard and there's no guarantee and I'm almost twenty-two and I've never properly touched. And I'm exiled in the country that's held up its nose to randy Lawrence but enveloped as its own, with a scraping reverence, the dry, sexless Eliot. *It's a land strangely lacking in desire*, Rebecca wrote in a letter to me once and I dread the contagion of that. Every book in the cottage of possible interest has now been read and I haven't taken to the television, it just hasn't stuck, and I lament in letters home the absence of my Wednesday larders of fresh stock, the new novels and chocolate biscuits and glossy maga-zines and girly chat. I write to Ed of my longing for London, and a man, and out; I ask her how she's managed for so long the secret life of Silk Cut cigarettes and Scotches on the rocks seeping into the hours beyond midnight and the letters pages of men's porn magazines and cashmere stoles. Mail order, she replies, there's *such* delight in that.

But I want shops, and skin, and smell, and touch.

−7−

What I Do

Cedric is in London, he's delivering the first draft of his manuscript to his agent. He's refused to take me with him, of course, despite a campaign of fresh pleas: *I couldn't contain you, your mother would never allow it, there'll be other times, other trips,* but his confidence isn't matched. My mind's made up on one front. There are a rumoured several thousand volumes in Evendon's library and if it all goes to plan I'll soon be flipping my fingers along the lovely spines and spoilt for choice.

I look at my fearlessness as a young woman and wonder at it. It seemed back then that I'd do anything, stride anywhere, with anyone. I've lost so much of that, little one, I've become closed over by cautiousness. You see, there I was striding to Evendon at last, anticipation thrilling through me and also that lovely, churning delight at doing something wrong. Why is it that only when I'm doing something bad does that feeling of absolute power, and control, come tripping back?

I draw close. Can barely look in the eye the blank shock of the house's stare. It's like a once-magnificent thoroughbred of a woman now elderly and bedridden and lying in her own crap. I pause, the beams *do* look as if they might crash, the walls fall. But I'm pulled on, by fresh books and a red jumper perhaps and a knowing that this is possibly my only chance.

An old tradesman's entrance is jammed ajar and I'm treading

warily through a rabbit warren of Evendon's damp-welted little rooms and then a wider door opens out into a hall of the great house and I'm bathed in a creamy light from tall windows and I'm smiling and spinning in the lofty dimensions of it for I *knew* it would be this. The walls hold in the rain, I can smell it clamouring to get out and there's a clattering from a far wing and a clinging cold but I won't be pushed from it. I move briskly from room to room, fingers trailing, searching for the library while gobbling the sights in a lovely, still light. But hundreds of sacks of potatoes bobble the floor of one frescoed room and grain's heaped dune-high in another and empty petrol drums are methodically stacked in a third and I quickly realize that the building's now a succession of silos, it's the owner's dirty little secret, and my heart's affronted by it, and by a whirly shell of a spiral staircase climbing to the sky, by birds rising out of the rooms with great, startled flappings and by their droppings inch-thick on parqueted floor which my footsteps slip through like wet paint. By the detritus, still, of transient wartime occupation – notice boards and signs in Polish and Dutch, iron bedsteads, broken tables, upturned helmets. By the piracy of indifference, for it's a building in a state of rigor mortis and there are mysterious stains like old blood seeping from under high doors and grime bruises clotting walls. Finally I step into what could have been the library but I don't know, surely not, and my heart sinks.

Chaos. Like a lost dog shelter where all the animals have rotted in their cages. The few books that are left have mostly fallen or been thrown across the floor and there are only foreign languages, mainly Latin and Greek, and in the hundreds not thousands and the only order is on the shelves of one bay where twenty gas masks are obediently lined up with tin hats propped on each and too much thought has gone into that one, it's too much a thumbing to the house's wilt. I tread across a strange, white flaking on the slippery, book-strewn floor and recall a story Cedric told me about low-flying RAF planes, how every time they passed the ceiling would flake like snow and eventually the pilots were redirected but it was too late for by then there was hardly any paint left.

I'm treading to a last, disappointed view from a tall window and then stopping, the sweat's scuttling across my skin like too much chocolate too quickly gulped for tucked into a corner of the sill is a *New Yorker* from the previous month and two orange-spined paperbacks and my fingertips brush the shininess: here, now, who? *The Great Gatsby* and *The Outsider* and I trust the choices and think of nabbing both, there's no owner's name on either but a dog-ear on the Camus so I slip *Gatsby* into my coat pocket but in the taking feel watched, someone else is here, close, and I put the book back and turn.

Who's there?

Sharp into the room, but only wind sighs from some faraway wing answer back and empty-handed, and spooked, I'm clattering out.

Beyond Evendon there I am, gulping the air and the fresh light and all cross at my fear, how silly I was to flee. I'm walking back along the cliff with the heave and bash of the water below me and flushing my lungs clean with the push of the wind and the wet. A storm's coming, there's electricity in the air, I can taste the thundery day sparking me alive and I'm holding my hands high and clasping my palms and twisting them outward as if I'm pushing up the broody sky and then I'm dancing a ten-year-old's handstand that's all dragged down by my coat. I'm hurrying home along paths overhung by branches that are bowered by the garden's press and I'm looking back to Evendon and searching its window gaps for any sign – I haven't finished with it yet. A reader, and good choices, and now that I'm outside in the whipping air I'm trusting all that. And wanting to go back. But the light's dropping, Cedric will soon be home.

He believes that if one must have a relationship then it should be conducted in a shade of cool cream, he read that in a newspaper on the train and he loves it and I'm telling him no, no, a relationship has to be vividly blood red and he's saying that it settles it then, we're hopelessly unsuited but he always suspected that and we settle into a comfortable silence and he turns to the window and says absently that he's stopped looking at the sea or even hearing it any more and I don't answer because I dread ever succumbing to the contagion of that. Yet my trip's sliding now into its very own stillness along the sure path of routine and there'll be more of it: Cedric's returned with the latest draft of the book approved, there'll be few road trips now and ahead I can see the rut of my last weeks. But there's someone in the house, a reader, a discerning one, and on that night the tantalization of it is with me too much. I'm singing inside, giggly with it. The wind wheening in the windowpane is as mournful as a distant aria and a tree shakes its leaves like the mane of a recalcitrant pony and I'm listening, all restlessness, to the pummelling wind and the surf pounding the sand, to the booming smack of the water's weight. Slick black leaves plaster themselves to the glass, wanting in, and we hug our Horlicks close to our chests while Cedric tells me of my maternal great-grandparents, they both died in 1916, he killed her and then himself and I gasp at the horror of it for I never knew, Rebecca had never said.

No, no, Lillie, really, it wasn't terrible at all, they were madly in love and they had a pact. Now *there's* a blood-red relationship for you, and look how *they* ended up. She had tuberculosis and couldn't be cured, and so he overdosed her with morphine and then injected himself so that they'd always be together. He'd never have been happy by himself, they both knew that. You used to be able to buy morphine and heroin in kits from Harrods, to send to the boys on the front.

I close my eyes and imagine: such a consuming love, the suck of it, the strange beauty and it's my dream, my goal to have something as vivid as that and I climb the stairs to bed and wonder at the people who go through life never knowing love, and what instead they might find. Later that night I don't realize it's been raining until I looked up at the window and see the spatterings of wet, for the sturdy little work pony of a cottage hides the weather so well, unlike the great shell of a building nearby. That has someone sheltering in its beam-webbed rooms.

Who, I have to know, it won't let me go.

In the stillness after the storm has huffed itself out there's a light in a wing of the darkened house, a torch beam flitting and I don't feel fear for I've put the book back and they've seen me do it, I've felt their watching. They didn't harm me and they're a reader and it could be the man who disappeared from the beach, who knows, it could be another chance. My breath clouds the glass as I stare at the dance of the light and I cup my eyes with my fingers and press them to the pane, trying to read the arcs: someone moving from room to room, examining, or signalling, and I lean close, my nose to the cold glass and fingers impatiently wiping and the torch beam lingers longest in the library, *my* room, examining, or signalling, I can't make it out.

I creak across the coffin lids and down the narrow stairs and try the front door for the first time since I've been in the cottage and it's locked from the inside of course, foolish hope that it wouldn't be. All the downstairs windows are firmly jammed shut, they won't budge and I retreat, exasperated, to my room.

The torch beam settles, pooling its glow and I'm imagining the scene, the person reading an orange-spined paperback and there are more by their side just waiting for a borrowing and I'm lying in my bed owl-awake and listening to the heavy thump of my blood through the pillow's skin and to the saliva in my jaw and I'm not catching sleep until the morning light, can't.

And no clothes, a long time, so long, since that.

Cedric is all city energy as he talks deadlines for the Christmas market and thirty-two title suggestions and pictures and copyright costs, but there, scatty at the hub of it, is my ragged attempt at solid work and precious little is done for there's a reader, a new friend, they're waiting for me in the great house.

That night there's the torch beam again, the strange play of a glow on the walls and then oddly, absurdly, a flash from room to room and I fling wide my windows and winter rushes in and I can hear soft music, perhaps, I can't tell, it's some murmuring borne just above the quiet sea, singing me into restlessness and singing me out and I hurry on my mother's coat and slip a notebook into my pocket and tightly wind a scarf. Dash a spray of perfume that Ed's given me as a parting gift: Be Prepared, she'd said, always, and I remember her smile with the knowing in it that I didn't understand yet.

You need perfume?

Oh yes. And lipstick, and condoms, and a cab fare home.

My bedroom window is the only way out and I've never attempted anything so high and I balk for a moment, there's slippery slate to be slid across and scratchy brickwork to be dropped from and all in silence and sky-dark but it has to be done at night for it's the only time for the reader to be caught, I need their torch glow as my guide. I sliddery-scrape down the tiles of the cottage's jutting kitchen extension and turn and dangle, all fluttery-queasy, from the gutter at its edge, my knees grating on stone and then I'm willing myself and holding my breath and dropping to the ground, there's a thud, my feet tingle, it shoots up my calves but, beautifully, nothing stirs in the house.

Free.

So there that young Lillie Bird is, walking along the muddy cow paths to Evendon with her face to the strange heavens, the constellations she cannot make out, all shivery with expectation and her instincts singing for they're a reader and implicitly she trusts that. There's a silver path of moonglow across the water and she's thinking of what Ed told her once, that to walk across it is a Chinese form of suicide and she's smiling, remembering, and she's musing on how much her friend is with her that night.

The loose parquetry shifts under my feet, wooden blocks lift with the suck of the greedy, snail soles and then settle back resigned with a plop. I walk towards the wing of the torch beam, I don't feel fear, for soon a book's to be borrowed and a friend's to be snared, someone new, clean, with whom I can create myself afresh.

There's no music, just the gentle clacking of the blocks and a flapping somewhere of a distant, woken bird even though I tread quietly. I don't trust the electricity, don't know if there is any, don't dare a switch, the moonlight will have to do. There's no torch glow now, damn, that didn't work, but I can feel the waiting house, the expectancy in it and I climb the curving bones of its beautiful main staircase and feel the calm, sad breadth of it in the dark and stop midway, breathing in the great stillness and then continue on, my breath booming and my ears tuned, trying to catch clues, and my eyes straining, trying to remember the library way and I step into a room of flapping birds that's facing my far bedroom window and open to the sky and a hand slams across my mouth.

Fingers clamping my eyes. Pods of tightness blacking my sight. Glasses clattering to the ground and skidding across it. Physically I've never been held down and I'm like a person drowning as I claw for air and light, I'm scrabbling, scraping at the hands and kicking at the bulk but I can't shake the ferocity of that hold, the body's too firm and I can't make a sound, I'm writhing and lashing and there's a man's sweat and his smell as he tries to clamp me still and I hate it, hate it. I'm panicking and then suddenly he changes tack and behind my ear he breathes *shh* like he's trying to soothe a spooked horse, *sshh*, and I listen for any threat in it, *shhh*, and I stand very still and our bodies are tight and the seconds tick and the hand suddenly loosens the brace of its holding, I'm not making a sound and then gingerly the palm slides to my chin and cups it in readiness for a springing back, for it all to begin again if I want.

Don't touch me.

My voice seizes the slackening and comes out cold into the dark and the palm drops and I turn, afraid, furious, ready for a fight, for I wasn't expecting the tenacity of that clamp. The red jumper of course, who else, the carrier of the piggybacked woman's joy and up close little more than a teenager, as tall as Tiriel but bulky with it, a shining face of fresh vegetables and milk and an odd smell on him, a strange diet staining his skin, a vegetarian, perhaps. The jumper's hand-knit, badly so, but with some kind of love in it, I can tell. It needs a wash. As does he.

So, the fourth sighting. The prickle of it.

Face to face I'm wary, he's too close, I step back. An uneasy, assessing silence and his eyes gulp my affront and then his hands are in his pockets and he's leaning forward like someone pausing to watch a local cricket match on a Saturday afternoon stroll and there's a challenge in that relaxing as if he wants me to do something next, his eyes flick to the torch by his side and back, he's waiting, wanting me to comment on the signalling or spring at him or do something and so I do nothing, I stay very still. He hesitates, stoops, not taking his eyes from me, he scoops up my glasses and hands them across and we brush a touching and I remember again the clamp of his hand, his body's butt and the presumption in it and my indignation's all out.

You're trespassing, you shouldn't be here—

He holds up a palm and winces his eyes tight, telling me to be quiet, telling me that my voice isn't gentle enough for cats and I catch the languid flick of a tail out the door and roll my eyes for I've instantly read the flattened vowels and I'm scarcely believing, not wanting it, for everything's changed by that.

Crikey Moses, this country's full of us.

Well, well, so you too, and he's leaning back, he's rocking on his heels with a smirk I don't like.

Yeah, but I belong here, mate, and you don't.

Lifting my chin, jutting a challenge and I'm all deflation, all interest lost, for someone from my own land is just too close. And there's suspicion, I remember the prickling of that – how on earth have we come to be so near, in such a remote place? It's too odd, I don't like it, I want him gone. His body's no fireman's and I'm not attracted one bit and so I'm cheeky and blunt and bold, too annoyed for awkwardness, or shyness, or flirt. And anyway he's taken, consumed by someone else, I saw his woman on his back and her content and yet he's pressed me close, I can still feel the hand across my mouth, can still feel his chest and his groin pressing into me, learning me and I don't like it, the presumption in it. I brush my mouth and feel again his touch and his smell is threaded into my fingers and I wipe my hand on the side of my thigh.

He's a photographer, he's obsessed by decay, that's why he's in the house, Is it yours? he asks and I don't answer for I don't like his stare or his youngness or his cat. Or his tease, for he knows that I know he's already woman-locked. I look at my watch, it's late, I want this wrapped up but he's too full of telling and showing, it's as if he's trying to snare me with talk but I don't need a netting and the disappointment is deep through me: how can he be from *home*, anything but *that*. He pulls an old Leica from a worn leather bag that's all webbed with tiny cracks, It's my most treasured possession, he says and I hold out my hand for it and Can I trust you? he asks, stiffening back. I don't know yet. Blunt. He shuts his eyes and presents the camera on the platform of his palms and he's teasing and I don't like it, he's playing with my affront and I say nothing and take the object and finger its beautiful, odd flatness as he tells me he uses a Polaroid too.

Why?

Because of the accidents with colour that you get with them, I like accidents the best.

He's got to go, it's late, I've had enough, I want to borrow one of his books and get back to bed but he's plastering every opportunity-gap with his talk, all the while looking at me like I'm a mannequin pedastalled in a shop, pushing me with his tease, walking around me, assessing, delighting in my hair, my fingernails, my coat and even daring a touching from which I flinch back, it's as if he's never seen a woman up close and I don't like it one bit, the arrogance, the oddness, the front. I drape my arms across my shoulders. Back into a wall. Assess.

The nails dirty and unbitten, the mark of grime around his wrist and a startling white that flashes under his loose watch and it's all too backpackery for Evendon and too close to a homeless tramp. But there's a strangeness to it all, it doesn't sit quite right: his face and his hair are too clean-cut for a ragged cloth bracelet around his wrist. What's he playing at? I wonder who he really is and if

I'd ever be able to strip him back, but would I want to, he'll be gone soon and that prickle of suspicion just won't stop. I hand the Leica back and he holds it tenderly, his actions careful and not matching the grubbiness of his hands. His fingers brush mine, there's the quickening catch of it and I snap my hand away and begin a cursory digging before the final kicking out, wanting to know just two things: the woman and how he ended up here, that's it, no curiosity for anything else.

He's been travelling the country from his London base, seeking out ruins and photographing them, he's never seen anything like them, he can't understand the size of the old houses and the wastage of them and he'll be in Evendon for a couple more days, God willing, because someone told him about it once and he hasn't finished with it yet but that might change, who knows. And there's a sudden trembling of a grin under the smooth bravado, I catch it, it's a nervousness quickly wiped and he's talking too much, trying to wile his way in and I can't relax with him but can't pinpoint why.

Have I noticed how shiny and new the cities back home seem now that I'm in this land? I don't answer, my stance is arm-crossed, walled, I can still taste his hand on my mouth and the press of his groin, I'm still furious at the audacity of it. This place is fantastic, he's gabbling on, just what I've been looking for, and he's sliding his hand down a door edge with a proprietal air as if he's claiming for himself the whole house. His backpack and bedroll are neat in a corner, settled and workmanlike.

I should be calling the police.

Ah, but you won't.

The lopsided grin, one side up, one side down. How long have you been here? I ask and Days and days, he replies, I've been waiting for you to pop over and say hello, I've seen you around and I've wanted to meet you, and you're from home, God, don't you think it's fate that we've met? He's seen me from a distance and can't let me go, the lady of the manor, so aloof, and there's a shiver, I can't tell if he's joking or what, if he's stalking me, his fascination is so intense, I've read about those men but I don't feel fear on that night, not that yet. I roll my eyes with no gift of a softening and it pushes his nervousness into faster talk and I let him meander now, I'm here because I have a psychiatric disorder, he's telling me, it compels me to take risks, it's a documented case, and there's his laugh and my eyes giving nothing back. How do you keep clean? I'm snapping, looking again at the nails and wrists and he's telling me he has an accommodating friend in the village, Is she your girlfriend? I'm snapping and There's nothing in it, he's tossing back, it was only one night, and I'm swallowing his brushing off with veiled eyes, not believing him but it's pricking, not sure why. A pause, another grin, like a schoolboy waiting for the photographer's class shot and too smug by far and nothing to be smug about.

Where are you from?

I can hardly remember the response, in the middle of nowhere or something, it doesn't stick, he likes travelling and that's where he's living now, on the road. So, a nomad, a wag, an intruder, a probable thief who's cheekily declaring after twenty minutes together that our lives are fated to be entwined and who's wilfully refusing to allow any gap for his pushing out. Someone who's happy to let the world form around him, with no problems, no worries, no settling, no ties, a man some women would consider to be golden with that skin and that smile and that face, but not me, oh no, he's too normal underneath it all and I've always been suspicious of that. And he's too young, he can teach me nothing, and there's a confidence lack and boy-lips still, despite the height, there's something about him that a mother would still wing a protective love for and I don't want any of that. He jumps onto a low window seat and points his camera and tells me to smile.

What?

Oh yeah, yeah.

You got this at the gatehouse. You don't need it again.

Not replying, just clicking, winding, clicking, winding and I huff and turn my back, clicking, winding, clinking winding and I throw up my arms and glare. Click.

Oh for God's sake, I snap, mother-old.

I *love* photographing faces before the expressions have all congealed, it usually takes a couple of seconds so you've got to be
quick, he says, jumping from the ledge and imping another click
before I stride to his lens and shut my palm over it.

Touchy, aren't you?

I think you better go before I call the police.

OK.

Sunny, like he expected it, I'm not ready for that.

What about one last request before the firing squad comes?

What?

The suspicious, downward slide of my voice, I remember it so
much. His grin.

A smoke.

I remember it so much.

Watching his fingers smooth his tobacco and all daddy-long-
legs-delicate roll it out neat and watching the tip of his tongue
slide across the paper from end to end, his eyes at me all the while,
not moving from me and watching his fingers daintily removing a
sliver of tobacco from his tongue and then I'm taking the matchbox
and holding it, feeling it, softly rattling it and he's asking if I want
to do the honours, if I want to light the cigarette. My breath held.
Panic. For a moment, lost. Can I remember how?

The sharp smell pierces my nose, there's the spurt of flare that
settles into beautiful flame and my fingers waver and hover it under
my nose and draw it back and I breathe it in deep and he reaches
for my hand and holds it still and the flame finds its calm and I
smile at its halo of blue for I've forgotten the loveliness of that.
His hand holding mine moves to his cigarette tip and he keeps
on holding my trembling, clamping me still but I don't like the
presumption in it, the owning of my fear and I withdraw my hand
and shake out the flame and wipe my fingers clean on my coat and
he watches me all the while and smiles, changed, the bravado gone,
all the bluff, and something gentler in its place. Quiet, and pure,
and frank.

*

He hates England and I hackle all over again at the certainty and say in return that I'm loving it and the emboldened cat pads onto his lap and settles and I stare at the sensuality in his fingers and his really quite beautiful wrist, the only thing I'm attracted to in him, as he rolls and rakes the animal's fur and it thrums its purr-oozed bliss.

The little bastard hated me too at the beginning, and look at him now.

The lopsided smile again and a contentment, a sitting back, happy to watch now, as if he's *amused* by me and relaxing, as if he's sensed that something has firmed. He's changing so much, it's as if he's making himself up as he goes.

He tells me there's a label on a brand of local mineral water that reads *gently carbonated* and he says only the English could write that sort of bullshit and he hopes that one thing he'll never be is *gently carbonated*, thank God you're not, he says. He stands and the cat spills from him and he picks up his Polaroid and probes plaster scrolls and door handles and cornices, all the while lulling me with nuggets of talk that keep me reluctantly held, telling me that he wants to settle some day, that he wants his dream house to have the quality of a lit candle, something as warm and quiet as that, telling me that it'd be somewhere back home, deep in the bush, away from other people, in the clean air, a loved place. Not like this, he says, running a hand across a water-stained wall like it's a horse's flank, it's not cherished, I've salvaged three doorknobs already and no one will ever know.

You've *what?*

Snatching up his torch, glaring the light onto him and he turns his head sharply from the sting of its glow. I don't let up, examine the face, don't trust it.

I want the doorknobs put back and I want you out of here by mid-morning.

Moving to the doorway but he's ahead of me quick.

Come to London with me.

What?

Run away, just for a couple of days. I need a playmate, it'll be fun. I'll be your guide.

Shaking my head in astonishment and catching sight of the light-stained dark and flurrying past him, his torch still in my hand.

I don't need a guide, thanks very much.

But how does he know that London is the place where I'm concentrating all my hopes, how does he know *that?* The door has no handle, there's a horrible, blunt gape and a fresh swamp of anger and I'm saying colder this time that he has until ten a.m. before I tell Cedric and my fury's now entrenched.

Who's Cedric?

He doesn't have to know. You won't tell him, he bounces back and there's the rub of his voice, the certainty in it and I don't look at him and I've forgotten to ask for his books, *damn.* Run away with me, come and play, it's sung one last time at my back and I don't turn and I'm certainly not giving him any more talk but he doesn't see my disbelieving smile or my shaking of my head because within all the teasing he's managed to hit something on the head, the fear I have now that I'll die before I ever know anything of the world, or even, perhaps, a man. But I can't abandon my stroke-slowed grandfather in the cottage, I've already resolved that, I can't put him through the trauma of it, I've grown to cherish him too much. And anyway, how ridiculous, this new boy in my life just isn't the running-away-with type, God, can't he see that, he's no dreamed-of rescuer and I'm not attracted full stop, he's from home and too irritating and too young. I've made this trip to be a student of the world and to fall in love and he's no good for any of that.

Hey, think about it.

One more cheeky, laughing yell but I've turned down the stairs, I've gone.

But there that Lillie Bird is, fury now spent as she strides back across the fields and her heart singing from a strange haunting, for that teasing grate of a boy-man is the only person she's held a long conversation with over the past eight years who's treated her without any admonition or distrust, who's shown her the possibility of an untainted friendship, who's proved she can begin afresh. And he's somehow wheedled under skin, not sure how, maybe the lighting of the match. And should she be so quick to fling people from her when she needs every experience she can get? She's thinking of a quote, she doesn't know from whom, *if you break, break going out, not in*, and she's thinking that perhaps, perhaps it's worth keeping, all this. She cannot push him from her, the fingers on the cat and the flame finding its calm and the grin and the wrist and she's sure he'll be there beyond ten a.m. for she hasn't finished with him yet.

It takes half an hour of hauling, grating work to climb to her room and once Lillie's inside she shuts the window tight, battening herself into the warmth. The wind tugs and the glass rattles but the window holds firm and protesting on its latch and she slips under the heavy bedcovers, naked, and can't stop thinking of the prickly boy alone with his books under a roof of cold stars and how she cups his fate, in a way, in the palm of her hand. She could go back, or leave him alone, or call the police – well not that, yet. Again, she doesn't even have a name and she bangs her head on the pillow, she's hopeless at this and he's so vivid in her head, she can't scrape him out, his certainty, his tease, his sudden tremble, his taunt.

Come to London with me . . . come and play . . . I'll be your guide.

Cedric's snugly slippered feet creak outside Lillie's door at eight on the dot and she wakes with a start and all ragged, for it seems as if her head has only just settled into the pillow before it's being forced out. In that mewly hour she makes a cup of tea and can hardly hear the wind outside the jammed-shut house but can see the protesting trees, it's a blustery, squally mongrel of a day and the local radio says several more are to come and that not even the fishing boats have put to sea. She glances across at Evendon, wonders if his piece of fluff in the village will help him out.

Cedric is precise with a fresh list of rewrites and she strains at his jottings, resolutely desk-bound and more and more jittery as ten a.m. crawls close for the boy's crowding her thoughts too much.

112

She's not allowed to walk into the wind until midday but by nine fifty-five, head snaggled, she's abandoned all work.

Walking calmly along the path to Evendon until the cottage's sightline is slipped from and then running and running and splashing mud up my legs and as I get closer to the house I can smell the lovely perfume of an open wood fire and soft rain in the cold and my heart's lifting at the building being cranked into a working once again and I'm bolting two at a time up the stairs and in the room of flapping birds there's a grate of glowing ash that's softening away but there's no backpack, no sleeping mat, no note, and not in any of the rooms near it.

Hello? Are you there?

Only emptiness answering back. I can't believe he's vanished, just like that, and I head home, my temples thudding with disappointment, for I thought I'd worked him out.

Hey, you, stepping from the trees and his camera pointing at me and I'm all smile, filling like a glass.

I thought you'd gone!

Yeah, well, I'm not very good at sticking to the rules, never have been, ask my mum. Hey, come and have a look at something.

What's your name, by the way, so I can give a full account to the police?

Dan. My father calls me Daniel, but Dan's what I like, and there's the distinctive grin and the extended hand and I take it and hold onto it for a touch too long, curious, nothing else and he slips it back.

OK, Dan, Daniel, Daniel-in-the-lion's-den, show me what you've got.

You have to tell me *your* name first.

Lillie. As in the flower.

God, that's much too pathetic for someone like you.

Raised eyebrows. Nothing more.

*

We enter through a bower of branches overhanging a fragment of a path and almost swallowing it complete and swiftly we're gulped by a new world, there's a distant wind-roar and closer birds somewhere and scurries of low animals but I can't catch what and at one point we have to crawl, Indian file, on hands and knees under a toppled, moss-heavy branch.

Do you want to go on? Tell me if you don't.

Oh yeah, as I stand and brush myself off. Huge tree trunks have twisted to get at the light and we stop at the great groaning grooves in one of them and run our hands up the curves and stiffen back a touching and the path darkens and the world closes over us with a jumble of vine and ivy, there's no bark or dirt, it's all green, the canopy of cover is complete. *Hey look*, and my hands are tearing at the undergrowth, scrabbling at an old gatepost that's as beautiful as the curved leg of a Victorian table and with both of our hands it's freed. And then an enormous stone wall is ahead of us, it's bowed out as if it's been bloated by the sun and crowned with tenacious weeds that have found footholds somehow on its rim. There's a gate, Dan yells and I quicken to it and it takes the strength of both of us to heave it open, to break the lashings of brambles on the other side. Inside is a circular produce garden, its beds are still there amid a blather of weeds as tall as a child and on the far side, askew, is the peak of a greenhouse, its beautifully carved wooden apex straining from nature's clutching like a man reaching from quicksand or an earthquake-sunk church.

We look at each other and smile our secret. Nearby is an old tree whose branches curve gracefully into the ground and we stand close to its wide trunk, marvelling at the bark that echoes the stone of the wall in some crazy Darwinian adaptation.

I feel like we're standing under the skirt of a Victorian giant.

Woohoo, Lil, I like the sound of that.

Steady.

And I look across at him, smiling, for he hasn't lifted his camera once. Well, aren't you going to use that thing now? He looks down. Fuck, I forgot, I was too blown out, God, I feel so happy, I feel like this is one of the happiest days of my life, and his face is all filled with beam and light.

I step back. To spill himself so much, I'm intrigued by that. Perhaps there *is* something to be learned, perhaps he *will* do for now, but I won't tell him any of that. I watch him close, in repose, when he's forgotten to act and there's a sudden melancholy in his eyes and a kindness in his mouth and yes, there is something worth pursuing in all of that.

I need to speak with someone for I feel fit to burst and my only trusted confidante is Ed. *Letters mingle souls*, she had told me once, quoting Donne, and I'd loved it so much that I'd bounced the quote back. But I can't speak to her of this morning, only to my journal can I confess about the fluttery newness that's in me, the tug, the wet.

I write this out now, for you. What do you see in there, in your warm little cave? The thump of red? Pulsing dark? Streakings of light? I hope it's red, ruby red, I hope that.

— 8 —

Growing Her Up

He's holding a small waisted glass, inside is a golden liquid, he flicks a match and lights the surface with a flourish and she gasps and claps her hands in delight. There's a blue swirl of fire and smoke and he blows the flame out and hands it across and there's the glass softly hot and the tang, still, of a freshly struck match, it plumes through her and she nibbles a sipping and languishes the potency in her mouth, languishes the flavour of hazelnuts and luxury and something dangerous and something delicious subtly stinging it. He chuckles as if his child has taken its first step.

It's called amaretto, I came across sixteen bottles in a cupboard, and one glass, he says, as he takes the glass from her and finishes it off. He tells her he'd love to have a go at growing her up. She looks at him sceptically and laughs, too abrupt. It's beyond midnight, she must get back.

She grows bolder, does daylight now too, when there's time to steal from Ced's fret.

Dan's left little notes for her to find him, tiny pieces of him on white cards, they're in strategic places around the house in his beautiful architect's hand that doesn't match the grubbiness of his bracelet. *This way, Miss Lillie. You're doing well. Follow the arrow for the next book.* The cards lead her to a conservatory, she's never seen it before, it's all brown, brittle plants and dirty glass and winter light. He's sewing, patching his socks, barefoot. She sits on an old iron chair and they say nothing, they're comfortable within their

116

silence and she loves that, that they don't *have* to talk. There are his sensuous feet, the high arch, the rake-splay of bones and the small, neat stitches and she's intrigued by the hands so swift and precise with their tiny work. It's erotic, she doesn't know why and yet she feels nothing for him, she's not interested in that. He's still telling her they're fated to be together, that he's fascinated, struck. It's too easy. He's young and from home and she wants anything but.

The first massage by a man, he's ploughing the skin of her T-shirted back with a plastic comb and its teeth are slipping down her bare arms and he's reaping goosebumps and swiftly he's enslaved.

Come to London with me, Lil, come on, I'd love to have a go at growing you up.

She looks at him sceptically and laughs, a little less abruptly now.

You can't teach me anything, mate.

Oh yes I can, you just wait, he's laughing back.

There's someone else. Anna Sarah Henderson, who's unlike any woman I've encountered in my life. Rebecca told me once it was as if her younger sister had been invented by someone with too large an imagination and I wonder if it had been a contributing factor in driving Rebecca out, that she had to leave the country to escape her sibling's glow. My aunt smells of strong coffee and fresh bedlinen and men's aftershave and she's as calm and distant as a trickle of cool water and she's been permanently thirty-six since the age of ten. She's a corporate lawyer, in London. *A pirate of a woman*, Rebecca had written, and she was a little afraid of her, once.

Anna smartly drags out the rubber band that claws at my ponytail. Ignores the yelp. Webs it around her buffed fingernails. Her eyes are flinty and her face is sharp, all bones and angles and her hair is bobbed blunt and the colour of midnight.

There's an old saying, Lil, that the first marriage is for love, the second for money, and the third for friendship. Seb's my husband and he's also my best friend and he's been hanging around for, God, *so* long, bless.

She holds my chin firmly in front of the mirror and lifts off the glasses and snaps them away because contact lenses must be worn from now on, no one likes a clever girl, especially in England, and I'll feel taller without my glasses and bolder – as knuckles are dug into my lower back, as they work my reader's spine into straightness. My world's a sudden blur and fingers scrabble for a bedpost and I feel as shorn as a sheep under her nurse-brisk hands and then there's a trickle of the softest satin before me, it's brazenly adult, ankle length and sleeveless and dipping low in the back and it's flourished before me and floated over my head. I gasp. It's mine to borrow if I want. The dress's fabric is the palest turquoise – it is *exactly* the colour of the inside of a quail's egg, Anna says – and I hold its slipperiness close and catch in its folds the ghosts of lovely smells and shining parties and men close.

My aunt stretches on the bed and tells me, grinning, that the best thing about the dress is that it doesn't need ironing because ironing is terribly working class, there's a man who's to inherit half of Scotland and he constantly wears crushed shirts and it's magnificent and irreverent and sexy, for men obsessive about ironing are anally retentive, they're not good in bed, they're stiff in the wrong places and I laugh through a blushing. Oh God, I'm such an appalling influence, aren't I? I'm actually considered the golden one, the one that turned out all right. Lucky you, and Anna uses her fingers as a comb and bunches my hair and tells me that no, it's exceedingly boring being the good daughter all the time. Why? Because the more children make their parents suffer the more passionately those parents will love them. Her father's always mooning about his lost daughter on the other side of the world and because she's the successful one and he doesn't have to extend himself with her, it's too easy, so she's ignored.

Your parents must adore *you*, she says.

I don't know.

Oh yes you do. You have a quality of mystery about you, Lillie, and it must drive them absolutely crazy. We *all* want to know why you did it.

Thinking of Dan too much.

Laughing over something I've said and then leaning close and kissing me awkwardly on the cheek and staying with my skin as if he's trying to hold on to my smell for a fraction of a second and I'm tightening, feeling nothing, but how can I tell him that? Without another word I'm gone from him, giving him nothing back.

I slip on the dress. Anna jiggles it straight. Pushes straight my slump. Steps back.

Style is what you do with the mistakes, Lillie. You know, Barbra Streisand's nose, Audrey Hepburn's neck, that kind of thing. The trick is to accentuate them. Your mistakes are your weird yellow eyes that stare too much so I've brought them out and made the rest of you very plain. See. Nothing detracts from the face, it's perfect. The goddess Coco Chanel said that elegance is refusal and I live by that.

Transfixed by the blurred, barely recognizable woman in the mirror, for it feels like an anointing, a hauling into adulthood, or at least a journey's departing.

I want to show Dan, to see his face, I want him circling *this*.

Anna says the old quilt on my bed is soaked in stories of the family's life and her fingers run along a scrap of kitchen curtain from the day Rebecca was born and her mother's old maternity dress and her own school uniform and I stare at her, all softened, and wonder at the scattering that's befallen four such painstakingly sewed lives.

What happened to your mother, Annie?

She walked out when I was six, and of course instantly took on all the glamorous qualities of a film star because I never saw her in her old nightie and she never did the washing up.

How often did you see her?

Four times after she left, and that was before I was nine, and then it stopped.

I wonder at all the scattering within Dan's life, but he's clammed about that. What's known: he loves comic books – *Richie Rich* and *Phantom* are the best – and Steinbeck and Greene and the Beatles, still, and jazz, a lot. His surname is Smith and it tells me nothing, half the world's called that, and he's a policeman's only son and he hates it, there's too much expectation in it and I suspect it's all tied up with the boyish face and the endearing grin that to a tight nuclear family can do no wrong.

Yet I can't work him out, can't grasp him, there's something not quite right. There are motorbike posters on his wall at home but nothing of photography for he doesn't want it let out. He tells me he never really started anything 'proper' with his life because he always wanted to be the best, never a beginner, never awkward or gauche. With photography he could make his mistakes alone and that's how he likes it, being apart, observing, just mucking about.

He isn't a typical policeman's son. From his father there's no tolerance for something as flimsy and pansy as a photographer's life and even this trip has been frowned upon. His mother's hope is that it'll straighten him out, that he'll return to a set path rid of all the strange fractiousness that's never publicly spoken of.

He loves cartons of coffee-flavoured milk and his body reflects it – it's not fat but well-fed and he's redeemed by his height which stretches it out. There's a beloved kid sister and a home surrounded by a beloved bush and an empty swimming pool where he learned to skateboard when he was eight.

Why was it empty?

Because my father hated cleaning it and eventually it went green and one day he just pulled the plug. It made a great ramp.

So, a respectable upbringing and golden looks and yet the doorknob stealing and the squatting, the boldness and the cheek and it doesn't add up, why he's here, and it doesn't add up why I'm not demanding any more that he get out. It's charming, and dangerous, how the clarity of first impressions can so easily be wiped, how a prickle of suspicion can suddenly be gone. For most nights there I am, imagine it, sliddery-scraping down the roof slate and striding along the cow paths and looking back for any lights snapped on in Cedric's house.

Such wanting of a friend, such lengths. And a falling, but into what?

Ced is having some people around for dinner, for the first time in ten years.

It's not one of those dinner parties, nothing as fancy as that, but yes, my dear, you may dress up.

The doorbell rings and before any of us can answer Richard bursts into the room, clasping Cedric's hand and bowling up to Anna and kissing her on both cheeks and then catching my eye and stopping, lost, for a second too long. There's the stately bow of the head and another blush and it floods me tall with composure, enough for us both, there's his how are you and the shocking intimacy of it in the public place.

I'm fine thank you, Mr Daunt.

You look extraordinary, I hardly recognized you, he's speaking as if we're the only ones in the room.

Was I that horrible to start off with?

Just a little sunburnt around the edges.

He turns to Cedric and says he hopes his granddaughter is sitting next to him, she must and Cedric smiles and tells him that he should've replied to the invitation because he hasn't been included in the seating plan, Oh come come, you can improvise, returning his face to its normal state and then sidling close, you *will* sit next to me, won't you? a little-boy-lost look on his face.

I will, but I must warn you that I'm blind and will have to be guided. Anna has removed my glasses, she says it's something to do with looking taller and I'm not to complain under any circumstances and that it's better to be blind than brainy.

Well, well, I never thought we'd agree on anything.

*

Dan will never see me like this, transformed, with the hair and the dress and the new face, the new eyes.

The other guests are arriving and I'm sitting in a corner, I like it like that, I'm not quite ready for the social-mingle thing and I'm soaking up the vibrancy of the chatter and the blur of cold, buffed faces and then I'm swamped by Richard, his consuming attention and Anna hands me a champagne in flitting passing. It's my first, the drink in books, at last, the drink of parties and weddings and toasts and I hold the fluted slimness at eye level and stare at the lovely march of the beads up the golden liquid and taste it, tentatively, the soft honey fizz and it's wonderful, gone, so quick, and I'm beginning to float in a sweet champagne high as Anna tops up the glass again and again with her wry grin. Richard is close beside me, his knees are nudging mine and we're slipping into talk of travelling the world and of exploring lives, of my mother and the bush at Bony Mountain and the sanctity of silence and people are filtering into our sphere but I'm hardly seeing them and in the thick of his thieving concentration upon me I'm feeling beautiful and sparkling and centred and watched. And I've grasped that night the essence of his gift: that when he focuses on people he makes them feel absolutely wanted, absolutely unique, and I can feel myself being drawn under like a swimmer in a soft, insistent rip and in the thick of it I'm calling him Rick, for the first time, I've only heard my mother call him that.

At one point Anna's voice crashes too loud into our talk, mid-conversation to someone else: Well, I never would've got where I have with a trust fund, every person I know who's inherited large amounts is utterly hopeless, don't you think? And Richard's raising his glass and saying loudly, Thank goodness *I* didn't inherit then, and Anna's replying that yes, he's normal, but only just, and throwing me a glance and there's a smile crumpling down the corners of her mouth and I'm seeing, suddenly, another side of the woman permanently thirty-six, a chasm quickly shut, something brittle and vulnerable and snapable and I'm turning back to Richard and I'm watching myself tell him from a distance, from a champagne headiness, that I think I may have a crush on him.

Really?

He's splashing out another glass of red and telling us that when he first met Cedric he wanted him sent to Cambridge to be bottled because he was just so delightfully unique. Oh yes, a collector's item. That at Ced's first ever dinner party, for dessert, he'd tipped into everyone's cereal bowls chocolate-covered peanuts from a brown paper bag and it was probably because there'd be less mess to wash up because Cedric can't cope with that and one by one the table's drawn to the talk and Richard's egged on. He tells them that at the age of fifty-two Ced went back to school and learned some theory about the conservation of energy so only ever used one light bulb for years and undressed at night by the white noise of the TV and hated cupboard doors because they wasted time and so took them all off, but his oddity has mellowed, hasn't it, Ced, and my grandfather is nodding and smiling pale but I can read his discomfort and there's a crackle of sweat, I'm necklaced by it.

There's a form of public school bullying, Lillie, that the upper class has perfected, don't be alarmed, it's harmless, Anna's explaining to me, Richard's a master at it even though he never went to a public school himself, he's like a magpie, he'll pick anything up and the table's laughing and then Anna's asking, So what do *you* think of Ced, you're in cahoots with him now, but my breath's tightening and tightening and I sit back, wanting out, Come on, speak up, say all the mouths around me and I haven't yet learned a smooth talking back and I'm stumped, mouth dry, I want to yell stop but Come on, they all demand, spit it out, and I say, suddenly harsh, I'M NOT A PERFORMING MONKEY, and the hubbub drops to a shocked hush and I look around, bewildered, needing escape.

Cedric teepees his fingers and places the apex at his chin and asks mildly if there's anyone in particular to hate at the moment, he needs catching up, and I sit rattled and mute through the story of the Asian cadets who'd bribed the officers at Sandhurst with gold watches for better grades but the cadets had complained because the officers were taking the bribes and not changing their marks, Why should they? someone says, haw haw. I sit mute through vivesections of facelifts and priestly affairs and divorces and stare through my red wine, my first ever, as the strutting talk, the glutton-chorus gathers pace and I wonder where Dan is that night, if he's in the house, I want to light his cigarette, I want quiet and the calm of all that and I stand, needing air, needing out.

But Cedric needs me, and I can't walk away from that.

As I steel myself to return to the dining room Richard walks towards me along the narrow corridor and there's his smell, close, and he leans into me and kisses me, a snatch, it's the first time my lips have been touched by another's, there's the nub of his tongue, the enquiry in it, his wine-mellow breath, the scratch of his skin, his taste. There's the sweeping of my mouth as if he's searching for something, there's the question in his kiss, there's his hand firm in the small of my startled back and the hardness between his legs and then he says excuse me, and smiles and continues on. I walk back to the table flooded, trembling, changed, the kiss savage through my blood.

How are you finding our weather? someone asks and I'm replying, stumbling, I love it, the rain and the cold, my cheeks flushed and not thinking straight and there's talk of water being used to clean the stables and it freezing in great sheets to the walls, talk of the woman in Scotland who killed herself rather than face another long dark winter, It's a disease called seasonal affective disorder, a depression triggered by lack of sunshine and she was sent south every January but it did her no good and I'm only scrappily listening for there are Richard's eyes straight into me on his return, asking me, challenging me and I feel wanted, flooded, it's begun.

Not that she'd ever complain, he says. Lillie, we Brits have a habit of not speaking up, it's why our actors can never get Tennessee Williams right, it's just not in our blood to be emotional or spontaneous, and his eyes are warm at me as Anna's voice shoulders into the looking, as she tells us about an elderly couple who had pneumonia and died within a day of each other because they didn't want to disturb their doctor, as she tells us about timidity, the English disease, as she attempts to work out the red that's vining my face and my neck.

Someone asks me what I want to do while I'm here and I say too loudly, Oh, be in a girl band and then have a solo career and write my autobiography at twenty-five, and there's a chill in a weak smile and an awkward pause and Richard swoops.

You must always remember, Lillie, that whereas success and naked ambition are applauded in some parts of the world, we English tend to look a little less generously at boldness. We don't venerate stories like Oprah's and if we had a Michelangelo around now I think he would have been laughed down long before he got to the chapel roof.

Hear hear, Anna claps.

You have to move to London, he says, you'll never do anything from here. His eyes are straight at me and I try to brace my focus, to work a way out, London, the dream, but I'd never be allowed and I can't leave Cedric and I have no way of getting to it by myself.

Ced, what would you do if you found a tramp camping out in the great house?

Shoot him, Lillie, right between the eyes.

Another drink? says Anna, flicking the air with a flourish of her arm and several more bottles are brought, wine and mineral water and Cedric places the latter firmly in front of me and *Gently Carbonated* declares one label and I think of Dan huddling right now in the house, alone, and *Delightfully Still* says the other label and yes, I look around, and I know that I have to live in that great city, somehow, I *have* to. I'm taunted by the thought of just that one tantalizing car-glimpse and I look across at Richard for in little more than a month I'll be on a plane home and time's leaking fast and I don't want all this crumbling into a never-scrubbed regret.

You have to move to London, you'll never do anything from here.
Yes.

Back in my room Anna's whipping a cigar from a slim wooden box and lighting it with a tall flame and snapping her lighter shut and the smell's stinging the small space. I'm walking to the window, all restless, and staring out at the silhouette of the great, black building and wondering about Dan, is he asleep, warm, is he there, and I'm asking my aunt, tetchily, why everyone refers to Evendon as a house when it's anything but, it's diminished by such a humble, suburban word.

There's a great love of understatement in this country.

You're telling me. Do you reckon there'd ever be campers in it?

Lord, no, it's too cold. And unsafe. Only a madman would stay in it for more than one night. Ugh! This cigar is so tight it's like smoking a pencil, I can't draw from it.

Anna rolls the tip delicately on a newspaper and I ask her to come out for a walk the next day, to take a look at the grounds and she says she just doesn't get that rambling thing, England isn't deeply in her blood, she doesn't know why, she has no respect for gardens or baked beans or the countryside or dogs and all in all she's exceedingly odd.

That's why I love you, Annie.

She smiles, lies back, slips into a lesson – your first, girl – on how I must to get on in this land. Air-hair-lair. Get it? Air-hair-lair. Oh yeah, and a chuckling from us both. My evil school taught me that, Lil. It was a horribly repressed, single-sex boarding school that your mother and I stupidly won scholarships to. We were taught how to speak, and how to conduct ourselves with good old-fashioned British reticence. For example, if I wanted the water at table I'd have to say 'Would you care for some water?' and pass it to all the others first so that by the time it got to me it was empty – that's what being a lady was all about. Propping her feet on the quilt, whipping out a cigarette. Bette Davis taught me to smoke, Lauren Bacall to drink. There's a book you must read, I'll lend it

126

to you and there's the tall flame again, don't tell Dad, drawing deep, or, heaven forbid, your mad mother.

She never talks about her school, I don't know why.

Of course she doesn't, that's her way. She hated it, it was one of the things that drove her out of this country. She was always looking for something a bit more exotic and . . . red-blooded, I guess, and that's why she loved your father. He seemed such a dare. You see, at school there was the banana rule, which meant that all the girls had to eat bananas cut up on a plate in the dining room because eating one whole was seen as sexually suggestive and I tell you, that type of thing drove your mother crazy. So, my dear, you missed out on nothing being schooled at home. In fact, I think you were rather canny.

I do too.

We smile, a friendship sealed. Watch that Richard Daunt is the last thing Anna whispers as I'm kissed goodnight. Why? Because he eats women up, with a smoky smile, and in stockinged feet she has left. We must get you some contact lenses, as she makes her way down the creaky corridor, tomorrow, don't forget, night night.

With glasses firmly back on I'm staring at my changed self in the bedroom mirror, at the watery, adult folds of the new dress. I'm tightening my tummy and sucking in my cheeks, thinking of Richard and the fireman's thighs and thinking of Dan and his fingers and his feet and I'm cupping my hand under my belly and trying to still my body's churning tug and the grip in my groin, the sweet pull of it and there's something new through me, something brazen and womanly and it's rich and deep and dark red. The rhythm of rain against the window is a soft spattering of rice and I'm thinking of the sanctity of love and a sealing kiss and the insistent light is arcing in a window of Evendon again, calling, urging me out, but I don't go across, I've been going across too much, and I now have a kiss holding me back.

Asleep, the world is transformed.

A snow-scrubbed day has absorbed all sound, even the sea is

meekened, there's a gentle swell in it, a slow rise and fall like a giant's slumbering breath and the sky is milky and I don't know what it's bringing next and I run out into it and there's the lovely crunch of my sinking footsteps and all around me white-laden trees like strange, still coral and a hovering quiet as if the whole world's waiting for God knows what.

I walk through snow as resistant as a frozen grape, I'm collecting the milk, it's too far for Cedric. The birds have a habit of drinking from the silver-topped bottles and the milkman leaves a piece of tin on top weighted down with a stone, and there in the cleanness of that wondrous morning, freshly stubbed on the rock, is a familiar, self-rolled cigarette. I flick it away, my fingers retracting at the wet lip and under the tin are two brand-new books, *Doctor Zhivago* and *Breakfast at Tiffany's* but I retract at them too, don't need them, he's trying too hard, I don't want a binding, I have Richard now for that.

Gone off reading?

He falls into step beside me and tries tugging the wire basket of bottles from my grasp but I won't yield and I tell him, I'll get my own books, thanks, for he's too jaunty, he's getting too close and I don't want to be ensnared in some bribe of kindness that'll have to be repaid down the track. I can feel complication coming into all this. He tugs harder. I firm my grip. He yanks the basket from me and the bottles clang their protest and I sense then what I've sensed before, but have forgotten, it's a violence in him that I suspect could break me one day if I don't watch out. It was there as he clamped his fingers across my mouth on the very first night, as he held me tight, as he welted my arm. Sometimes I can't see any gentleness in him but it's not vindictive or deliberately aggressive, it's unknowing, and in a way all the more frightening for that. He doesn't realize his strength, how he could snap me with a grasp, how all it would take is for the golden surface to crack and something else would come spilling out, I'm not sure what.

Come and have a look at something, quick. Beckoning with his camera, all intent.

Shouldn't you have finished with this place by now?

Nope, not yet.

I hold back. His brow clouds. He comes close. Reaches out for me and his fingers are hurting as he tugs me into the garden, he's leaving his welts, stamping the imprint of his fingers, he's twisting skin and there's the determination in him and I don't like it and he won't let me go no matter how much I pull from him and I'm laughing at the start but then I'm not, it's all snuffed, for I don't like the ownership in the grip.

It'll lure your grandfather back to the garden, I can guarantee it. *Come on.*

And that, reluctantly, is what gets me. I soften. His fingers loosen. He hands the milk bottles back. I set them gently on the ground. Follow, not too close.

A path of snow-streaked loam lifts back like a carpet to reveal a pale gravel underneath, waiting for a waking. Guess where it leads to? as the smooth dark shuts over us, come on, don't be afraid, drawing me in, but I don't come too close and my hands whisper along grooved trunks and moss and I listen to the faraway funnelling of wind that's the sound of the sea as I mull over Richard's question in his kiss and my grandfather's hover and Dan's hurting grip. We pass rhododendrons startled through ferns and lichen-covered tree roots like giant, slumbering lizards, it's all protected from the snow by a roof of green and then we stop in a small clearing, isn't it incredible, see, and he's gently holding my hand and this time I'm not drawing back.

Hey, I'm sorry for before, he says.

Nodding, giving him nothing.

Before us, a flower garden, almost completely whiskered by snow-weighted weed. An old summerhouse with three arches veiled to the ground by vines, facing an overgrown hedge high before the sea. This is where proposals would've been made, this place is soaked in old love like the lace curtains on the wreck of a house my parents had found once. I push through the vines, expecting a lovers' seat perhaps, but there's just a honeycomb stacking of old terracotta pots in the dank coolness. Dan brushes a touching and I flinch from him and walk to the garden's edge and stare at a darker band of cloud on the horizon that's nudging the water and looks like a sudden new land.

You'll get there some day, he says behind me, too close.

Where?

France. I'm going there soon, why don't you come too?

A shrugging. It isn't as easy as that, I say and there's bitten silence: not everyone lives as loosely as him. I have to get back to the house, I say, my grandfather's waiting.

I think I should pay a visit to him. Ask if I can take you on a school excursion or something, because, you know, I'd really like to see you out there one day.

Attack in his voice for the first time.

Where?

The real world. You're so sheltered, so cautious, you don't know *anything*.

I don't answer, I huff from him. How dare he say he's going to bowl up to Ced.

How old are you, Lillie? Twelve? Fourteen? Don't you *ever* want to grow up? I just want to see you out there, in life.

Not looking back as he yells after me that with life, you just have to go out and grab it, and not looking back as I crash my way home and he's not following, there's just a frustrated crack, he's flung a rock against the summerhouse or kicked a brick, I don't know what but he's not crashing through the undergrowth after me, thank God for that, and my head is with his taunt and a kiss and a quail-egg dress and a house probably without any doorknobs left.

I sweep through the cottage door and crash the milk bottles on the table, clenched. He's gone too far, and he's getting too close.

A phone call, no introduction just Do you mind if I chase you? and there's the warm, confident ooze of his voice and it's silking me back to a calm, *this* is what I need. I want to see you again, Lillie. But how, my grandfather won't— and there's his urgency,

Can we get you up to London, can we get you out? I'll have to think. Ring me, I'll ring you, if you stay at Evendon I won't see you again and then you'll be back in Sunshine and lost. The question in his kiss is singing through me still, something's all awoken, and there's no insistent arm grips and no accusations and no intensity, no swamp.

Fuming, still. I want a winning, I want Dan's arrogant, knowing, boy-grin cracked. And I want to get an idea of how he plans to go to London, to see a way. I want Cedric to come with me to gravity the command, to meet him on my terms, not his. He's got to move out.

Evendon always makes me think of a martyr with its tongue ripped out, Lillie. I don't know why you persist in wanting me dragged across to the corpse. I'm too old for that.

Cedric will not be budged, it's in his face, it hurts too much, he doesn't want the mess of all that.

So there that Lillie Bird is, walking Evendon's rooms through broad bands of light filtering from half-closed shutters, alone. The house is alive with sound from too many secret places where the wind's found wending ways in and there's the fear, again, for the first time since she's found the books in the library, just a touch, she's not sure why. There are ceilings gently bulging like ripe, pregnant bellies and parqueted floors spongy with moisture and tapestries falling into nothing and in one room there are the fine mahogany legs of a table robbed of its top and in another a billiard table that's just a turf of rectangular green, its legs sawn off. There's no sign of Dan and the house seems resolutely empty and she feels a flutter that she's been trumped: he's stormed out, and no address, no goodbye. He's so difficult to pin down, so slippery, ungraspable. She hurries to the library and searches the window seat and the shelves for any sign, thinking of a promise to one day photograph her before noon, or just awake – over my dead body, mate – the best times for a woman he'd said and yet now he's gone and she could've sent the photo to Richard and she doesn't know where he'll be next, London or France, or when he'll head home and he's her first untainted friend and infuriating as he is she doesn't want that lost.

Ced, would you ever allow me to have a gentlemen friend while I was here?

Goodness no, he says from behind a tall paper and then flips down the headline and peers over it. Don't look at me like that, Lillie, you're not here to chase the opposite sex, you're here to work and be safely delivered home. You can worry about all that when you're back.

I turn to the window and Cedric comes behind me and puts his hands on my shoulders and tells me that when it does eventually happen to seize it and not let it slip by. Why? Because when he was sixteen he'd met a woman he'd felt strongly about, but he'd never followed it through, and not a day goes by without him thinking of her and what, perhaps, could have been.

Who was she? Where were you? Ced?

But he wouldn't say.

Back again, one more try, every single room, no luck. At the end of it I'm pushing through a revolving mirrored door into a ballroom that seems as empty as a shut stadium and I'm standing in its centre, very still, and turning and listening and it feels as if Dan has disappeared into the air and it feels that my life all of a sudden is a leaky wooden ship finally giving way to the water, with all of my dreams rushing out.

−9−

The Leap

Sitting on my window ledge on the wild finger of land with the ocean all restless around me and the faint smell of diesel or oil carried on the breeze, murmuring the industry of a wider world and then I'm pushing the windows wide to feel the day and there are birds circling, they're dipping and soaring and calling me away. But I've no idea how to go and just a handful of weeks left and in that softening day I'm thinking of all the things I could do to snare Richard and all the paths to London I could take, yet I'm goodness-bound, held by it, have been for most of my life. But something is making me contemplate once again a magnificently irrational act − love, its promise − and I gasp even now as I reread my journal, at all the undoing that infatuation can flame. For suddenly there I am, all rush and hunger as I contemplate a spring-cleaning of the duty-stilled life, before it's too late, and I'm back.

A phone call from Anna, she's sent a package to be opened in my room and kept under the mattress and never shown for she's decided to take over the growing up. *The Story of O.* The guilty, hot wet of it, the swiftness in my turning and the hand clamped between my legs. Not understanding it, not able to put it down. Every night, revisiting.

Richard rings, late, his voice more insistent now. London, *when?* I don't know, I don't know. There's to be a party at his new house in the country, a chance, in a room overlooking the topiary garden and the bushes will be lit with two thousand fairy lights and we're all invited and I must come, I *must*, Thursday week. I'll be there, I can't wait, and there's the memory of the budge of his soft enquiring tongue, there's my wet.

Cedric's straining to catch the identity of the caller and I'll be ringed by watching family at the party and ringed by them until I board a plane home and as I convey the invitation to him I know I could never go against his wishes and I kiss him softly goodnight and climb up the stairs to my room, feeling a tear now permanent in my calm, for my grandfather's whole life has been a movement towards perfection, a gradual tightening of the screws and a polishing of all the locks and I couldn't ever thwart that for I care for him too much. And Dan's disappeared, fuck.

Walking restlessly from the room-bound stillness and searching for a seat facing skyward and then turning to the great house, abandoned and stricken and lost, as if it's waiting for a lover that'll never come. There are vague plans to plough the estate up to the walls or turn it into a convention centre or a headquarters for the Hari Krishnas and Cedric, of course, would be turfed out but he won't speak, much, of any of that.

The sun blooms briefly and dances awake my forehead and cheeks and I smile into the sky for happiness is the sun and in England I know now that the sun can be bought. I've read that it means leisure and laziness and wealth, something the rich can always have just by hopping onto a plane and jetting to somewhere bright. I've read that endless grey skies and drizzle are only for the people with no money to buy access to the heat, and yet in my own land there's the great egalitarianism of free sunshine and in those last days at Evendon I'm missing it achingly, there's such a longing for its thaw for my spirit seems to soar in the baking warmth and soon I'll be back. But do I want it just yet? I'm swamped by the indecision of it all.

I walk down to the sea and think of Dan and wish he was here to talk it all out for he's from home, he'll understand. Even the cliffs are tinged a moss green and there's lichen piggybacking on the trees right to the water's edge and black prows of the grim rocks jutting out of the water like battleships and grey sand as if a permanent wash of coal has been stained into it and I don't understand such a beach, such a sky, such a land.

I walk restlessly along the old cowpaths above the cliffs with my dreaming daring to tread beyond Richard's party and into the glow of the warm London lights. All dangerously impatient with my grandfather's battened living now, with his steadfast refusal to walk his old gardens or inspect his hedges or respond to my chatter about the wild place that grew me up, the place whose spirit is snug under my skin. I'm all restlessness, and love-brinked.

I perch on the pebbly coldness at the back of Evendon's beach, there's one small wave at land's edge and the rest of the sea is flat, lake-tame, and I want to peel off my clothes in the feeble sun and air secret parts of my body to wipe out the nestling of the long winter damp.

Hey, race ya to the water.

Jumping, turning. Dan, all sun-flushed before me and I'm laughing and laughing, so he's back, and wearing a ridiculous fisherman's hat. Well, if you're not going to get off your butt then you can just sit there and have a cup of tea, and he holds out a flask. Lovely, yes, all stammer-startled, where have you been, I thought you'd gone? From the house, yes, but he hasn't quite finished with it yet, he's staying in down the track, in a fishing shed of a mate's and it's four hundred years old and God does it smell like it. He's making his way to London with a backpack full of doorknobs of course and he grins and ignores the hands stern at my hips and clatters on: he'll miss the accents but he's going to keep his own vowels no matter what, because the English are so much into conformity and not standing out in any way and it just makes him want to fiercely hold on to any difference that he has, he's always been like that, he's the kind of kid who stuck sweets up his bum as a child and then offered them around to his classmates, he was that bad.

Yeah? We had someone who did that.

Ah, one of the great schoolboy habits, like Chinese burns and cracking eggs.

Cracking what?

Eggs, eggs. What planet have you been on, girl? Close your eyes.

And he smacks his hands over my head and dribbles cool fingers down my neck and goosebumps pelt across my skin as I slither and squeal from under him.

All right! All right! I remember now! Get lost, you, stop.

My furious thinking: London, a way to it, and I stare at a gull on the sand and it doesn't move as a wave rushes all greedy around its ankles and do I dare ask? The gull holds firm and I think of delightful stillness and will myself to leap but I'm not sure I can and then deep in the conversation there's the braced nonchalance, *Hey, Dan, can I come too?* I remember even now the exact tone of it. Silence, for a fraction of a second, then a blush. Only teasing, I say, I wouldn't inflict myself on anyone, and I'm laughing it off and shutting down tight with my cowardice and frustration but very faintly shining through it there's a protectiveness for my family, for their calm. Dan says I should be doing it, says he was just about to ask me again himself, says I'll always regret it if I don't come. Why did I ask him in the first place and why did I change my mind but I just shake my head, splay my hands, grin.

What are you afraid of, Lil?

Nothing.

Really? My philosophy is that you should try two new things every year.

That sounds hideously impractical.

Well, yeah, but it's a lot of fun. For example, this year it's skiing and fudge. Remember, I have a compulsion to take risks. Now look, there must be something you're afraid of, come on, have a think.

Well, um, thunderstorms, just a little, because they seem to rumble right through me.

Uh huh.

There's a name for it, Brontophobia, a fear of thunderstorms.

His top lip curls with doubt.

It's true, my grandfather told me! I've written it down!

I thought Brontophobia was a fear of costume dramas.

I hit him in reprimand on the head, all laugh, and stare at him and can't work him out. Or my pendulum feelings for him. He's always goading, always wanting to know too much, the greed in his curiosity is too rich. He's constantly asking what I'm thinking and planning – hey, penny for your thoughts – and I can't stand any of that.

The light begins losing its vividness, the day becomes gentle at only three in the afternoon and we stare out to the chattering of the sea while Dan composes shots in a neat rectangle of thumb and index fingers, framing the ocean and framing the beached kelp and framing my thinking face. It's a blustery day still, the sun marches across the land from behind a cloud and then ducks again under another's squally fret and then it's out again and there's a patchwork of light and shade across the sea's blue.

I really do want to see France some day.

You never will from here, Lil.

Well, yeah, some day.

I'll race you to it, come on, it's just across the Channel. It's been swum before, you know.

I put my arm around his neck and yank it tight – ow, you, fuck off! – and when our laughter settles there's a long quiet. The light grows cold and Dan swoops up his flask and tells me he could meet me down on the beach, on the Friday morning, for the long-promised shot. I can't, I have a party to go to the night before at another country house and I'm staying nearby and all the house's doorknobs are firmly secured, mate. Dan grins, one side up, one side down and he leans close and kisses me awkward on the cheek and stays with my skin as if he's trying to hold on to my smell for a fraction of a second and again I tighten back and turn from him, no words, and he's gone.

Sitting alone for a while longer, staring at his receding figure and then closing my eyes and listening to the endless sea noise around me and a lone bird calling into my thinking in a wide slit in the cliff behind me, it sounds like it's trapped in a high concrete room but it isn't at all, of course. The sun's elusive, it doesn't firm sufficiently, doesn't hold, and I don't have the courage to go with Dan for I know exactly what'll be in my grandfather's face and I don't want my days tarnished by that. I'll not be going anywhere, I'll be returning soon to the sun; I walk back in a fading, butter light.

Miss Lillith Bird.
    Lillith! Is that your *real* name? I feel like I've just seen you naked!
    Blushing a nervous smiling as Richard swoops a kiss on both cheeks and sweeps me to a terrace and kisses me deeply on the mouth, drinking from me, and he's hammering into my heart and I pull back, looking for any eyes catching us out. It's OK, he's laughing, cupping my face and smoothing with both palms, Anna's on the other side of the room and her husband's at the bar and Cedric's seeing to his coat, and his hands are wondrous on my back and my shoulders and they're not letting up, it's OK, shhhh, it's all right.
    Richard's signalled away by a man's discreet tap and I'm suddenly next to a lone woman called Cin, short for Cinnamon, she tells me and Where's my journal? I'm thinking, before I forget, she has a head too big for her body and brittle-thin arms and she's bubbling with too many cocktails and questions and each one I can barely answer before another's fired off. What's my accent? How long have I been here? Do I have a boyfriend, is he hairy? That's my father over there, she's telling me, see him smiling so sweetly at everyone? He has the serenity of a man who has three mad daughters but then he's got this totally bonkers party trick – in restaurants, if a waiter ignores him, he holds up the menu and sets it alight, it's the quiet ones you've got to watch the most.
    Anna floats to us in a cloud of grey silk and matching tulle and dances me away and tells me that she needs a change of image because everyone knows her too well and a woman has to keep recreating herself as she grows older or else she becomes invisible,

like a mother with a child and oh dear, tonight is just not working, she's saying, hitching up her gown unceremoniously at the bust. It is for me. I'm relaxing, my nervousness is melting, I can do this, I can handle a crowd, belong, and I feel buoyant with it, my movements are loose and natural and excitement's trilling through me and I can read the assessing in the men's eyes, instinctively I know it and my joy's scudding high as I excuse myself for the toilet.

Don't get stuck in there, Lillie-bet. There are lots of strange men lurking about.

Your eyes are greedy, they suck me up, says Richard in whirling passing, handing me a glass of champagne and I'm laughing and squeezing from cluster to cluster as I make my way to the back of the room and I'm sipping my champagne and then Richard's back, grabbing me by the waist and twirling me, arm firm, before he's waylaid by two elderly, thickly powdered women in heavy jewellery who need a cab home.

Are you in love? asks a lone, middle-aged man beside me, pale and stupendously fat, and I throw back my head and laugh. No, just happy. Yes, I can see it, he says, your face is all light, most people have shadows but with you there's this wonderful light. You're not from here, are you? Are you enjoying it? Oh yes, very much. He looks surprised and I ask him where the toilet is and he shuts down, embarrassed, he cannot meet my eyes as he mumbles directions and I laugh my thanks and then kiss him spontaneously on the cheek, tenderly, warmly, and his hand instinctively moths around his head, batting away touch, and I'm thinking of the film *Brief Encounter* I saw with Cedric only the other night and the line about the English being so reticent and shy, how they'd all behave differently if they lived in a warm sunny climate, how they wouldn't be so withdrawn and remote and it is easy, too easy to play up to it as a visitor, to be cheeky and brazen and bold.

Richard comes up behind me and holds me firm by the waist and I don't turn, I just smile as he whispers into my neck that I have the most beautiful innocence, a radiance, he could never do anything to hurt me, doesn't want to push me; adores me. And I head to the toilet, passing Anna's room-skimming eyes and cannot stop the smiling and stare into space, lost, is this love? I don't know, I feel maddened by sex.

And then I see him.

Baggy-suited, tie askew and deep in conversation with Cedric, of all people. There's the ease of someone who's comfortable, who belongs, God, the boy with the cheeky grin who can charm himself into anything and I just stare at them both and smile at their easy chat and he catches my eye, he's cut his hair, it looks self-administered, only I can tell that. He waves his camera and clicks a shot, says something to Ced and comes over.

You look like you've brought the sun and the sky with you in your face, Miss Bird.

Swirling around me and reeling off shots and I protest, laughing, and feel a flood of tenderness for him: he's got in, the little bugger, he's found out. I demand to know what he's been discussing and he says secret men's business, and winks and asks how he looks, tells me he hasn't tied a tie since school and I say it shows and he tells me that he's wearing his special shoes, the ones that make him feel like a gentleman and he grabs me by the waist and mumbles a few steps.

Come on, let's dance, right in the centre.

No, I can't.

Dance as if no one's watching, that's the secret.

No, no, I'm laughing and feeling his hair to distract him, feeling it gravely like a farmer testing fleece for he's lost his wild and woolly youngness, he's lost his arrogance with his magically shorn locks. And then he's grabbing me by the hand and propelling me outside, stemming my protests that I've had too much to drink and must get back and there's the iron in his grip, the control of that.

You're not drunk, Miss Lillie, I can tell.

Oh really. How?

It's the way you hold yourself, the way you walk, you do it differently to every other woman here, he says, and I roll my eyes and prop my chin on my hand, mock interested, as he tells me that I walk without fear, it's like the new staff in the White House, he read it somewhere, after every change of government they walked boldly down the centre of the corridors but it doesn't take them long to start hugging the walls like everyone else and then we slump against a wall like two teenagers outside a corner shop after school and stare at the topiary nodding its lovely light. I tell him I can't believe he's got in and he says, gravely, that he's a member of the international press and I'm ramming him sideways on the shoulder, almost pushing him into a pot plant and then I'm catching Richard's keen, enquiring gaze from the other side of the room and without looking at me Dan's slipping his hand over mine, threading his firmness through my fingers.

I've got a cab waiting outside, and a spare ticket to London.

My heart tumbling to my stomach, the serene smiling across at Richard, the nodding of my head, the smiling, the nodding.

What?

Heady with champagne and not thinking straight and trying to grasp what he's saying and there's his insistent hand vine-entwined in my fingers and I've heard of a strange disease where the victim loses their balance through some disorder of the middle ear and feels as light as a feather and always has to hold onto doorposts for fear they'll fly away and I feel it as Dan speaks to me, feel as light as a feather as he holds me firm. He says he's discussed it with my grandfather, Cedric wants me out in the world and travelling and living life but can't see a way of doing it and my parents do too but none of them can see a legitimate way. Except this. Shaking my head with the magnificence of it, oh he's good, he's good. I don't believe it, I say, floating, smiling, nodding.

Trust me.

Looking across the room to my grandfather and catching his eye and he's winking and waving and I'm raising my champagne glass back and is he telling me to seize it, is it a sign? Dan's insistent in my ear and firm with his fingers: if I don't do it now I never will, it's my only chance, have I ever done anything really naughty and I catch my breath, tell him no, not really, and deeply blush.

Have *you*?

All the time, Lil.

He presses the train ticket into my fingers and I glance at the words, *London Paddington*, the magic destination, the golden pass to a new life and my head swirls with a champagne lightness and the words that are singing me into a leaping. But the casual cruelty of it, the casual cruelty of a child if I go ahead, could I? I don't know.

We have to go right this minute, my entire life savings are being eaten up with the waiting time on the cab.

But Cedric—

Dan faces me square and holds my upper arms tight and he's welting the skin again as he tells me that my grandfather wants me to do this, he really does, he just can't find a way of organizing it himself and yes, I think, yes it *is* deep down what he wants and my parents too and you know, I decide in that split second that I don't want to be a supernaturally contained person any more because to prove it is chaining me to a life of entrapment and dishonesty and nagging want, it's all nibbling away at me like so many little tongues and it has been for eight years and the experiment's over, it's been a burden for too long. The locking away has become a great sadness that's settled at the core of my family like sediment on all of our hearts and this is a chance for it all, in one swift night, to be wiped. I'll let my grandfather know, he'll not be blamed, he wants it deep down and I'll let my parents know and there might even be relief, yes I'm sure of that, and I'll be free for Richard, I'll be solving it for everyone, Dan's right. The cheeky, shorn, charming little bugger, he's shown me a way out.

OK. Let's do it.

Firm, the exhilaration of it, the clean hit.

Excellent. Come on, then, quick, before you change your mind.

I just have to say something to the host.

Him? Why?

I have to, it's polite, you know.

God, watch yourself with that one, he's as sleazy as a pair of woollen underpants.

I *have* to.

All right, but hurry. I'll be by the front gate, don't be long.

Cedric's nowhere to be found and Anna's deep in mortified conversation with Cin, the coast is clear and Richard goes to kiss me but I pull away, almost involuntarily, for I hate those cheek pecks now for it's to be bang smash on the mouth or nothing.

I'll see you in London, I say, can't resist.

What? Where? Lillie—

But I've gone.

It was a cold that blew into the bone as I ran past the wind-pitched topiaries in Anna's spindly heels and red silk skirt – I'd forgotten a coat in the haste – and looked back for one last time to the floodlit shell of a house and then too swiftly and too easily my life was barrelling down a darkened road to a sleepy train station that I knew nothing of, not even its name to this day. The car's windscreen was pinged by frozen rain pellets that had spite in the drive of them, in the headlights they looked like styrofoam balls bouncing off the road and the triumphant man in the back seat beside me didn't know what on earth to do beyond the train and I didn't either, and what have I done, what have I done? I laughed in disbelief, sliding down in the seat, my arms wide and my palms up.

Ma'am, the world is at your feet. Your wish is my command.

Well. Gosh. I've always like the sound of a town called Wing, it's somewhere to the north of here I do believe. Pray, sir, what do you think?

You can go further afield than that, if you want.

Well, there's a Texan town called Happy I'd love to try out. And a snowfield in the Alps, and the Red Sea, and, oh, crikey Moses, too much.

I drop my head onto his shoulder and laugh.

There's a place called Home that sounds pretty good to me too.

Hmmmm. Well . . .

And I remember we chuckled softly and fell into an agreeable

143

silence and the slap of the windscreen wipers was like an urgent heartbeat and then the car drove into clearness and the wipers were turned off and there was a silence where I didn't want to think too much.

Dan had arranged tickets for an overnight train to the city, five non-express hours, stopping all stops, two upright seats, It's all I could afford, he said and I looked at him doubtfully, feeling as if the watertight life was already unravelling and we sat suddenly subdued side by side, tiredness now sucking talk from us. And then Dan was asleep, as easy as that, and the heaviness of his head flopped and was hitched and then fell solidly onto my arm and I didn't mind its sudden trust, I was hesitant to disturb him if he needed the shelf of me that much and there was the sweat on his skin and his newly flushed cheeks and deep in the journey he woke, as bewildered as a child, and I wanted to hold him in that moment and soothe him tight. He glanced without seeing and slid back, hitting my shoulder again and I lifted up the seat barrier and stretched him out in a jumble of sleep and he briefly woke with the arranging and smiled at it. There are rules, I said firmly, no talk, and rigorously clothed, and toes to nose.

Phew.

Wagging a finger at him and smiling. It was the first time I'd slept beside anyone and I was determined to stay awake for it. Imagine it, the first time, and I tell you I couldn't get enough – his smell, his breathing, the heavy heat of him my blanket, his arm flung, the pale vulnerability of its inside skin, the marbling of blue, the river-map of veins. And yet there were all the questions too, scratching at my calm deep into that night, for on that journey I was like a small wooden boat whose anchor had snapped in choppy waters, I was lurching and dipping and almost capsizing. *But I was free.* And at some point the simple clarity of that swallowed all my fret, and I fell, and as in a dream I saw the night flit and wasn't sure where I'd wake next for it seemed that my path would now be planned like flares shot from a gun, powering through the dark, and I just had to trust the brightness and its landfall wherever that would be.

A woolly sock at eye level, a toe-prodded hole.

And there that Lillie Bird is, rubbing sleep from her eyes and raising her head like a fairy-tale princess waking from her thousand years. Her pillow, somehow, his hip, and she's not sure how that came about. Out the window is the last of the green with mist on the fields like cloud kissing the land and soon they're in the scumbly outskirts of the still-sleeping city and powering through the vast swell of it, past the humble house rows and council towers with their slumbering window lids, past the railway yards and the graffiti and over the criss-crossing tracks and all her late night-fear is rushing back. For in one spectacularly impulsive act she's brought crisis into her routine, for the second time in her life. As she stares out the window she tells herself again what she'd told herself the previous night, that people create crises to speed up their evolution, that rupture is good. But to put it all into practice . . . For in the flinty light of that morning-after, and in a new, panicked soberness, it's the hardest and loneliest decision she's ever made. And yet on the balcony the night before it'd been so slippery-easy, so champagne-quick. She isn't sure now that she has the courage to carry it through for it's been ingrained into her that to be free is to be wrong: as a woman of Sunshine she's been taught her place. It was why she'd once before, spectacularly, tried to change the path.

A sleep-crumpled smile from Dan. Don't even think about it, he says, crashing into my thinking. I smile weakly. My grandfather will be frantic, my aunt will have guessed. Richard, God knows. And all it's taken is the question in one kiss.

Hey, trust me.

The day's finding its feet, behind a first scrim of cloud there's a higher heaven and I smile at the optimism in the sky and it dawns on me then, as the train slows through the city that's never clean, that this freedom should be seized and not worried at. For my life's about to begin, my real life. I smile across at Dan for I've come to a decision, whether it's the right one or not.

Trust *you?* Yeah right, mate.

Did I ever want to go back, on that fragile morning at the very start of the new life? There were people who disappeared, who vanished into thin air, I'd seen them on television in the nightly missing-person's slot and there was the tantalization of that for I owned a freedom now, for the first time in my life, and God knew what to do with it. But *don't we all crave a binding in some way,* I took out my journal, I wrote.

And now I'm bound to you.

You pull me from my ruby wine and peanut butter and limpid cheeses as you brew in your vat, as you float in your lovely, blood-dark. No knowledge, but intent: to feed from me, to suck. Do you ever want to come out? I can't imagine you wanting it gone, that warm, thrumming sac.

–10–

Look At Them

On a last Friday of winter Lillie and Dan walk up the ramp from Paddington station and into the thick of a London fog and Lillie holds out her hand and it feels as if a kernel of absolute stillness is contained in each bead of cold. She smiles, for she can smell even in the early morning the exuberant energy of the city, it's all there hovering in the wings and she lifts her chin to it in expectation. Her future's slippery, the only certainty is that she's been an observer for too long and it's now time to own her destiny rather than have it shaped for her and she looks across at her partner in crime, turtled by his backpack, and he sways and grins and points on. They're like two young puppies on that fog-stilled morning, all silky and soft and butting blind eyes to the light.

Just four talismans accompany Lillie on her journey into the new world: a notebook, a ballpoint pen, a wallet and a vamp-red lipstick from Anna that's deeply whittled into a saddle by use. They're all tucked into a beaded antique bag too flimsy for daylight. Her hair's plumed out with the sway of the train and a troubled sleep and Dan's wondrous touching that she doesn't know of yet and his jumper obscures the splendour of Anna's skirt and she's like a shipwreck survivor on that morning, there's something splendid about it, for she's grimy and bedraggled and a sight but like a shipwreck survivor she's determined to seize her life now and not waste it, to live it fully, to cram it while she can. Yes, a vast grabbing now.

*

147

A cafe with tired lino and egg sandwiches in a counter and the smell of baked beans in the air.

Can we take a tour in a cab? Can we see the city?

But I've hardly any money left.

Please, Dan, *please*.

He asks mock-wearily if there's anything I've always wanted to do and I whip into a list I've carried with me for so long, the Reading Room and the Greta Garbo mosaic and tea at the Ritz and a dozen oysters and the Tower and an abandoned underground station and Fleet Street and the palace and Dan stops me, hands high in horror, and says a lot of those things can wait. Nothing can, nothing, for what I don't know is how long this snatched freedom will last. He says I'm allowed just one thing for now and I say all right then, the heart of the city, the stinking guts of it and he says he'll oblige me with a few running sores, and perhaps a favourite park. If I'm good.

Always.

Why are the houses painted all the same colour? Because the English are really conservative, and often just one person owns them. They must be so rich! They must be millionaires and I'm staring like a child from the taxi window, fists balled at the glass.

What's the best way to approach it Dan, what do you think?

If you're contemptuous of the place you'll do fine.

No. What? Never!

You'll learn. This is the only place in the world where we're hated. They think our accent is ugly and they're irritated by us, we're lower than the low.

Really?

At best they condescend to us. At worst, they loathe us. You see we come from a nation peopled entirely by the lower classes and it gets right under their skin.

I'm backhanding him on the shoulder and smiling for the underdog's lair has always been my preferred launching pad, I relish the element of surprise that's possible from within it and nothing can blunt me on that morning, nothing, for love will be found and work and a settling and a new life.

The taxi sweeps by the heavy pull of the Thames, its surface is all fluttery as the wind skips up it and its water reflects no light, sluggishly it sucks it in and there's no dynamism to it, just weight. The taxi drops us in Fleet Street and the sky has a dirty, steely, black lung taste and the air's crammed with layers of noise that are trapped by the close buildings and I stare up at tall windows and steep slate, at gargoyles and chimneys and spires and as we walk deep into the city there are patches of war-cleared space, still, there are churches obliterated and gardens for pews and I feel in those few hours that all the angels have tumbled from the bombed churches and are flitting and skipping their joy through the streets. The creaky, growly, vividly alive cram of it all catapults my spirit for London's so scuffed, lived, scumbly, human, accepting and I love all that, all the life in it, centuries of it, fifteen hundred years of a city.

Again and again I slip from Dan's bemused watching and swallow the look of the people, the pasty, cloud-sallowed skin and the shock of dull teeth, even in the young, and the black people, so many, their wonderful hair and Muslim women in triangular black and gypsies on corners holding children too large and homeless people blank from cardboard box bits. All around me is the weight of humanity and the weight of the air and I feel invisible within it and utterly invigorated by the buzz of a metropolis soaking through me. A gull cries somewhere, a ghost-call from the city's maritime past and I wonder if the wind ever worms its way along the streets and licks them clean, if it ever perfumes the alleyways with the memory of salt water and ships, with the marine air of a small island that's butted on bits of it by a vast ocean to its left.

Dan catches up and cups my elbow and steers me to a tucked park and we sit on a bench, stilled by thick peace, and read the plaques that commemorate humble braveries of lost, nineteenth-century lives; the boy who saved a brother from drowning, the local policeman flinging a woman from a bus's path, the grand-mother rescuer of a fire-trapped child. A middle-aged couple sit entwined on a bench nearby, not speaking, just holding, as if a long-dreaded separation is speeding upon them and what's the story in that I wonder, how can they kiss for so long, don't their lips get tired, their breath stale, and in this city of extraordinary rush? Brimful I turn to Dan, brimful I hug my gratitude, it's the first time I've voluntarily reached out a touch and he smiles and ruffles my hair.

Come on, let's get going.

I'm all smile, because for the first time in my life I'm utterly unknown and already planning a new history for all the people to be met and the jobs to be sought and for the man ahead of me and the man by my side. Dan knows little about me and I'll not lie to him, I'll just be oblique with my chat. I'm starting afresh with a new life, a new past and with nothing of the blot of home. I nod at his carefully explained directions to his flat, what tube to take and what bus and barely absorb them for I won't be needing them for long, he'll be distanced a little once I've found my feet for there's something about him, now I'm out, that reeks of the old life too much.

Cedric will be frantic, Sunshine has perhaps already been contacted and panicked and I need a phone to staunch all that. Dan puts his hands on my shoulders to still the fret, We'll get home, we'll sort it from there. Home, whose home is he talking about?

All right, Dan, let's just get there.

Your grandfather wants this, remember.

Shaking him off and walking in silence, not sure any more if I trust his plan. Walking into a different London, past shops with their shutter-lids padlocked tight and vomit pools that don't even smell, it's so cold, and past peeling posters and eyes staring too much. A lurching red bus takes us to where he lives, an almshouse in the city's north-east and it's lonely at the end of a treeless street and there's the jolt of poverty in that: luxury is the sun, and tree-green. Rubbish spills from gutted garbage bags onto the pavements and graffiti stains house walls and grime accumulates on paint-work and drops in great streaks from roofs and suckles into cornices and looks as if it'll never be prised loose. So this is the future, and in the land all the world's meant to learn from. What's happened to Tiriel's dreamed-of country, the quiet, homey place that's soaked in a cherished heritage? The suburb we're walking through seems to be flinching and cracking under the weight of its age, to have given up, and Tiriel would never understand. Dan's building is U-shaped and grimly bricked, Victorian in its breadth. The Catholic charity that runs it hires out the front flats and in one of them is crammed an assortment of young exiles, travellers all, islanded in their new city and brash with their own code.

So there Lillie is, standing in front of Dan's building on that last winter-Friday, gulping in silence its grim sight and thinking of her settled and confident older man. What on earth can this boy at her side ever teach her? How to take a photograph, and massage with a comb, and crack an imaginary egg, and say the alphabet in a burp. Great. It wasn't ever in the plan.

His sliver of a bedroom. I sit gingerly on the edge of his bed, clutch my bag to my chest, tell him that I'll only be staying several days until I've found my feet but he's crashing in too eagerly that I might be lucky because spare rooms are always coming up.
Why?
Well, you know, because here isn't home.
Sunshine, I know, will never be home but he doesn't know that, I can't explain it, I don't even try. I have to ring Richard but Dan's swamping me too much with jobs and bank accounts and trains to France, he's already the guide, telling me to use the bathroom quick, to get in first because there's a towel queue every morning where everyone lays their towels in a line by the bathroom door and just waits until it's their turn and he's babbling plans for us both and I stand. How many people live here? It varies, the record's eleven but the hard core's four, all visitors from home. How many are here now? He says no one's up yet but there's some guy on the sofa and I'm lucky, it's not a full house and I'm swamped with a feeling of finding some stability somewhere else and of finding the

London of my imagination and the man who'll firm my life and none of it's here, in this cramp of a room. I ask if I can have the bed since I'll only be staying for a day or so and yeah, yeah sure he says. You're used to the camp mattress I add. An assessing silence.

You did tell me that you're an only child, didn't you, Lil?

Yes. Why?

You've got the expectations of one.

His grin and my swift neck-flush, I remember the heat of it and Dan seizes it, he takes another camera from the shelf and shoots my hands pale against the skirt, the knot of my fingers pollened in travel grime and all my irritation's back like a rash. And there's something else, he's nervous, he's afraid, there's a glimpse of it, it's like the sudden tremble I caught in his grin on that very first night and he's hiding his uncertainty behind the camera, it's as if he can sense his hold on me slipping now that I'm out in the world and he can't, for some reason, have me lost. His viewfinder roams to my feet and he tells me I need some new shoes and I snap that I can't afford them and he pulls a screwed-up ten-pound note from his pocket, with pocket lining, and hands across the money and tells me to find an old pair of shoes in a charity shop and if the soles have holes in them not to worry, to place a piece of cardboard over them because that's what Charlie Chaplin used to do. I won't take his money and the trembling in his hands is raw now, exposed for us both, and he snaps it away and I stare at him with his own photographer's searching gaze, I'm close to the real Dan, I can smell it, and I stare at the new manner, the sudden, unhinged stalling of the larrikin strut, it's as if I'm thwarting some master plan, God knows what.

Why are you doing all this for me, Dan?

I dunno.

Why do you always take photos?

A sullen, schoolboy pause. His face to the window, I'm close to something.

I'm interested, I guess.

It's like the shots are your trophies or something. I don't like it.

Dan turns and without another word he puts the camera down

and I stare at him, at the transparent wanting of me here, now, firm under his wing and I remember thinking on that first morning that I can read him like a book, my head in such a knowing cloud. I give nothing back. Pull the sleeves of his jumper down over my knuckles and ask for the phone, firm, cold, held. He tells me that no one must know I'm here, that it'll all be for nothing if I'm found out. This has got NOTHING to do with you, I say, hard, loud, and my frustration finally out. Being here will never work.

Are you, like, in love with me or something, Dan?

No.

His astounded laugh. I throw the antique bag onto the bed and push out. No one has ever vexed me so much.

But there I am, waylaid in the kitchen by a gaggle of sleep-mussed, pyjamaed, twenty-something tenants who accept my presence in a matter-of-fact way as they post-mortem their previous nights. All the fume is laughed from me as a woman called Ishbel Letissier talks of a pub party to celebrate her one hundredth fuck. Her newly blonde, brittle hair – *it used to be Nicole Kidman* – hangs limp, as if in shock. She flicks a photo from a fridge magnet to show the natural brunette, it's of herself and a girlfriend in an advanced state of pregnancy, they're both bikinied and tanned on a deserted beach and 'Cunts With Attitude' is emblazoned in lipstick across their bellies. What are cunts? I ask, wanting it for my word book and how did I miss that one out? But the other woman of the household swoops for Miriam Morgan, with her banker fiancé, rules the roost with a parent calm. She has beige written in her face and in the hunch of her shoulders and she tells me that the word will be explained later, along with the type of woman that Ishbel is, and the latter rolls her eyes and puckers her lips and hugs us both.

We're going to have so much fucking fun, girlies. You'll love it here, Lil. The cheese makes your nails grow like crazy, I'll paint them for you after brekkie if you want.

Oh yes!

I splay my nails and Ishbel examines close, the sides of her upper lip swallowed by her mouth and just the bow of her top lip remaining and I love her chatter and her butterfly tattoo on the nape of her neck and her attitude, her front. She uses the word *fuck* instead of *very* to great effect as she explains that her old uni mate who's still asleep on the couch is fucking hot, they met in drama school but she hasn't fucked him and never will because it'd fuck them up no end and he wanders in, hair sleep-sprung, and raises a palm and swigs from a carton of milk and wipes his lip with the back of his hand. Ugh, Miriam says, I'm throwing that out, grabbing the carton from him. He extends a hand.

The name's Laith.

The quick iron of the grip.

Pardon?

Laith. It's Arabic, it means courageous as a lion.

Everyone joshes at a telling heard once too much and as the laughter bounces across cereal and coffee and toast the household senses that Dan's foundling new friend in her borrowed jumper and grubby skirt – wondrous, intensely listening, drinking them all in, not saying much – is odd and sheltered and different, I hear this later from Ish, they sense that the new arrival is from some unexplained cloistered world and glowingly innocent and to be protected because of that, to be treated tenderly and coached in their ways. Dan's unable to explain for he's jumped on the phone, wheedling his way back onto the rotas of a local photo shop and bar if he can to pay for another trip.

What's it like, living in London?

God, where to begin? says Ish, crumpling a smile, and I'm told that the English don't put bread in the fridge or plates in the kitchen and there are no wolf whistles from the building sites – well, Hallelujah for that – and no sun in the summer – it sucks – and the mosquitoes are really slow and my only friends will be other foreigners like themselves because the city's deeply unfriendly and no one meets your eyes and the country's straining under Third World conditions with Victorian plumbing and a bureaucracy that can't cope: When in pain take a plane, Miriam smirks. I'm told I'll only be invited into a Londoner's house when I'm leaving the country, because the locals are jealous of us tosses Laith. *Us*, a disbelieving laugh, *why?* Because we're bigger, stronger, fitter and smarter than them and we beat them at every major sport known to man and we're God's own country and we're not arrogant, and he grins, I'll take you for a walk later, give you my guided tour. Yeah, a tour of all the pubs, Ish says, cupping his chin with her hand, you watch him, Lil, he's the guy who had a collection of condoms under his bed that the ants all marched away with and you treat men like him with a very big stick. I smile sweetly at Laith, extricate myself from his proprietorial arm and tell him it's not a walk that I need right now, but a phone.

On the answering machine is the lovely, firm roll of Richard's accent and I hang up, bitten into shyness, and walk away. Return, rehearse, ring again.

I'm OK, I'm in London, I'm waiting for your call, tell everyone I'm all right.

All rushed and then I'm leaving the number and asking him to keep it to himself, telling him I know exactly what I'm doing and hanging up not knowing what I'm doing and refusing to leave the almshouse all day and all night, in case of a call.

Late on that first day there that Lillie Bird is, walking as far as the communal garden, still in earshot of the phone and collecting four black winter leaves and borrowing four envelopes from Miriam and addressing them to her parents, and Edie, and Cedric, and Anna. No note, just a leaf, in each. Willing them not to worry, there's method to the madness and she hopes they see that. But she's not seeing any magnificence in it now, in herself or in Dan, and she doesn't know how to go back.

That first, unanchored night, lying on his double bed and staring until late at the pages of one of his books but not reading, can't: Richard hasn't rung. I've called thirteen hours ago and then again and I need the voice to still the rattling, the smear of the guilt, I want confirmed my grandfather's wanting of this way and yet I lack the courage to speak to Ced myself for I don't want any devastation in his voice, I'm not sure I could bear that.

Dan barrels into the room late after a drinking session with his mates and I can smell the city soaked into him as he flourishes two pairs of stripy men's pyjamas from a Woolworth's bag and tells me they've been purchased so that my delicate sensibilities won't be offended and he tosses across a pair and they hit me square in the face and despite myself I laugh. He flips out his camp mattress on the skinny strip of floor next to the bed and asks how it finally feels to be free, Miss Runaway? I'm not there yet, bristling again and looking down at him, lying on his back, hands behind his head and all plumped with well-being from his too-many beers.

I won't be here long, I told you that.

Later, my eyes are closed but I haven't yet caught sleep for my arm's draped over the bed and I know where Dan's looking, I can feel his eye-greed and I draw the blanket close to my shoulders, and turn, and curl. Yet deep from sleep I wake to his restlessness on the hard mat, his groan, and then there's a crack as he hits his head on the underside of the bed – *fuck* – and it strums at my guilt and I say, Come on, shhhh, and open the blanket and he climbs sleepily into it and I clamp both of us into the warmth.

We don't speak, we don't touch, I've never lain in a bed with someone else, and so close. Slumber and heat concentrate Dan's smell and I slip deeper into the pocket of his warmth and listen to the vulnerability of his breathing and breathe the soft sourness of his slumbering and do not sleep, too wired for that. Jiddered owl-awake by Richard's indifference and yet I'm guilty also, for I'm indifferent to this too-attentive rescuer and his kindness, irritating that he is, and he's so trusting by my side and with no knowledge of any of this. He's sleeping soundly now with the abandonment of a child, limbs flayed and mouth wide and I smile at the endearing mess of it and move closer and breathe in his sleeping. I need them both.

*

The city that I'm swallowed up in has a population the size of the country I've left. Has parks that are reluctant and in those first glazed days of arrival I walk around and around the squares' empty green, trying to find a way in, but the gates are locked and the fence iron's spiked and can't be scaled. Has stone that's harder and sharper and smoother than the honey-grainy, soft village sandstone from the mountain I've left far behind, a mountain that scrapes a tall sky; the new stone's fine and cold to the touch and it stains black the tips of my fingers. I walk cobbles whispering of old smoke and blood and horses and spit and pass statues weeping great pollution tears. The city I'm swallowed up in is set low, its buildings are sullen and squat, they seep wide from thick river sludge and I can taste air stained by cars, the cram of exhausts, I can taste the slam of industry from cold seas. My lungs have been coddled for most of my life and they know best air so pure that it hurts, but in this new place my breathing shallows and my walking slows and my sleeping balloons in the tenacious cold. I'm lonely in it, I've not known the intensity of it before, it walks with me as I wander this place.

Each day of those first days Lillie leaves a message for Richard and each day there's no call and her messages are softer and more hesitant each time. Swiftly she knows every word of his message by heart and panic's seeping into her, she's shell-shocked with the not knowing and the tenuousness of her new life and with the closeness of the almshouse, the pressing curiosity of its people and their constant TV yabber and the hammering on the bathroom door and the continual stream of visiting mates and the lack of thinking space and she's wanting, increasingly, silence and focus and stability and alone. She wasn't expecting it, that the transition into the world would take work.

Dan reads the swamp and prods her to step into life, not tolerating a wilting now she's got this far. He walks the neighbourhood with her and coaxes her to spill any ideas for how to begin a fresh life. She can't count on Richard, it's a certainty with each slipping day, she wants work yet she doesn't know what for she has typing and curiosity and nothing else. And each night the two of them sleep sibling-close but rigorously not touching, Lillie makes sure of it, scrunched rigidly and not turning to him on the very edge of the bed. She's fierce about that, the not turning, even in sleep.

Day four, he rings.

Can't see me for a while, he's swamped with a new contract in Russia, he's extremely surprised I've done what I have and he wishes it hadn't happened at his house and there's a new tone in his voice, businesslike and brisk. He assures me he'll pass on that I'm safe and yes, he won't say where I am. Talking thought: they're extremely worried, your grandfather hasn't told your mother, hasn't had the courage, how are you going to live? God, I feel like a father now. My contracting as he speaks: so, no hope of the fairy-tale rescue, and no going back. I'll get a job. I'll send you five hundred pounds to tide you over, what's your address? No, I want to do this *my* way. It'll be interesting to see how long this little experiment lasts, Lil. Annie, especially, can't believe it, she never thought you'd have the courage and she's furious she wasn't told, I'd hold off contacting her for a while. I wasn't planning to anyway, I want to do this by myself. Humph.

My grandfather's sent up a parcel and a suitcase is to follow and I swallow a crumpling as I imagine him alone, going through my drawers, and then I whisper to Richard that I have to see him, when, and my groin's tightening and my body's sliding into the wall, when Rick, when, and my hand's knotting the hair at my forehead, hurting my scalp and Not yet, he's replying, I'm tied up with work but soon, I'll call, and like an anemone that's plumed under the water's silky attention I am shut.

How did Cedric take it? I ask, businesslike and brisk back.

He was stunned.

Ugh huh.

But I wouldn't say he's totally against the whole thing. I think he actually likes the idea of you being out in the world, as long as you're looked after, and keep in touch.

So perhaps, yes, Dan was right and I cling to that, that it's all, secretly, what they've wanted for so long. It's the only way I can soldier on with the alone.

Richard rings Evendon and Sunshine and says he's been contacted, he doesn't know much except that I'm well and have money and know what I'm doing and that no one, apparently, is to pursue me or involve the police because then I'll disappear, I'll never be seen again, he has my word on that.

As soon as the news hits, Ed shuts the library early and speeds across to the farm, to the pale shock in my parents' faces, to Tiriel saying that I'm now like a balloon climbing high into the sky and he doesn't know when, or if, I'll ever come back. Rebecca's more trusting but her eyes now seem permanently creased as she says that my English interlude has taught me how to sip a sherry and recognize an orangery and say air-hair-lair, and not much else.

So there I am in that brave new world I've always wanted, with my dream man all abrupt, and no prospects, and stuck. I'm swamped by a loss of esteem that's fuelled by a lack of purpose and a lack of work.

Well, what do you want to do, Lil, more than anything else? Settle into London, make a living somehow and one day write, I guess. OK. But I've got nothing to write about, I don't know anything. Let me help you, *trust* me. Well . . . But Dan won't take no for an answer, he takes upon himself all the responsibility of smoothing my way, it's as if he's lowering a toddler into its very first swimming pool and gentling her through the cold's shock.

I'm loosening with him and haven't moved out yet – there's nowhere to move to and no money. And one night he comes home from the pub all fevered and flushed, there's a friend of a friend who's going home, the cold has got too much, I have to ring her, right now, here's the number, quick, she's been working in a poster shop and she's just quit and she's been asked to suggest a replacement and Dan's bagged the job for me and I can feel the outsider's network beginning to hum and a joy stirs at the chance of a settling, for I want a firmness, so much, in my febrile new life.

There's something in Lillie that encouraged a mothering in others back then, that prompted people to tuck her under their wing. Ish took her shopping on Dan's borrowed money and styled her for the interview and Laith and Miriam rehearsed her on what to say. Miriam was a BBC journalist and told her that it was much easier in England to create herself afresh, to make herself bigger than what she ever was back home for she was now in a land of reticence that was cowed by hierarchy and foreigners like themselves could use that to their advantage and brazen their way around the rules, could talk themselves up, be cheeky and confident and bold.

It's not in our blood to meekly follow the leader, so just walk into that shop and dazzle them, girl, with your enthusiasm and your smile.

Yeah, don't forget the smile, they don't often get that.

Laith, winking and grinning, and his arm settling over me too much.

I wasn't sure the advice was needed in the end.

A dusty shop on a side street in Islington with just one other person working spasmodically in it – Jeremy Clax esquire – the owner and occasional boss. My first sight: a man behind a long counter, reading a tall newspaper with a frown in his left eyebrow and a thin wrist and Radio Four in the background and he did not stand to greet me and the sight of him stopped me abrupt.

Miss Bird? Come closer. I don't bite, you know.

But he was beautiful, I wasn't expecting that. Lean cheeks and a high shine of a forehead and a remote, abstracted air that clouds some men of extraordinary handsomeness and yet as I stepped closer I saw that his looks had atrophied, they'd sunken and paled from years, perhaps, of sitting too much in a dingy shop when he should be out somewhere dazzling and chatty and bright, some-where else.

He put down his paper and told me he needed some help for

he was at the peak of his decline and couldn't I tell? No. It was glaring, surely, for he still used buses and he was well beyond thirty and for that he considered himself a failure, there was no mistaking it, and I didn't know if he was joking or not. He said we must celebrate the successful job interview with a little glass of something and there was a whisper in his voice, a sibilance in its wake.

But I've hardly told you anything yet.

No matter. I've seen enough. You do drink, don't you?

Well, yes, a little, I'm learning.

Splendid! My father never drank, and I'm sure that he would have been happier if he'd taken an occasional glass, as I do. I feel sorry for people like that, because as Frank Sinatra said they wake up each morning knowing that it's the best they're going to feel all day, the poor pets.

I'd never met anyone with a voice so bereft of wonder and I stepped closer to such a delicious new life. There was the full force of my smiling and a hand thrust for a shaking, as Miriam had taught me, and with surprise and reluctance the hand was met, just.

There, coy on my pillow on the night before my first day of work, is a slim, flat box wrapped in a page from *Vogue* and tied with two shoelaces that I quickly scrabble off.

Oy, miss, I want those laces back.

Inside, a fountain pen. I gasp, feel its agreeable weight, snap in a cartridge, scratch nothing onto paper and then shake the pen into a working and it glides over the page and I sign my name in a sweep from one side to the other and look up. For all the things you're going to write, says Dan, moving the camera from his face. I throw a pillow at him. I thought that thing had been banned? But this is an exception he explains, it's like the night before your first day at school, your mum and dad will pay me in gold to see a record of it some day. I poke out my tongue, unable to clamp my smiling.

One day I'll be thanked, he says, grinning and snapping another shot.

Why do you do all this, Dan? What do you want from me?

Oh, just your total, undying devotion. For God's sake, Lil, can't you accept that someone can be kind to you?

I'm *much* too suspicious for that, mate, I laugh.

Deep in that night and still back to back but there's the arch of my foot on his calf, the perfect fit, and I'm not moving the touch.

There was something so slope-shouldered about Jeremy Clax esquire, restful. His shop opened gently at eleven because he liked spending mornings in bed and this enabled him to wake mid-morning, to half an hour of poetry and it was how everyone's day should begin. He showed me the ropes with a pen in his hand that had beads of dirty red ink congealed in clear plastic, a replica of a syringe, and I wondered at his closed-off energy and the rigidity of his muscles and the drawing back, it was as if he'd been gazed upon so much as a child that in middle age he'd retreated, relieved, to the comfort of gloom. His beauty would deepen as he aged and God knew who would see it for he was a person I couldn't imagine with anyone by their side, he was someone never meant to be completed by coupledom, sexless, contained, apart.

Do you have a girlfriend, Mr Clax?

Goodness, you are bold. But since you ask, no, I do not. There's a girl called Finty but it's all very complicated. I knew I was in too deep when she started organizing salsa classes for me. And you, Miss Bird? Are you stepping out?

No.

The sting of it, the reddening through a nonchalance and Jeremy nods and smiles for he recognizes it, he tells me, the readiness spilling from me for he had it once.

I miss the head massages the most, Miss Bird. Did that mother of yours pass on her secrets, by any chance?

Well, it's funny you should ask.

I find massages exceedingly pleasurable. I must have been a cat in a former life.

*

And so from Tuesday to Saturday, eleven to six, young Lillie worked in the poster shop and with it came a firming to her new life. Her biggest seller was a print called *The Singing Butler*, of an upper-class couple from the 20s blissfully dancing cheek-to-cheek on a deserted beach and canopied by the blustery umbrellas of two servants.

Now what does that say about my country at the turn of the twenty-first century, Miss Bird? It cannot be good.

Mr Clax's favourite: *Tennis Girl*, the 70s blonde with a hand on her bare bottom that only style magazines were interested in now.

Gabriel Garcia Marquez said that every person has a public life, a private life and a secret one. That poster says something about my secret life, Miss Bird, and you are very fortunate to know that. Finty most certainly does not.

Lillie's favourite: a black and white shot of the Sahara with a swirl of sand that looked like the navel of a sleeping giantess. It reminded her of that fluttery squeal of a girl just six months ago, in her first high curving across the world. She still longed to see all her deserts and mountains and Red Seas but God knew when now, or how.

You're stuck here, Miss Bird, I have you for life. And let me warn you I'll be living to a ripe old age. The secret to my longevity is placidness. I'm going to live to one hundred and one by simply not worrying about anything, I have it all figured out.

And she'd laughed at that. For by the end of each day she was wilting with fatigue from standing too much but brimful of delight because her life had the prop of purpose now, the tonic of paid work. Dan was chuffed, as if he personally owned her triumph, You owe me big time, he said and she frowned for he was hovering too much and she was wary of anyone who might get too close, who might discover too much.

London was learned with my feet and I felt gloriously absorbent, living close to the surface of my skin. I shook off the offers of flatmate-company for I'd discovered a guilty secret: I had perfect fun, I was at my most perceptive and keen when I was utterly alone. One journal was swiftly filled and another.

I tried to understand the psyche of England and couldn't, the way it was so tightly held in and defensive and clammed whereas once, in its empire days and before that it had seemed so outward-looking, so rambunctious and bold. I couldn't understand the shyness of the people or the burdening past or such little hunger for a new way. It was a place that was obstinately foreign, a despairing country that seemed to absorb meekness and mistakes and shoddy service and queues and I didn't know why, I needed it explained.

I stared at three tall, healthy-looking homeless men walking slowly abreast up a Soho lane, blankets around their shoulders like Massai warriors and all their worldly possessions in plastic sacks and I couldn't comprehend the life choice. So many homeless, and always white, never Asian or black. And in a television report on a council estate a grim voice-over declared *this community will never prosper* and I was struck, it would never be said in my homeland, they had the gift of optimism and there was the innocence of that, there'd always be a way out, not this hopelessness and frustration and seepage of confidence and utter acceptance of a designated place.

I needed a sounding board and Dan couldn't provide it; his presence had become too sticky. There was his hovering greed for my new life, for the work and the wandering and the fresh people in it and I was still focused on Richard and he didn't ring enough and I hadn't seen him yet but each day the promise was still there, for despite work and the addiction of this working life I was still a hostage to my hope.

OK, so we've done Fleet Street, guillotine and tube station. What's next?

I don't know. Gosh, um, a dozen oysters? There's still that, mate.

Rolling onto my stomach and giggling and cradling my head in my arms.

*

A slurp of the sea, like being punched in the mouth with a wave. For him, a whole week's wage. Dan, I just do not get this. Shhhh, relax and enjoy it. And at moments like these there's a softening to all his quirks and his kindness, I can feel the seep of it and I forget all the suspicion and grate. But it's only in moments.

We're very similar you know, Ms Bird.

Oh yeah? Is that why we drive each other crazy?

Well, perhaps. But we're both pretty weird.

Excuse me, Mr Smith, you are *much* weirder than me.

We're both left-handed.

And he demonstrates on a very expensive-looking napkin that I write oddly because my wrist curves around the script, protecting but smudging it, whereas his hangs underneath it like the string of a balloon which is much more neat, see and he pushes his pen into my hand and moulds my arm, Come on, try it, he insists. And he subverts the knife and fork when he eats and he's right and I'm wrong, I'm just not bold enough, look.

Uh uh, you're *much* weirder, mate, with a snorting laugh and another sea slurp.

I cannot work him out, the devotion is too gluey, too much.

And then the summons and I hang up the phone and breathe my joy through fluttery finger wings. Who was that? Ish asks. Just a friend. Your eyes are the eyes of a woman in love, and she raises her coffee mug like a champagne glass and blows me a kiss. Soon I'll be moving out and settling and finding a firm footing in this new world, it's all locking into place.

You'd better give me a name and a number, Lil, just to be safe.

This has got *nothing* to do with you.

He grips me by the arm and I remember in that moment the clamp of his hand across my mouth and the vice of his fist pulling me into the garden and there's a darkening in his face and the grip as if he'll never let me go and I wrench my skin from him.

It's got everything to do with me. I'm looking after you, I'm protecting you.

You're not my husband or my father, you don't *own* me, I'm not in *love* with you.

Shaken by some need that he will not voice and I storm out and he yells after me to sleep in someone else's bed then, to get my own room and my own house and my own life and there's a crash of his door slamming and it's so forceful that it shakes the whole flat and there's a thud of something and then my pyjamas are ejected, and my clothes, and my journal, and my shoes.

Thick quiet.

I sleep in Ish's bed. Her hand strokes my hair into sleep but it takes a very long time on that night.

The next morning, a note under her door, an apology. I can stay in the house, I mustn't go, he doesn't want that. Signed Dan boy, nothing else. Curt, and blunt, and giving little back.

The knot of him.

– 11 –

A Still, Deep Cold

A still, deep cold has clamped down the city and the cab driver tells me there's impending snow and he asks where I'm off to tonight. A date, I've never said that before and my face burns with the new word and the cab driver laughs. Well I hope you end up marrying him, love. Oh no, tense-quick. You'd be good for my son but he'll never tie the knot, he's too selfish for that, too tight with his money, you know what I mean? And the car enters a curve of white houses, the London of Mary Poppins and Henry James and prams wheeled by nannies in parks and it slows and it stops.

Who is he, love? The Sultan of Brunei?

The shallowing of my breath, the damming of my nerves, as I lift the heavy knocker on Richard's door. The heroine's life, at last.

There's a tightness to this wine, Lillie, it has to bud. Let's leave it for half an hour.

His long, spidery fingers blooming like a flower into loveliness and my smiling through the champagne and the bubbles curling into my head, too golden and too fast.

It was so big! Every time he came close to entering I jumped back because it grated, it scraped, it was stuck and eventually *get it off* I yelled and that was it as far as I was concerned and then he propelled my head onto it and told me to suck. What? Suck, *suck*, like an iced lolly. Oh. And then he cried, Take me, Lillie, take me and groaned, like he was on the toilet and I had no idea what it looked like, no idea that it squirted out. You're lucky that's my favourite thing, he said afterwards and there was a kiss as if he were trying to steal my lips, it hurt, there was the hard suck of him on my neck and the shiver of him across my belly and I love every inch of you, he was saying with his great hand running over my skin and his palms, child-soft and there was his assessing touch and I was not in the moment but looking at it, watching it all, shell-shocked, struck. And afterwards I was curling instinctively into his chest, I knew that bit, I was curling, cracked, and he was brushing the hair from my face and tucking it behind my ears and asking me to sleep beside him that night but No, I was saying, I can't, I have to get back.

He called a cab and gave me money for it as well as Cedric's parcel and I caught glimpses of the sterile, interior-designed loveliness of his rooms as I left, utterly scrubbed of the spill of life and resolutely without books – they're all at my office – and I'd always been suspicious of houses like that but this was my chosen man, he'd change, I could make him, I was sure of that. I had him now. And money left over from the cab. And hurt.

So there that Lillie Bird is, raw and dishevelled, her hands sweeping into Cedric's parcel on the way home, searching for something familiar within all the new trembling, searching for some ballast, something from home, there's her passport and some toiletries and a few clothes and a blush at the underpants and a note in the familiar, tight hand and there's a wave of tenderness as she skims the terse words, there's a tug at what she used to be once.

The biggest mistake I ever made with my life was that I didn't do what I really wanted to do, but you know all about that.
C x

She doesn't feel very heroic in the cab, with the insistent hurt between her legs, with the sour tang in her throat.

*

Late that night I'm waddling up the almshouse path straight to Ish's candle-cluttered room and flopping on the end of the bed and declaring that at last, at last, the deed's been done. You don't need to tell me, sweetie, I can see it in your face. Don't tell Dan, I'm imploring, not sure why. And she's saying fine, whatever I want, but everyone knows that he's madly in love, except me of course, and there's a raised eyebrow smirk and a half-eaten chocolate block thrust at my doubt.

But he told me he wasn't.

Her duck lips, her lowered chin.

Men, who knows, darling. Fuck, if I did, I'd be a millionaire.

Consumed by caution, perhaps, yet isn't he the man who always takes risks and I just don't understand, I cannot work him out but it's lost as Ish launches into a dissection of the night: condoms first, were they used? No. How old is he? I'm not sure, mid-fifties, I guess. Mid-*fifties*! Holy Jesus, you do like a father figure, don't you? The older generation always hate to use condoms, they just don't understand and then she's grilling me about the details of what exactly's taken place and declaring that I'm still a virgin no matter how much I hurt and asking if I'm in love – yes, I've adored him since I was fourteen – and she's rolling her eyes and flopping back on the bed and saying the only man she's ever been allowed to adore is Jesus, she was taught it at school and she literally fucked her way out of her Catholic upbringing and was all the better for it in the end.

I was expelled, Lil, because the Mother Superior believed I had more influence over the students than she did.

The next day I feel aching, split, and he hadn't even entered and he rings late that morning, at Jeremy's shop, bubbling holidays and dinners and operas and says tongues will wag and is that all right?

Yes, *yes*, who cares, as long as we're happy!

He tells me the previous night was beautiful, beautiful, and I clench my hurt and smile my glee for I have, finally, my man. At the ripe old age of twenty-two I'm on my way out.

*

Dan grills me: Who is he, is he from work, where's he from? but I will not tell him and I can feel his fume and I worry at what he might do, at the intensity within him.

Nothing you can do can change this, Dan.

He's saying nothing more, he's putting on his coat, he's out all night.

Richard rings every day the following week, through work and dinner and into the jaggedness of early mornings and I jump at his calls and drink all his talk, his alarming honesty, *I feel nervous, I feel like a little boy*, and it's flattering and empowering and I marvel at his ability to pull my focus so triumphantly from friends and from thinking and from life, to bunker me down. The gossip worries him but I tell him I'm strong and he says yes, I'm the strongest woman he knows and he has to stop ringing me so much. No, Rick, don't, I like it. Feeling a falling, soft in my belly, is this love? I don't know. The stomach-flip, the conscious steadying of my talk, the flutter, the nerves, the sweat. For as soon as a man has put his arm around me it's as if I've forgotten everything else and I marvel at that, the wipe.

There are Dan's eyes through it all when he comes home from the pub and when he leaves for work in the morning, knowing, not knowing. There's the intensity of his stare and his silence and his wilful not helping any more. No gifts, no talk, no night laughs. In the end there's indifference, as if he doesn't care, as if he's found something else. And he's all darkened down, he's losing his impishness, his glow. The nights increase when there's no one in the bed beside me and I miss the warmth, I have him in the sheets and the pillow but there's no talk of that, or of anything any more.

So there that new Lillie is, with her glide of smooth restaurants and operas long into the night, with deep carpets and smiling doorman and a panicky ramming of the silences with more talk, there she is in empty church visits when Richard comes at her hungry because he says she's at her most pure in church and he has to sully it, get her dirty and she pushes him away, schoolmarmish and giggling and mock-curt, there she is perching on his desk as he discusses over the speaker-phone restorations around the world and his hand is cupping her crown and pushing her head onto him, there she is beside him in the back seat of his car with the driver a tactful blank and then at his house there's the tussle of kissing and nibbling and sucking but she won't let it go all the way, she's always forcing him to stop, saying no, not yet, it isn't her community's way for she wants some sort of permanence for the gift of that, it's deeply ingrained in her, the holding off and Ish has instructed her to stick by it.

I won't ever stay in a situation just for the sake of it, Lil. So many women put up with things just because they don't have the confidence to make a choice. Remember that.

It's the lunch hour when Richard knows I'm busy but he can't wait, he has to see me – please, Jeremy, well, all right, just this once – and the sleek panther car dispatches me to his office, making me hurt and stealing me from work.

No of course I don't mind, Rick, I want it.

Nina Simone wailing through the fret.

Just a small gathering. A few old friends.

You will come?

Acceptance at last, the relationship aired, and Ish supervises the dress and the face. I step into the conservatory and the knot of the two middle-aged couples stops talking and they glance me over and turn their backs and resume their conversation and I stand silent and waiting with a foolish smile of hello fixed on my face and I feel vividly alone in a new cocktail dress that's suddenly wrong, the skirt too short and I want to tug it down and the shoes too high and the lipstick glaring as is my awkwardness and my panic and my too-gobbled, too-grateful talk to the spotty young man serving drinks. Will I ever smoothly slot into this world? My eyes smart with the sting of it and the evening snails on and I overhear Richard describing himself as spectacularly single to some shiny woman from Singapore and I catch his eye and he smiles, unknowing, and a distance is blundering between us, I'm lost.

Why do you never introduce me as your girlfriend?

Later, to his bewildered stare.

Later, collecting my coat and walking out of the door without saying goodbye because I don't know what I'm meant to do in a situation like this and I'm sure no one notices except the young man attentively serving his cocktails with his knowing eyes that in the end I can't meet. And as I walk down the quiet streets with their tall, rosy-glow windows, searching for a cab, the growly cold pesters me and judders my lips. Love isn't meant to be this, surely? It's meant to be a rescue, I've read that, a haven, a port.

I've not really spoken to Dan since the night of the fight but it's all forgotten as he bustles about me, brisk with gentleness. The old Dan's back, what he's read in my face, God knows. So how was it, really? as he hands me a cup of tea but I turn and shake my head, too full of shame for talk. Hey, come on. It was horrible, finally, my blurt. Why? Are you all right? Silence, my head turned, my eyes shielded and I can't bring myself to speak of the pain of it and Wait, he's saying and leaping up and returning with two handfuls of chocolate cookies and shimmying them under my nose, your favourite, madam, you've never been known to refuse, and it gets me giggling in spite of myself – the kindness in a cupped hand! He goes back to the kitchen and returns with a carton of iced coffee and plonks himself at my feet. Grins, one side up, one side down and says, Ready now, shoot. It was horrible because no one talked to me, it was like they all hid their hostility behind this mask of absolute politeness and it was humiliating and rude and, and – and I can say no more, all wrong in this new world and ready to ring home but Dan kneels before me and puts his hands on my knees and tells me not to lose heart, because I just have to remember the magic words if ever I'm invited into an English person's house.

What?

Would you like another cup of tea?

Staring, blank. Why?

Because it actually translates as would you go now, please. It's true, they never say what they mean! It's the signal to piss off, and there's his delighted grin and the old, sunny Dan is well and truly back and I'm laughing through brightening tears, suddenly grateful for this funny prickle of a friend within the unanchored loll of Richard and all his talk and I close my eyes, jamming fresh tears and a tongue hits my lid and laps up my crying and it's trembling and tender. *I'm sorry*, his whisper, and I do not move from under it and more tears come and there's the tang of salt on my lips and his kiss of them up and then without a word I'm standing, I'm walking out.

Dan like cool water on that shrill night, soothing me down, but Richard is my future and I'm sticking by it for I've always stuck with the plan and I'm not going to risk a leap into the dark with a man who wilfully isn't in any book I've ever read, or imagined.

Later in bed I apologize for getting angry several weeks back when all he'd asked for was a name and he says, No, it's OK. Why? Because I'm magnificent when I'm furious, I'm raw and open and honest and he loves it. Why? Because it's close to the real me, and he never sees that.

So there I am being hauled into a growing up. The love-wrong is making me all sour of spirit and there's a longing for church-calm, more God in me. I'm visiting Richard's office on snatched, lunchtime dates and the tap tapping of the keyboards, their pitter-pat, is like soft, sad rain as I'm walking through the curious worker-rows and I'm feeling wrong as I'm kneeling on the deep carpet of Richard's office and undoing his zip, wrong as I'm leaning back on his desk and parting my legs, wrong as his fingers search and thrust up. But I have that obstinate hope: of endurance, stability, a lifelong mate, and I marvel, looking back, at the resilience of it. It's as tough as a plastic toy rolled in by the surf and I tell you, it just wouldn't be cracked.

London itself souring too.

Feeling hemmed in on the tube and on the street and there was coughing all over the city, it was worst on the buses and no one covered their mouths and I constantly shrunk from it for my resistance was down and everything bit. London in that love-fret was being chipped in the head by the pointed spoke of an umbrella and it drawing blood and the well-dressed woman who did it not even stopping, not even looking. And it was the black people who seemed the polite ones, who apologized for bumping into me or stood back to let me before them on the bus and weren't suspicious of my smile and my curiosity and my keenness to be liked, who reacted with a smile when I thrust out my hand and told them my name and instantly responded with their own but I didn't get it enough and I was thinking of Sunshine too much for I was faltering in my new world, I wanted the old trap back, it was all, suddenly, wearing me down.

As was the collective regret of the almshouse travellers. There was a whining negativity among most of them, an indignation at the reality that scuffed so much at the dream. We'd all been told from an early age that our own land was not beautiful and England was, we'd all been told that our own land was uncivilized and England was, we'd all been trained to hear an Englishman's cultured voice and think *that* is the way our language should be spoken and its bureaucracy was a modern wonder from which we must learn. And I knew now that history had conned us, for I was seeing at first hand the pedastalled nation that my father had always spoken of so proudly and nothing had prepared me for the shock of it: a land soaked in resignation.

You must go to the library.

You come too, you take me.

No, you have to see it by yourself, I'm too busy.

He wouldn't have been once, but I step into the Reading Room and feel the aroma of waiting words; all of life is there. I uncurl and smile for Dan has found me a sanctuary of a place and I want to stretch out right there and then and breathe in all the words of the world. This could be a retreat in this city and I tuck it away. And thank him again, for there are many things I need to thank him for and he doesn't get it enough.

But I'm sucked under, the swimmer in an insistent rip.

Richard's fifty-something birthday comes and goes and there's no proper response, just a stunted thank you to my too-expensive tie. Rebecca's right, it's as if he's never learned basics like the receiving of gifts, has never been shown, and I wonder if love, too, has to be learned, if it has to be known before it can be passed on.

Rick, do you think we can work?

Three weeks into the relationship and a strange calm floating over me. I don't know, I'm a very complex man, most of my life I've spent alone and there's his blush and his faltering as he rams his tongue into my ear and pushes my head down. And all I want is for him to allow a seeping of love, to let it in.

I never expected such a weight. Love isn't making me gentle and generous and kind, it's making me prickly and fretful and sapped.

Is he really that good for you, girl? You look so pale, it's as if he's draining you.

Of course he's good for me, Ish. Don't worry.

Ah, you would say that, wouldn't you? You're young and that explains everything. When women are young they see all the good in men and ignore the bad, but when they're older they see all the bad and ignore the good.

Dan's indifferent too much now and there's a sadness in the back of his eyes and a too-wilful not coming home and a smell on him sometimes of another woman and I don't like it but won't talk to him of it, won't let him in, for there is something broken between us. He won't compete, he just retreats and that's worse. I want door slams and arm grips back, God, I can't believe I'm wishing that now, I want fights and urgent letters and shouts. I don't want passivity and the smell of someone else, don't want a giving up.

From somewhere near Dan's high window a child practises a recorder and the sound slips often into squeaks, it's tense with effort and the noise is unbearably tugging for it reminds me too much of a childhood abruptly cut off, reminds me too much of home.

Imagine Tiriel and Rebecca alone in their kitchen, waiting for any news, hastening to the letter box and jumping at the phone. Imagine them in their office with Shiners ringing and asking if they can speak to the advertising manager or the sports section or the motoring section and whoever answers saying Just putting you through, and handing the phone across to the other, it's a community joke, and I wonder if all the fun's been drained from that now. Richard feeds them drips, all they know is that their daughter's in a city and working and getting on with her life but it won't calm the fears, I know that.

They begin to get letters, they're scrubbed of any pinpointing location but still with leaves of long winters and low skies. I say nothing of a relationship but Ed tells me later she's guessed for there's a new vulnerability in me, a strange fluttering, and she's known for so long that I want more than anything a man and she recognizes the new tremor because she's seen it all before: a strong woman brought to her knees by sex.

Not ringing for ten days and there's the strain of the not-knowing, the fragmenting. Gnawing at past conversations and offhand comments, gnawing at silence and at what everything means. I ring Constance, can't contain it any longer, have to know. Coffee.

He chases skirt, you know that, don't you? He what? Oh love, and the older woman shakes her head. I'm awfully fond of him but he's like an empty cardboard box with nothing inside. *No.* He doesn't love women, he destroys them. *No.* Folding my arms, sitting back, what would this middle-aged, blousy woman know?

He was my first relationship, Lil. I was twenty-three, a virgin, from a traditional Catholic family and they'd never have understood. I always knew of all the others, they'd ring the office, he had a woman in every port. The sex between us only lasted a month.

But I love him.

She rolls her eyes and smiles.

Romantic love is the most ridiculous myth a woman can ever fall captive to.

I don't listen any more for I can teach Richard love, I *know* it, I can alter him, rescue him. If only I knew where I stood in the relationship, how much pull that I had, for I'm strength and serenity without him but with the not-knowing I'm eating chocolates and stuff-cramming my face and pestering the answering machine and learning a sloppiness and not liking myself. I crave the return of the known, of control and focus and my early work-joy but I'm netted too tight.

I meet Constance again. There's a peculiar sisterhood bonding us now, a strange collusion, for I've become one of Richard Daunt's women.

There are hundreds of us, Lil, scattered all over the globe.

He rings, just as I'm stepping out boldly again and refinding a firmness and he asks, almost shyly, if I can see him, he says that he burns with want.

Oh! Oh!

Running around the house, leaping onto lounge chairs and touching the ceiling and dancing with Ish and twirling in delight. I can plump him with love now, fix him, cherish him, teach him presents. I imagine a togetherness: children, Anna's raised eyebrows, the return to Sunshine, the church, the stares, Brother Sleet, his peeved face. Oh yes, the little brat would have well and truly won.

Dan watches it all, sullen, indifferent, mute. He knows he can't compete for it's what I've wanted all my life, knows he can't steer my course, I have to do it myself. He used to talk of us travelling to France and the Italian Alps but I don't want any of that now, I want to stay put. I'm islanded in my new country, exiled and a fugitive and fearfully alone and not a single person, besides Dan, knows anything of the ferocity of that love-hope for I'm used to masking myself too well and deciding rigidly and sticking to the plans and stopping anyone from getting too close.

No teeth. That's it. Yeah.

Until my jaw's aching and my chin's butted by his frenzied hand. That's it, that's it and then Richard comes, forcing my face into it and splashing the creaminess over my cheeks and smearing it triumphantly, blooding me and laughing and wiping the last of him onto me from his dripping fingers. I bob up, bravely smile.

As I'm curled in his chest he tells me he hates going down on girls and I ask him what that means and he says reciprocating, and smiles, he tells me he hates the smell of vaginas, they almost make him gag, there's no sexual pleasure in it for a man. He says he's repulsed by the body of any woman over thirty. Why? Because of their skin, their teeth, the sag of their bellies, and it's as if I'm never going to become old myself or I'll be long gone from him by then and it splits the man open, who he is.

An ageing man leaning against the cold marble of his bathroom to relieve his eczema, pressing his back into the cool slabs with a young girl just out of a fundamentalist religious community who was all newly minted once, she's naked, lying on the soft carpet outside his door and asking again does he think they can work and he's saying that during the week he feels sick in the stomach over the two of them because it feels so good when he's with her and that scares him so much because he's never felt sick in the stomach before. And she's thinking of a blush by a crypt and smiling at that until he's telling her that life has always come so easily for him in every way, except for love, and profiles in newspapers have always spoken woundingly of his personal problems, he has to confront his fears in terms of relationships, this is the way his romances have always gone, not developing, just meandering, never making the next step and he's telling her of the deep loneliness of the nights spent at home, between seven thirty and nine thirty is the worst and early in the morning, and Sunday, all of it, and her smiling has stopped and it cannot be flicked back.

She clucks to him, says the soothing words and sees stark now the maxim's truth that great men are the only things that diminish as you get closer to them. For Richard Daunt is a little man, caught by all kinds of fears, and she pities him now.

Hey, Lil, come up to the roof and watch the stars. You can actually see them tonight.

Dan's gently tugging at my ponytail, guiding me to the knots of stars we do not know and we stand side by side and little is said, I can remember hardly anything of it but that pull on my ponytail as I stare into that sky, thinking of home and its lovely night breath.

I'm whispering somewhere behind his ear to his neck that I love him, trying for the last time and That's beautiful, beautiful, he's saying, his reply utterly detached and not in the moment and I'm feeling raw, stripped. I draw back, a faint smile hiding the chasming hurt and again there's the floating calm and I'm standing and saying goodbye and that I don't want to see him again, not even in Sunshine and I want to see him broken on that night, see him hurting, cracked but there's just his calm smile and a deep blush and with careful, even breaths I'm walking, filleted, from his house. You have to care, to crack.

Walking the streets through soft rain dyed orange by the glow of the street lamps, gulping that London night and not wanting yet the home that's not home, not wanting its curious people cram. Walking and walking as the city drops away into sleep and my toes are finally pinching me into a stopping and I'm squatting on a cold step and feeling utterly alone in the mist-wrapped city and wondering what on earth could be next. So much love in me, wasting away on no one, and so ready. It's all turned, just like that, and my rational heart is knowing now that it wasn't love at all but infatuation, and with a man who doesn't like women very much. If he did he wouldn't treat them so recklessly, he's sloppy with his love and he's left me confidence-sapped. I slump my cheek into my hand and it feels on that night as if only my clothes are holding me together, that if I didn't have the binding of a firm bra and a coat I could split apart, crack.

Not sure any more who I am, or what I want, or where I should be.

Close to home I stop at a coffee shop in a cavernous concrete hotel with a nearly empty wallet and wonder how many hours I can make the cash stretch, sleep dragging through me like a slow rake but I'm fighting the pull of it, wanting to hurt myself, wanting to slam myself with tired and there's the persistent attention of a softly drunken businessman and the suspicion of a waiter as he brings me my second teapot and asks me again if I'd care for the bill, grimying the sit but still I cling on, notebook on the table and three of yesterday's papers well thumbed and staring at the lonely street and the halo glow of the street lights and at two or thereabouts I see him. The searching eyes, the tall shoulders scrunched, the hands deep in his pockets and the floppy hair that doesn't see enough of a cut and the face too pale for by then he's been in the city too long but he won't be going back, not yet. I'm too much in it, and too unanchored for that.

I'm almost going to turn from the window but something makes me wave, listless, I catch his eye and he smiles sadly and stops, looking into me with those speaking eyes with his head on one side and he walks up to the glass and mouths am I all right and I nod yes and he comes inside and says would I like another cup of tea and what I ask, brusque, knuckling my forehead and he tells me it means would I go now please, would I go home and oh I say and we chuckle and OK I say, OK, for suddenly there's not one single atom in me that can resist.

Ishbel said you were probably out somewhere close, indulging in one of your mad midnight teas. Come on, it's late.

I fall against Dan, I trip in my tiredness and he picks me up and holds me to his chest and he carries me the last two streets home, my face damping the shoulder of his jacket as the silent tear-flood comes, and comes.

I'm not allowed to lose you, Lil.

Why? I ask, but he won't say, he just tightens me close.

And that night his arm wings my sleeping and I do not resist.
Broken at last by persistence, and kindness, the resistance all slipped.

As daylight bleeds into the dark our bodies are folded into each
other's, there's the jigsaw fit and I'm slamming my eyes shut and
remembering the sweetness of it, can hardly bear its intensity. To
be held so tightly, to stop the fight, to relax.

—12—

Entwined, Just Like That

I can feel you pummelling this story onward now, with your fists and your feet, you want it told, you want it gone from me so that my focus swings back. I can hear the question, little astronaut, so where am *I* in all this? It will come, shh.

It begins perhaps when he asks if I have a swimming costume for he needs to cut my hair, he used to cut all his family's, his mother had taught him but it had to be done wet, in the shower for he didn't know any other way.

What?

We need to disguise you a bit, you're too obvious. We need to find you a new life.

For I'm jumping at every phone, severed now from the one person who's the link to my family's calm and Richard's aware of all my haunts and not often walked away from and who knows what he might do next? But I don't have a swimming costume, I'm not a swimmer, I had been once.

Where's Ish, she'll lend you something.

Her eyebrows shoot up as she flourishes a bikini in one hand and a one piece in the other and tells us that the only time a woman has a drastic haircut is when she has a break-up or a baby or gets married.

So what's it with you, Miss Big-Smile?

*

His hands are swift and sure and I can feel all the weight of the past nine years being shed and then there's the shock of sudden cold steel at my neck and water dyed red, the thin snake of it from my shoulder to my breast and it's pummelled into nothing by the shower's strength. It's just a nick, sorry. It's OK, it's not going to kill me, and my fingers dam the red before it feathers into the costume's paleness.

That's what I love about you, Lil, you haven't learned to be neurotic.

As his hands sweep lightly over my shoulders and back, brushing away scraps and assisting the water and then he turns me to him in assessing conclusion and softly, accidentally, his fingers brush my breasts and a strangeness is shot through me, I'm gone, it's started, I can feel it from that point. Sorry, he whispers, smoothing a wayward curl on my forehead and smiling with a mother's chuff.

He tells me I'll have to go swimming with him some day and I say, I can't remember how, I haven't done it since I was thirteen and my swimming muscles have all rusted over. I'll just have to reteach you then, and he's stepping from the water and mashing his head in a towel and then gone, leaving me goosebumped under the shower's weakness, the bits of me not hit by the hot and I step out light-headed and light-haired and shake my blunted fleece into a towel and look at the mirror and smile: a new face, and no more knots. And a fresh seeing of the man.

Or perhaps it begins when I'm lying on my back in a park with my face wrapped in my arms, all closed to the sky, and Dan's placing his head on the pillow of my belly and my eyes are springing wide at the trusting weight, at his face pointing to my thighs, at his falling, gently, into sleep. For in that simple gesture some boundary is transgressed, I can feel that the dynamic of the relationship is changed. My breathing betrays me, it quickens in wonder and I try to even it out so as not to wake him, so as not to let him know.

*

Or perhaps it's when we're standing on his roof, staring up to the orange glow of London's night that's skyless and starless but then in a swiftly cleared space there's the shock of a full moon and I so rarely see stars in this place, rarely look up to the sky and Crikey Moses, I'm saying and Dan's swift with a kiss and this time I'm not pulling back, I'm nudging for more, trapping his smell for a fraction of a second before my lips slide across his skin and I catch his lovely scent on his cheek and in his hair and temple and neck.

Well, look, I just can't pinpoint it but suddenly it's there and I'm all changed. Some have said it's rebound, some have said it'd always been there and was too hesitant, too shy and just needed a coaxing out, all I can say is that what should've been for so long, now was. It was an uncurling that had crept over me throughout several days, or weeks, or months, I don't really know but my God when it found its grip it would not be shaken loose. I'd relented, relaxed. And I thought often during that time of the only two men that I'd known: Richard, all Protestant, all prose; and Dan, all Catholic, all poetry, and I smiled at what I'd grabbed first. All the irritations softened or gone, or perhaps I just understood them now, had learned to laugh them off. And Dan didn't even seem so young any more, he'd gained confidence with the knowing that he had me, he'd firmed. God, love, the clean slate, the blinded fresh start.

And there I am, seizing it complete. Finally, a vivid blood red. An unwavering love then, just as my love is for you. There's no lapsing to it, no slippage, it's pure and intent.

Dan put down his camera and took no more photos of me, he was no longer the pursuer, no longer frantically cataloguing me as if every photo was to be the last and it was a fundamental shift. For he told me that a photograph was an attempt to hold on to something that wasn't present in the flesh, to have the essence of it long after it's departed and there was no need, suddenly, for that.

OK, so the Garbo mosaic was the last thing on the list. Anything else, madam, that you request?

Um, a new bed, a wider one. And proper jazz, at that club, and a concert where you have to dress up, and an ice cream in a cone. And an orgasm. Yes, that.

Madam, the challenges you set.

Oh, and a closer park.

So you want to move out?

The split of the grin. I had him then, had him tight. Reciprocated love – what could be sweeter than that?

So we began flat-hunting, and the growing up was speeding upon me swift.

The carpet was laid the day President Kennedy was killed, said Mrs Green, the twinkly landlady, as she showed off her inner-city nest. If I got new carpet all the furniture would just laugh at it, so it's better in the long run to stick with the old, you know what I mean?

Nature didn't reach the shy window of the bedsit at the bottom of a tall alley, the city grew over the building, clogging it in, and I had to twist my head until it hurt to catch the sky but it was convenient for Jeremy's shop and cheap. God, it just cements me to this city, said Dan, throwing up his hands and laughing. But hey, it's OK, it's a direct tube to the photo shop, I'll be all right.

And over that spring of vivid happiness we had precious little, such a frugal life, but the little we had we possessed graciously. The sheets were always clean and the sink always sparkling and I basked over that season in a great, spreading warmth for the city was brightening, the sunlight was firming and there was a lovely, new lightness in the sky. I became womanly, motherly, all of that, it was something that was awoken in my bones. A sprig of jasmine in a jar on the windowsill flooded our dark little poke of a room and in those newly washed days I opened the windows as wide as they'd go and the white curtains flapped and danced like a pair of hankies waving at departing troops. By late May the sun was so sweet on my skin and the sky had lifted and I was loving London afresh, I felt filled up with light, felt it singing in me and felt loved, properly now, it was a canopy of joy. I'd waited so long for this. And I wasn't sure how long it'd last, I had a foreboding even then, can't explain, perhaps it was as simple as knowing that happiness never lasts.

You need to get a post office box, Lil.

Why?

Because you never know when we might move again, and it's handy to keep track of your mail.

I'll just use yours.

No, get your own, I need mine for myself.

Why?

I dunno, I just do.

Why?

But he won't say and I taunt him with what Jeremy had said once, about a public life and a private one and a secret one and he laughs and says yes, he'll only be telling me his secret one when he's sure that I'll stay, that I won't run away.

Why on earth would I do that?

Tucking my lips into the curve of his cheek and neck. Never tiring of that body during that time, it was simple and smooth and young whereas Richard's was complicated, all wheeze and eczema and sag. And the touch was different too, Dan's was much more competitive and creative than the older man's, it was as if he was trying to wipe the memory of Richard's selfish ways, to stamp my skin with the permanence of his own stroke.

Tell me about your community, he asked one night and I can remember gabbling on about how strict it was, and God-abiding, and how they'd disapprove terribly if they could see me in London with an independent life and a man and there was his sudden gravity, his clasping of my cheeks in the muffs of his palms, his saying that I must never go home, I must promise him that and there was the intensity again, it had come back, like the mouth clamp and the arm grab once.

Why?

Because it'll snuff out all the happiness that's in you. You're too vivid for a nidderly place like that.

Nidderly? What does that mean?

He opened my word book and wrote down *cowardly* in his beautiful hand.

And what about you, Mr? Aren't *you* ever going home?

No answer to that.

I open the journal that catalogues that time, it's the only one I haven't dipped repeatedly into for there's something about it that keeps it from me and I can hardly bear now to read the words back. And yet during those first days all it's filled with is a neophiliac's wonder, it's an inventory of all the novelty that silked the long-lit summer days.

The first owned double bed and I'm spreading diagonally across it when Dan isn't there and feeling the luxury of flung limbs and plunging my face into his pillow and collecting his smell. The bed whose foot and head had once been gates on an Irish field and then reclaimed from the mud and the cows and restored to their rightful purpose and shipped across the sea.

The first concert at the Royal Albert Hall and there's a shriek as I enter the vastness of it, at the scale of civilization and its beauty and I'm closing my eyes when the music begins and basking in the sound of the notes pluming skyward and a smile is sealed on my face.

The first quail's egg, the mild, ball-dress blue of it inside and the shock of the taste, *it's just like a hen's!* Well, what did you expect? Dan's indignant response.

The first swim, awakening my body to the memory of the stroke and pulling away strong with my laps, seal happy. Leaving Dan behind and stretching my limbs as far as I can and feeling the crank of the sleeping muscles pushed into a working once again and in a flash, too quick, four laps have been done and Dan's already given up but I'll not be stopped now I've begun. His mock-bored grin, his rolling of his eyes, when I finally climb out.

The first jazz gig, at Ronnie Scott's. The single sax note on a

187

highway of music and the hum of the double bass in my feet and then the little bongo-boy like a featherweight boxer prancing out in his T-shirt and track pants with a towel around his shoulders and his hands are fast, a whirr, a hummingbird's wings and there's a whine of music like a bee arcing and circling and I'm leaping to my feet and moving with it, don't want it stopped. And on the return to the flat my skin's heavy with the smell of cigarette smoke, my hair's listless and weighted and I'm breathing it all in, smelling the heaviness of it and smiling at the growing up.

The first love, proper-way, and I don't know where it'll end, can't imagine how. I hold Dan's smell to my face like a mother does with a child's and *could it ever sour for me?* I write.

So there we were, stopping our working and dreaming in the sweetness of that summer and the journal is full of days and then weeks of vast blanks and Dan's camera is put down. And within that vivid happiness my outsider eyes are softened, I'm losing the sharpness of seeing in the thick of the falling but I don't care that love is stopping the hunger and wiping the thinking, don't care that I'm not reading the signs any more. *Happiness slows me*, I write and I want to bottle that ripe time, want it with me for ever. I feel absorbed by Dan, dissolving, floating within a wonderful morass and I ask in that journal, in a summer-fat, loopy scrawl, if it's possible to be diminished by happiness and I'm not really caring if it is.

What I learned of Dan Smith during that time: that he flossed religiously every night, ate bread until it sprouted blue spots, was cleaner than myself, loved reading all ten national newspapers on a Saturday and browsing in Tower Records and would sleep until one if he could.

Only a handful of things to recite, and nothing of his secret life or its churnings. How odd that you can be with someone for six months, or five years, or a lifetime, and never know them.

Touch is with me the most. A hand cupping my hip, fingers trickling down my back, a tongue on my eye, his lips on my lids and his palms muffing my cheeks and the ferocity in it, that I must never go back to the community, I must stay in the world, I must promise him that.

Summer shuts itself down and winter returns as abrupt as a garage door slamming shut on the warmth. We sense a city settling back into the chill with relief for London isn't comfortable with the heat. Darkness gathers in and the sky is so close and so cold, so cold becomes our juddery refrain. So cold that the steam from our tea dances into the air like a snake charmer's cobra, so cold that the duvet is too thin, too much a skeleton, there's not enough meat in it and our bodies steal its spread from each other in sleep, so cold that we're mutual heat-bricks as we ram each other each night, so cold that I make Dan warm his fingers on the hot water bottle for a full five minutes before he's allowed to touch my skin. We haven't yet learned to wear enough clothes, haven't learned the secret of layers. Winter means goosebumps under a shower's thin water and a flinching every morning when we step into the air and a constant shrinking into coats.

Home fills Dan's heart now that winter's back, I can tell, there's too much light in his bones. He's yearning for the sun and his people and his sky, it's in his talk too much.

You know, Lil, I looked at the man in the corner shop the other day and realized that even if I lived here for thirty years, I'd never get to know him any better. It's a lonely city, the people just don't let you in.

Oh come on, I'm saying, it's not that bad, but there's a flutter in my belly for he won't let up. This country leads the world in nothing but decline, he's snapping, it's the past, not the future and there's nothing for us here, there's no sense of community for us, no warmth.

I dread a return now, in the thick of this settling, dread the idea of community back home.

I find St Brides, the writers' church, it's a fresh sense of warmth but I cannot get Dan to it no matter how much I tug for he doesn't want anything of a God. It's obscured deep among offices and was built on the bones and shards of the wolves and Romans and six buildings has it seen over its two thousand years, it was bombed during the last war and yet still its spire soars. I begin to haunt evensong every Sunday night, wanting to cloak myself in its community, to quell the sense of alone that I have living now with Dan's hungry gravitational pull south, into past and family and sun, I can taste his veer. But every Sunday night I come home quietened by the calmness of the ritual, feeling a centredness and a soothing feeling that everything, eventually, will be all right.

It's OK, Miss Lil, I'm not leaving this place yet. How could I, you're in it.

Knowing I can endure as long as Dan's by my side, my ballast, my mate. For I'm beginning to hate solitude for the first time in my life when he isn't around, the old Lillie's leaking away, and when I come home I turn my face to his chest and he encircles me in his arms and it seems like a haven, a refuge, to rest from all the world as he holds me tight, as if he'll never let me go, and it's all that I want.

There's the writing dream still and I'm trying to fill my journal and too easily giving up for I'm addled by novelty and happiness and a partner's wants and the demands of work and a brand-new life. It's all my lovely fuel to creative inactivity and my dream's drowning in the sweet thick of it. *With happiness I've lost the will, it's pushed out reason and I don't seem to care,* I manage one night to write, and then for weeks, more blank.

I wonder if you could survive here by yourself now, he muses one night. Have I got you into the world enough?

And I'm hitting and laughing, saying, No, never, there's a long way to go, I still need help, and my fingers curl into his red jumper and snag it tight.

A new development: not taking our watches off before sleeping, not bothering.

*

Letters are sped home, I've finally given out a post box to reply to, *it's the itinerant's anchor, for I never know where I'll be next*, and Ed says she feels so close to me during that time that she can almost put out a hand. Can feel herself willing her palm flat on my back and pushing me onward and deeper into life and not home.

Why on earth do you think I'd be doing that? I write back. For somewhere in my journal is Baudelaire's great malady, the horror of one's home, and I know in my heart I won't be going back, that it will never quite hold me enough.

The cottage is rung. There's the joy in Cedric's voice and a glut of questions that stems a swift hanging up, it's as if he never wants me gone. Finally I get in my own asking, so much of it: his book's on hold, the old publisher has left and the replacement doesn't like the idea near as much and Cedric tries but doesn't succeed to keep the devastation from his voice.

They'll pay me of course, they just won't publish it. But that's the whole point.

His dream, his whole life.

Never mind, Lil.

No, no, we'll do something, we'll take it somewhere else.

No matter, dear, it's all gone now.

My indignation's fuelled by guilt for he doesn't deserve such treatment from his publishers, or such a long silence from me.

But Dan has a surprise, and all the plans for Cedric are momentarily swamped.

There's a bird from home in a Scottish zoo, but it's stopped singing, I read about it in the paper. I'd love to photograph it, do you want to come?

To the land of deep fried Mars Bars? Now what do you think, Mr Smith?

He hasn't talked about photography for months.

So that there that Lillie Bird is, her heart lifting with the voice of the flinty far-northerners as she steps from the train at Glasgow and she wants to drink their lilt, the music they make with words as meek as *time* or *far* or *nine*. Her heart lifting as Dan drives the hire car deep into the remote pocket of the Highlands, for this, finally, is rugged land, with hills nudging the belly of the sky and mountains pushing up into cloud and slopes rushing down into roads. Her heart lifting as Dan stops to take another photo and another, her heart lifting at his working again. Snapping a runnel of snow like a teardrop on a distant mountain and a hill cracked clean down the middle and tumbling water in a stream that's stained the colour of moss. Her heart lifting as they drive between soaring peaks in the whoosh of the valleys and she feels close to God and puts her hand on Dan's leg and raises her face in joy to a very wild sky.

I'm so glad we're doing this, she says.

The bed and breakfast is huddled far west, alone by a loch and close to the sea. It's a humble, salt-scoured place, flinching amid its landscape of rusts and wet-blacks and compromised blues and I bounce like a child on the high double bed and tumble Dan onto it, loving sleeping now in different beds after so many years of settling into just one. Ha, the girl addicted to new beds, I'm still that.

The sturdy walls of the stone cottage envelope us with reassurance, cosying us inside against the bash of the wind and wet and for most of that first afternoon we stay tucked in our room while the rain spits at the loch. From the bedroom window it looks like mist rising from the water and as the afternoon lengthens the stubborn wind buffets the house and every time I look the water's colour has changed in the shifting, windblown light.

Come on, let's go for a walk, you're getting as soft as a pocket, Danny boy.

The clouds move over a distant mountain like the drawing of a stately curtain, the weather's all symphonied as it rises and falls and thunders and repeats and I love how the Highlanders live so close to the weather in a way that we don't in the city, love how the sky orders their lives, feel taller and straighter within it.

God, I could live in this place, I say, breathing in deep. Could you?

No response, oddly quiet.

Dan?

No, I find it oppressive.

Oh.

His face still, and old, and unknown.

Lil, I have to go home.

My world stopping. A lightness in my hands and a sudden discon-nectedness in my fingers and the float of my belly and W-what do you mean? is all I can stumble out and I'm looking at the salt spray shunting across the rocks and the little, lone white cottages hugging the shoreline and I'm waiting for an answer but it doesn't come and I'm looking at those cottages so alone and reduced by the dimensions of the land around them and I'm looking straight into Dan and he's shifting, pale, I hardly know him, who he is, the other life that he's got and all my suspicion is ramming back. He won't meet my eyes and I stare at the disappearing huddle of the community living under the great thumb of the weather and still an answer won't come.

Dan?

Sterner now and forcing talk from him and he tells me, as if it's all been carefully thought out, that his visa's about to expire and he isn't like me, with an English mother, he has to go away from the country and come back into it again and there are things he has to tidy up, you know, before he can be back here for good.

My brightening.

Silly billy, I'll come too! Ruffling his hair with relief.

No. I have to do this by myself. It's the only way to make it work.

I step back. I rub at a frown as I listen, half-listen, he'll be back soon and he'll be leaving his cameras with me, as proof, a guarantee, what more do I need than that, and this is so hard, the hardest thing he's ever done and he loves me so much that it hurts. Lillie? Lil? Catching my arm, You must know you've always been the only one, and he's clenching me, he's pressing the colour from my skin with his firm finger marks and all my doubt's back.

I brusque from him to the water's edge and balance with the balls of my feet on a wobbly, wide stone and the wind fans the loch, it whips and butts me and tries to push me off the rock. I don't want to be left in Britain alone, I'm not sure now that I can do it by myself. I look across at him: the first person who loves me cleanly and I can't let that go and I don't quite trust that he'll ever return, for other women, other lives, could so easily spill across his path. I remember again that first time in Evendon when we'd both been haunted and I slam my eyes on a sudden sting of tears, thinking of the cocky boy-man from home who's somehow knuckled his heels into my heart, who's become beautiful and strong and right, who's been transformed into the only man that I want, the standard by which all others are dulled.

Please, Dan.

You can't afford it and you've got your life set up now. You can't leave all that. I promise I'll be back. For fuck's sake, trust me, Lil.

Shaking me by the shoulders with his words, there's a violence in their tone, he's pushing his love into me, I think, I'm not sure, I'm not sure about anything now. No people are as exasperating as those we love, remember that, and I want to walk away from him in that moment and never return, I want to stun him and scar him and prove it can be done. I haven't yet seen France or the Alps or the Red Sea, it was all, all to come. Together. I shun the held-out hand.

Walk for hours on that shutting day and keep getting whiffs of him as I move for he's soaked into my clothes and my hair and my heart. It's cold and the backs of my ears trap the chill and thud with its hurt and I walk through a scrap of a village with its tired store that sells everything and wonder if I could ever live back within a community like this, with its lace curtains cramming windows and its mothers picking up children and their pointed curiosity and know that I can no longer do it alone, I need people now, Dan's taught me that. There's the stately migration of clouds across the hills, there's a storm folding out to sea and peeling back and I just can't imagine a future without him, or facing my new land by myself, or going home.

I slip into the warmth of our bed, late, and Dan's arms lock across my body with a ferocious relief. Thank Christ you're back and he turns me to him, cupping my face in the brace of his palms and telling me he'll always find me, always, and he's sliding his lips along my eyelashes and damming new tears and slipping his hands up my nightgown and holding my trembling. I won't let you go, his whisper into the dark and I'm kissing him into quiet and he's blooming a smile as I draw back, there's the shine of his teeth, it's as if the touch of my lips is a gift he'll never tire of.

So there we were with a silence in the cottage that was distracting, demanding after the continual hum of the city's noise and neither of us could sleep for the quiet crashed into our tiredness too much. There was a bright moon in a mackerel sky and it called us from the bed and we sat in armchairs pulled up to the window with our socked feet on the radiator and cups of tea in our hands and watched in silence the moonlit loch, the path of shine optimistic across its length as we fluttered our breathing across the tea's heat. So, back to the sun-scoured place, and after the meekness of this land. But I could not scrub the fear that Dan would be swallowed under by it and would never come back, that I'd be softened from his longing like a fire dying from a hearth. I wanted to be there to always kiss him awake, couldn't bear the thought of someone else.

The two of us curved back into the bed and Dan's arm held me to his slumber and I listened to his quiet breathing and fell into his sleep, and from somewhere within it he whispered that he'd make sure I was always loved and my dreams breathed in his words and tucked them away. And then there was a fragment, so vivid, I was walking barefoot through a fern-bowered, Bony creek with the water up to my calves and the coolness of slime at my soles and I woke to a wave of nostalgia washing over me, flooding my limbs and dragging my consciousness hurtlingly home. For clouds like curtains brushing the high peaks, for wide fields and the smell of my earth but I forced the dream into the hard light: the prospect of home and all it meant. Yet there I was that night, bound by desire and *please let me come* I whispered once more into his sleep.

No.

Flopping back onto the pillow.

I couldn't do it to you, Lil.

The voice firm with finality, I remember that, no budging in it and warning now.

I'm doing all this for you, you know, I'm sorting out my life and coming back. OK?

But how long will you be gone?

I'm not sure.

And so in those hardening days we're snatching that leaking time, grabbing our love like the heat of an Indian summer before the winter of it all is to close over us.

Dan grew more hungry, creative, bold, it was as if he was trying to sear himself into my memory. Nightly now there were his nimble fingers and his flicking tongue, nightly now his kissing in four places – eyelids, lips, and then the dip below – and the nudging of my thighs with his chin and the first, slow lick and the implosions like thunder gentle across my belly and the clenched eyes and the warm, flooding wet. We talked through our skin, that was our world, we were safe in that. And only in sleep did Dan surrender his panic, he held me so tight, he thudded me into the wall, as if he were clinging on to a lifebuoy in a vast ocean of fear.

The bird was never photographed, neither of us had the heart for it any more.

How long will you be gone?

I'm not sure yet.

*

London, the night before he's to fly out and he's folding my fingers over a set of rosary beads, his grandmother's, and the ends of the crucifix are jabbing into my flesh as I shut my fist tight and we're holding our foreheads to each other's and then cheek to cheek and nothing more is said for everything has been said.

How long will you be gone?
Only silence now.

What will not be wiped, and I don't need a journal for it bites into all these nights: the wing of his arm cupping my sleep. Waking from sleep to his torso curled around me with his hand balled into the softness of my groin. The smell of him in the small clearing behind his ear, the close, secret smell of skin and soap. Reaping goosebumps with a comb. His laughing at my ear-rims blushing at his kiss, his hands trickling over the back of my shoulders like cool water on a sweltering summer's day. His finding of those ways for I'll never allow him to venture too far and there has to be something else. What will not fade for it bites into my nights: catching sight of him from a distance if I haven't seen him for a while and getting a tremor in my bowels deep inside me, like the beginning signal of an orgasm, because I'm aching with tenderness at the sight of him.

God, for it all to have changed so much and I would never have imagined it in those first, ragged months of knowing him.

−13−

Once Upon a Time

Once upon a time there was a woman called Lillie Bird who on a rain-bright evening stared at the sharp little bullets of wet smashing into a headlit road and thought of the prospect of home, of diving into sunlight, of moving from a congested island and back into the permanent light. Did she have the courage for that?

At Hammersmith station, as she scrabbled in wallet corners for coins to the airport, a young backpacker approached her, all weight and stain, and she tightened defensively as he handed something to her and began to turn from him, not wanting leaflets and not wanting talk but it was his all-day travel pass, he told her to take it, he'd finished with it. Oh, she said, and the cloud of suspicion was whipped from her face, thank you, she said, and she felt herself softening with the kindness of the grubby stranger and felt herself brightening for it was a good sign. Lillie had rejected someone once who'd been kind, and the lesson had been learned.

At the crowded check-in counter there were long, bag-swathed surfboards as cumbersome as canoes and there was the ragged, beach-blond hair of the young men of her land and she had never seen before such a concentrated clutter of them in London. So many Dans, so much optimism, so much keenness to be going home.

*

And then I saw him.

Standing a little apart and not optimistic or proud but lost, and I knew his body now like a bus route I'd travelled every day of my life and I felt in that watching that I'd never tire of it. He stood aside for a family and caught my eye, he propped his head, he couldn't quite comprehend, it was as if he'd just woken up. Then he bloomed his grin and there was that wild love for him, so huge, it hurt. I held my plane ticket aloft and nodded and he shook his head and smiled and he held out his arms and I walked into their folding.

Oh you mad, mad bugger, he said.

Mmm hmm.

So it's all decided, then?

Mmm hmm.

His heart thumping into me. That fire in my belly, that life driven by love.

Just remember that all the best love is remembered love, Ced had written with his cheque. *I'll prove you wrong,* I'd smiled back to him on a postcard of fifty thank yous. Knowing he was my best bet to lend me the fare – I hadn't specified the destination – for he'd told me once to seize love when it was close so that I wouldn't be haunted by it and for ever trapped.

The plane angled into cloud and my optimism bubbled now at the prospect of my homeland, of flinging sun into my lungs, of light that bashed at me as opposed to light that had licked me for so long. I wasn't sure what to expect, just knew I didn't want to make it as far as Sunshine, not this time, for home meant ambivalence and tenacity and fret and I didn't need any of that on this trip. I looked across at Dan and he smiled, drained now, all questions talked from him and he reached for my hand and kissed my fingers and held each digit in the hollow of his mouth and there was such a tenderness in each slow gesture that they're in my heart still. I slipped my journal from the seat pocket and asked if people should be scoffed at for aspiring to nothing more than something they could enslave themselves to, be that belief, or a goal, or a cause, or a man.

There I am, leaning and kissing Dan softly on the temple and he's saying from sleepiness that it's like a fairy dancing on his skin and I'm cupping my palm on his cheek in reply and smiling, remembering a lifetime ago on the cusp of twenty-one, a sun-smeared church and the dust motes dancing on their streams of light.

He asked if I'd thought about what I was going to do back home and I said flippantly, write. What about? But I couldn't say, I didn't know. He said I had to write what I'd experienced and he warned he'd be jealous of any old lovers threaded into my work for they'd all laid claim to my past in a way that he didn't and he was teasing but there was iron in his smile. I haven't done anything yet, swiping the curl of my little finger down his cheek, I'm an unfinished canvas. He said ah, so it was him that I'd feed from, for writers were all vampires with their constant need for fresh blood. And yes, I thought, all that selfishness, all that hunger for the world, and experiences and fresh lives and solitude and love. And I thought of the time when Dan had seemed so reduced, so dazzled out by someone else, and I knew now that love wasn't always shouted.

I still wish you weren't doing this, Lil.

Nodding, smiling, not paying enough attention to his doubt.

The plane begins its descent and out of the starred, plastic window is the beautiful spread of the city's lights and Dan asks me one more time why I'm doing this, for don't I know that it's dangerous to put all my eggs in one basket, hmm, and my fingertips press his lips to a stillness.

Above us the sky stretched like a vast spinnaker, it was a blue so sharp that it hurt and we screwed up our London-softened eyes at its blast. A breeze frolicked its welcome and in a too-shiny hire car we drove to the ocean and held our faces to the slap of sea air and stuck out our tongues and tasted its heavy salt and filled our brains with its rush. Dan took out his camera but I snatched it from him and aimed and shot, I caught the sun-blustered face and punched the air and laughed.

So how does it feel, mate, to have the tables turned? I'm the stalker now!

We peeled off our shoes and let the greedy surf play around us and could feel all the grimy grey being vacuumed from us by the sun and wind and spray. Then I stood very still with my skin drinking the sky, and the magnificent, light-flooded land brimmed my heart.

Yet in those first hours back in it I also felt a peculiar sense of removal, a slight queasiness experienced, I suspect, by many adventure-tainted travellers upon return, the oscillation of someone who sees a familiar world with a stranger's eyes. The known was made strange and I could suddenly see my blessed country as sparse and small-minded and parochial and still, on the very edge of the world, when I'd come from a land that was deeply *in* the world and there was such a seductive, fractious energy to that.

That feels like an angel kissing my throat, Dan says, as he swigs from a bottle of mineral water and I tell him he's loved for his talk rather than his tan for we're both brazenly white and it's wrong in our land. I plead with him to stay just a night in the sparkling, seaside city before the madness of home is to begin, before responsibility and adulthood close over us both, for there's skin to be tanned and shops to be seen before a day-long drive to some faraway place with a brand-new family in its midst.

Prove how much you love me, Dan Smith. Just a night, come on.

The robust English currency pays for a ridiculously wide bed in a five-star hotel. The service is lazy-friendly and nonchalant, infuriating if we were in a different kind of mood but we aren't. A wealthy Czech in the lobby cafe, loudly jacketed and thickly ringed, tells us he'd sailed into this city as a refugee in November 1953 and had seen its wharfies on the docks and its men in the bars and had known that at last he'd found a country that would always be free, because it was plain from the manner of its people that nothing would ever get them to cow to authority, to do a Nazi salute or a bow, they were just too laid-back. We laugh and step again into the glare to grab every spare minute that's left. Summer is my home, and sunlight. Bought: the first bikini and a straw cowboy hat and sarong and they're worn proud from the shop and on a wide beach boulevard I walk past a neat young man with a curious, spastic lope of a rolling walk, he's caged within a phalanx of robed Muslim women and he stares at my body and smiles wide and speed-jerks his limbs and there's his want as the women's eyes collectively speak to me: Away with you, girl a world apart.

I *am* a girl apart, I've fought for it all my life. And I have a plan on that afternoon to come back every cicada-shrill summer and flood my lungs with this light, to always return to thaw from some flinty other place. Back to this different sky, back to these happy, chatty people. I fling my arms around Dan and giggle my dream to him and he says I'll have to have a lot of cash for that. Where's your optimism, mate? I flick back. His mood has soured, I don't know why.

So there we are on that first night back, sleeping deeply and not touching at first, too tired for that, for we're slugged by jet lag and the emotional dumping of the past week and the relearning of our land and the scouring of the sun. I've opened the windows wide, I've forgotten what it's like to sleep in balmy weather, to be caressed by the air rather than huddling against it. At one point Dan rolls across and holds me tight, cupping my breast in his palm and thudding his love into me and trying to calm his racing heart and then he wakes with a start at four fifty a.m., jetlag buzzy and ready.

Come on, Lil, we can't put it off for ever.

Nibbled by anxiety, it's all jumpy through my sleep.

*

We take back roads into forgotten towns, petrol stops at shiny super-centres, ice-cream stops at wilting corner stores. My arm's wedged lazy on the edge of the car door and my fingers drum the roof and the sun's so sweet on my skin and I lean my head out the window and scrutinize the land: yellow-stained country, flimsy-looking towns, ugly barbed wire, sagging telegraph wires and fields never lush that always remind me, post-rain, of baby birds with their cavern-mouths wide open, newly-fed but not sated. Again and again there's a feeling that the inhabitants have given up, defeated by thin soil and a cruel sky and yet deeply I love it, the drive's reinforcing it, that it'll always be soaked through my heart. Without a word Dan places his hand over mine and lifts it to the gearstick and teaches me a little of the car's talk. Feel it's grunt, see, he says, as he accelerates and then releases the gears. Oh yeah! We pass the spouting whale sign of a car wash and I yell, Stop, quick, and Dan glances at his watch, his family's bearing upon him and shutting him down but I tell him I'll never forgive him and he laughs and slows, All right, all right.

The tentacles of the giant, felt kelp judder over the car and I squeal under the heaviness of its chugging dance and spume of the suds and mad spray and Dan kisses me into quiet in the shuddery cosiness and I wonder if I've ever been happier. Back on the empty zoom of the open road, bereft of other car company, I strip off my shirt and wear a freshly purchased bra that's all satiny-black and as sexy as a magazine and at a distance, I hope, as quiet as a bikini top. Dan whoops and swerves and I trail an arm high, butting the breeze and the car slows to a stop and there's a long kiss with my lips coming to rest in the soft dip between his collarbone and neck and I hold my breathing quietly to him, collecting his smell. In a draining-away day we eat spilling hamburgers-with-the-lot by a lake and then lie on beach towels on our backs, Dan's head on my groin, and catch in silence the scraps of conversation around us.

You've got a job now, you can go and get my hat.

Daddy, have you got a surfboard at your place?

I smile and say nothing, for come nightfall we'll be shut away tight within another family, with all its quirks. As darkness claims

the day Dan stands and reaches out a hand and hauls me up –
come on, let's get a move on – and we push on.

Quieter, and quieter still.

The car's powering along foggily familiar roads and there's an
uncertainty seeping into me: I know, vaguely, the geography of this
last leg. A scratch of panic in my throat, nothing more, soon we'll
turn off, a coincidence or what?

But an intersection.

A town hall.

A white statue of a soldier, head bowed.

An abandoned fruit stand and it's all from a childhood that's
now flooding back and my breathing's shallowing as the car pushes
on confidently to a surely-not home.

Where did you say you lived, Dan? Wet draining from my
mouth.

A place you don't know. Too swift.

Oh.

But the known mountain looms. Then the first sign to Sunshine,
Sunshine, the bluntness of that, and there's a creeping cold and I
grip the sides of the seat as I stare at the mountain outline and feel
like a blanket has been thrown over me, stopping all light, for
Dan's heading with intent like some crazed deadly arrow to my
home. Which means, and I can't comprehend, that he knows who
I am. And he's bringing me back into it. And he's known all along.
And he loves me, he's said that, but *who is he*, what? Smith, a
common name in our town but a common name in every town in
this land and I've never thought anything of it. There's the sap
in my mouth as the car powers closer to the mountain, there's the
slam of it all nettled in my throat as I scrabble with rationalizing:
he'll turn at the last minute and I'm being paranoid, ridiculous,
and he's never heard of a village called Sunshine or the secrets that
it holds.

But the road sign, the run of the river, the womanly, foothill
rumps, the shift of the clouds and the way their bellies scrape the
stark peak and there's no mistaking it as Dan turns left into the road

up the hill into the town and he's saying nothing, his eyes are rigidly ahead and his face is set and the unfairness of it all is ganging up on me and I can hardly get my words out.

What's the name of that place where you said you lived?

Bindle.

Never heard of and there's my yelp of relief, oh, I don't know that town! and I'm telling him, babbling, that it's just so weird because it's all so close to where my own family is and there's my laugh and the quaver in it and just a short, bitten hmm in response in a tone I don't know, it's a different Dan, a different voice. And a Brother Sleet catch-cry comes back to me *he that increaseth knowledge increaseth sorrow* as I look across at the man I've invested all my future in, and who I don't know one bit.

You're taking me back, aren't you?

Tight, cold, old.

Asking who he is through the swell of vomit in my throat and he's telling me that he's always planned to go to his parents and he's taking me to mine – *what?* – he's telling me it's the best place for me and the only place he can think of, he's doing it to protect me and keep me close until he can sort out what to do for he didn't ask me to get on the plane and follow him home, God, no and what a mess, the whole lot of it.

Well why the *fuck* didn't you tell me this before we got in the car?

I knew you wouldn't come.

Too fucking right, mate, and I'm nodding and nodding, mouth set.

I didn't know what you'd do, Lil, I thought perhaps I'd never see you again, I didn't want you storming out. I'm at my wits' end, I just don't know how to sort this out.

Not able to voice the next question, can't bear the response, what his place is in the community because all I can think of is the last kiss and the last sleep and the last twelve months and my hand's on the car door but he's winding the climb too fast and there'll be no stopping now until the farm's hit, God, the farm and my parents and a long, long night. A wailing's slipping from me, it's slammed shut but then fuck it, let him hear it, let it worm under his skin and it crawls through the car and curls into its far corners and tries to get out and reach the sky, it's a sound that seems to fill every inch of my body and there's an intensity of delivery I've never heard before and I want it through him so he'll never forget.

I love you, Lil, he's saying softly in defeat and apology but it's overwhelmed by my heaving to stop the car and let me out but he won't and I scrabble down the window and stick out my head and retch along the side of the doors just like I did in a lumpy streak when I was four and he stops and leans across to me and wipes my face with the end of his shirt and he's trembling, holding me tight. I can feel his racing heart, God help us, he's whispering but he will not let me go, God help us, he's whispering and the child safety-lock is still on and there are no tears from me, just shock.

Blind corners and dropping gears and branch-spattered asphalt and trees whose trunks leered drunkenly toward the windshield and then the levelling out and the turn down the Tanner Road, the drive past the basketball hoop with its wag of a sign and the cathedral of singing trees and then the final slowing at the too-familiar driveway and the car stops at the farm gate and its engine ticks. All hollow I tell him that if he knew me at all he wouldn't be doing this and he replies that it's for the best, to trust him and one day I'll know that.

You said you lived in a town called Bindle.

A place, a place called Bindle, that's the name of our house, I didn't lie, I never lie.

A snort in response.

I didn't want to lose you, Lil.

Smarting at his ridiculous, selective truths and old with my fury and not moving from the car and so he gets out and opens the gate and he's watching me all the while and driving through it with a jerk and then shutting the gate and closing the car door again and wordlessly heading for the familiar house in the distance, smaller than I remember and huddled too alone now in its crook of a hill. He drops me at the door with the promise that he'll contact me the next day, says he has a lot of sorting out and now's not the time for a proper talk and to stay put, to trust him, it'll work. I can't look at him. I want to marry you some day, I'm not letting you go, remember that, but I don't answer and the car pulls away and this was never, ever meant to be the homecoming, alone, sour of mouth, hulled.

It'd been showering, raindrops were balanced on a spider's web near the doorstep and I smiled through my heart-crack at the lovely clustering, the wet diamonds. I lifted the familiar knocker and imagined the thud in my parents' hearts at its late-night demand. There was the familiar pad of slippered feet, panicky-fast, and the tugging shapes of Tiriel and Rebecca through the frosted glass and only then did I realize I was still wearing the bra top with just a beach towel around my shoulders but there was my father's anxious voice – hello, who is it – and it was too late to scrabble on a shirt.

It's me, Dad.

All I could get out and the cry, the shock, the familiar sound of the key turning in the barrel and the arms swiftly enfolding me and my parents' faces creased with fresh ageing and vulnerable now and there was the shame of my nakedness and Rebecca's fingers already busy with their calming work and Tiriel's tears stamping tracks on my cheeks as he held me and held me and had I ever been held so tight?

They propped my sway and asked if I was all right and then I was wrapped in a blanket from somewhere, shhh, no talk, it can wait. Was I hungry, thirsty, what did I need, a cup of tea per-haps, and I was shaking my head and brimming a smile and then the quick hot tears came and came, would they never stop? My mother's arm was strong around me, propelling me up the stairs to the familiar room and its nurse-neat bed, a space small now and heartbreakingly young like a dead child's untouched shrine that was waiting in some expectant, unaccepting readiness for return.

We knew you'd come home, Tiriel was saying with certainty as he placed Rebecca's suitcase in the corner of the room and then he sat on a chair and read the marks of a mysterious journey in my face, read a new knowledge in my eyes, an adult's knowledge, and I felt that something was severed between us that night, there was his knowing that I'd moved on. He asked if I was cold and there was Rebecca's admonishing hush as she slipped off my shoes and kneaded my soles, her fingers enquiring over the hard ridges of skin on my heels and toes that were used to walking on concrete now and not dirt. I wanted to spill it all to them, my job and the flat and my heart too full and my life suddenly lopped but Rebecca said, Shh, tomorrow, it can wait, and beckoned to Tiriel and they smoothed my brow, one after the other, and tucked me in child-tight, and left.

Lying in the familiar dip of my bed and not able to fall under; sleep all stolen by Dan for he's in my head too much. There's a coolness in the air of Bony Mountain, an exhilarating crispness and I rise and fling wide the windows to let in the brisk evening air and to sweep away the distilled smell of childhood that's pooled for too long in the shut room. I've forgotten all those familiar night sounds from home: the call of cicadas and the veer of mosquitoes and the hum of the quiet, my mother's vigorous brushing of her teeth and my father's bedtime cough and none of the noises have changed over twenty years and they're all I have now to fill the bed-time dark.

Once, long ago, my little gilled breather, when I was thirteen years old, I wrote on the first page of my mother's journal a quote from Freud I'd picked up: *separation begins with the first secret*, and on that night of slugged homecoming I wrote it again. But the second time it was written in a journal from a far foreign land whose battered leather had absorbed the ringmarks and pen flicks of much vivid living and my hands fevered across it on that long,

long night, my nails worried at it, for God knew, now, when I'd be back.

I creaked across to the familiar mattress in the early hours and finally fell into sleep and Dan invaded my dreaming too much and the narrow, dippy bed lost its innocence.

The *Shiner Courier*'s set aside that next day and the story is begun at breakfast and the telling of it takes all of the day's light. We don't move far from the kitchen table until the relief of coolness in the late afternoon, when we walk the garden of sprinkled green that laughs at the yellow enviously nudging it on the other side of the fence. Rebecca says Dan must be one of the Elliot Street Smiths, a big Shiner family, established, the policeman's son, of course, and they both vaguely remember him, nice-looking lad, woman-watched, expected to follow in his father's footsteps, a bit apart, a bit quiet.

That's not the man I know. He's very . . . cheeky with me.

Well, he must be comfortable with you then, and that's good. So many of the young boys around here are so sullen and shy. It's a stoicism mistaken for strength, but it's not.

Tiriel, as Rebecca kneads my shoulders, and there's no chiding or remonstration over what I've done, just questions and speculation about how the future can work. And on that fragile day I begin a re-knowing of the two people closest to me, see them not as parents but as individuals, and there's an appreciation for the first time of their experience and tolerance and balm.

He says he wants to marry you? Well, a good marriage is as close to heaven as you can get, Tiriel says, looking at Rebecca, and I catch the tired smile and God knows, now, for my head hurts so much and I slump my cheek into my hand. Tiriel springs up, brisk with purpose, and disappears into the kitchen and returns with a cheap cooking wine in a child's plastic glass and hands it to me as if it's a medicine cup, he tells me to get it into me and raises his mug of tea in a toast:

He said he was bringing you here to protect you. Well, as a father, I've got no argument with that.

Resistance slipping from me.

Ranging back inside and relearning the still house, its tense spirit. Seeing now that Rebecca's equilibrium is constantly doing battle with it and the house is winning and wearing her down, teasing with rattling windows and restless cracks and becoming too much. With the child's energy gone the building's too boomy for just the one couple.

I flop onto my bed and think of Mrs Green's little bedsit I abruptly gave notice on only a week before: so much happiness soaked into such a modest space, and so much ignorance. A post box, of course, so I'd never see the postmarks on his letters, never catch a return address. Anger gives me clarity and I flip through my journals, the storeroom of our love, and methodically reassess the shared life.

You must never go home, you must promise me that, his voice is written down and the sweat sheens across me as I hear its urgency again, as I feel his hands on my cheeks. But here I am, back. Who *is* this man?

At eleven thirty p.m. the phone rings and I shout down to my parents not to answer it, I leave it to shrill and shrill and it rings off and begins again. Let him stew for a bit.

But that night he comes into my dreaming once again, will I never be rid of him? I'm cutting his hair on a stool in a summer park and there's the startling intimacy of it, my fingers on his scalp and the intimacy's publicly masked as my belly presses close into bits of his back.

The geography in my bones: a wind-scoured freckle of land where the sky talks. A farm where the breeze scrapes off, constantly, the scent of the earth – the locals say of the place that its wind could blow a dog off a chain. And as I walk it again on those early days of return I know that it'll never, easily, let me go.

There I am, little one, striding that land in a long skirt with a hem of old grass stains and scattering the white birds that snow the fields as I inhale deep into my memory the smell carried on the breeze. How can I carry that scent with me? I want it close, like the memory of air that caresses me like a warm bath and the certainty of sun and long lean shadows and a world stilled by twilight and everything hushed down, like the golden light washing like a mist over the land and the glow snuffed out and the night chill suddenly there. Oh yes, all that, but how to trap its smell. All I'll have is a memory of my lungs smiling in this walking of the land for as I'm scattering those birds I'm not sure when, or if, I'll ever live here again. The separation has begun. The physical beauty of it is a paradise in my eyes and yet *paradise* comes from a Persian word meaning walled garden, Cedric had told me that. And I don't know where I'll be next, or where Dan is, or what he's sorting out, and all the sourness of uncertainty is walking with me.

An approaching storm. The first ragged smack of the wet and I'm hurrying home.

That white-hot anger at him seeps away over the days, I'm good at forgiving now, I need people too much. *It'll all work out*, he'd said to me and I hold on to that but I'm champing at the bit, wanting to know so much. I toy with ringing the twelve Smiths in the phone book, imagining the ask, but something always stops me from taking the plunge. Thinking of someone else, and what I might soil, and whatever he's going through, perhaps.

Trust me, he'd begged, and I have to hold on to that.

Ed drives in fourth practically the whole way to the farm, scarcely believing. Mother and daughter are on the verandah to greet her and she tells me later that she's struck by the difference in both. Rebecca's face startled into youngness again, and yet in my own stride to the car there's age and fresh purpose and it isn't only physically that I've changed – as we walk the land Ed has to wheedle the fresh experiences out of me for I've learned a filtering, she says that I've finally gained definition, a hardening into an adult way.

The weather closes in and we move to the house and rain strafes the windows, demanding in, and we sit on the high bed in the attic of faded colours and I'm wrong in the room now, my energy only temporary, a visitor too much. We sip cups of tea from Rebecca's mismatch of a harlequin set and talk of the future, Ed still tossing up all the dreams from magazines and books just like we had when I was fifteen. I keep my cards close to my chest, steer conversationally to get my own way, shield the soft inner self and the afternoon ends up more about my friend and I want it that way: why has she chosen to stay in such a small town, in such a small library, when there's a whole world out there? Does she need any help? Is she content? What could she say, that she was afraid, that she was settled, that she liked what was known?

It suits me.

We speak of nuns, the few that we know, strong and luminous and self-contained women who draw others to their light and I tell Ed that she gives off the collected energy of a man-free woman and I've always been struck by that. What about Mike? And she says they have their separate lives, there's no light left in their marriage, ducking as she's learned to over the years and I remember putting my arm around her and being gentle with her, pouring more tea and offering more biscuits and she tells me later that she's struck by my mothering on that rain-slammed day, by the newly tender, adult way I have in me, as if I alone see her vulnerability, or respond to it.

Hey, it's OK. At least I've got someone. Isn't that the main thing?

I'm looking at her, imagining Ish's scorn if she were here, imagining the deliciousness of her walking down Sunshine's main street and her continual, wondrous fuck, *fuck*. And somewhere within it I'm saying that I still want to write, I don't want to hit forty and say why didn't I ever give it a go and even if I fail at least I'll have tried, there won't ever be the mind-nag of that. For isn't that the worst kind of failure, the knowledge that there was never the time or courage to have a go at the dream in the first place? I'm going to see the world, I say, and I'm going to write it all out, as my fingers trace a quote from Melville in faded, purple felt-tip pen that's sticky-taped to my old desk, trace the careful, fat handwriting that barely exists now: *Keep true to the dreams of thy youth.*

The old Lillie's sparking back.

Rebecca reads something new in me that Tiriel can't, a bottled stillness that's ready to explode. She tells me she's getting me out and my heart sings as she grabs her car keys but then she tosses across a baseball cap and it isn't caught.

They're not quite ready for the shock of you yet, chick.

We avoid the town.

Rebecca drives obscure mountain roads that nudge through the bush and seem on the verge of being defeated by it, she whips through ferns spilling over bitumen and under branches arcing low and there's an airy prance of leaves kicked into a dancing by the car's wake. She stops by a field eight miles from Sunshine and I think at first it's just a rectangle of stubborn dirt but then I see ridges soft at the far end – all that's left of a cemetery's graves. A quiet wow, and new care in my step.

It's not for us, it's for outsiders in the community.

There are weathered stakes with rusty tin-can lids nailed onto them and the names are handwritten in rough block, just surnames, unaccompanied by the luxury of a birth date or a death date or an inscription. In one corner there's a stake careless on the ground with its one precious word of identity long ago bleached from its lid and a few boxed enclosures of four old gates wired together, propping each other up, and one fresh, high mound covered with browned stems and branches, the skeletons of bouquets and rushes. I'm struck by the unyielding soil that pushes at everything alien, rejecting fenceposts and stone and tin and I pick up a freshly fallen white feather from the ground and it seems that it's the only thing gleaming in the field and I walk back to the car in silence with my arm around my mother's waist, knowing that I can't stay much longer in this place. I ask Rebecca where she wants to be buried and she laughs, she doesn't know where home is. Not Sunshine, or England, she just doesn't know.

I'm in this strange state of homelessness, and I wouldn't wish it on anyone, chick.

The words wrenching, for it's as if Rebecca has sensed. And she's speaking as a true exile now: home doesn't exist for her any more, memory is all she has left.

No return address on the padded postbag. Inside, a scuffed cream box that cradles a delicate web of an antique diamanté necklace. The piece's fragile busyness rests on yellowed, watermarked silk and I gasp as I lift it from its moulded stand. *One day your daughters will fight over it*, says the unsigned, fountain-penned note tucked inside, in the handwriting that'll never be wiped.

He's seducing you with words, Tiriel says, nodding, smiling, knowing.

The phone rips into the midnight and I shout that I'll get it and run down the stairs and on the seventh ring I lift the receiver and instantly read the hushed tones – he's calling from a household asleep. I'm looking at the conversation but I'm not in it as he tells me he loves me so much that he feels sick without me and I steal all the calm from him the nights we're not together because he stays up lonely and restless and craving, he forgets all sense of time and then there I am, melting, drinking in his voice in the dark, gone. It's good to hear you, I say and there's a smile in his *yeah* and a pause.

Lil, I've got something to tell you.

Oh?

My hand tightens on the phone, my breath shallows. I can tell that I'm close to the real Dan for the voice has dropped and slowed, it's from somewhere deep in his belly, there's no front and I slip down the wall and crouch in the cold in readiness for a long night.

Where to begin, gosh, and a weak laugh.

From the start, mate. That's always a good place.

Um, yeah, and again the laugh, and his smooth talking is fractured by tiredness and the desire just to push it out now, to have it all gone as he tells me of a little boy once who barely knew a girl at his school, she was bigger than him, and back then when someone was just three years older they could seem so incredibly grown up, remember that? She was different to any other person he knew, she didn't belong and she didn't make any effort to and he was fascinated by that.

She was so kind of luminous, and remote.

Uh huh. Doubtful, slow.

Yeah, he says, yeah, but there was a kindness there too for she helped him to choose his library books once, she was always in the library, it's the only time they ever talked and it wasn't enough even to know names and his narrative's all stumbling and picking itself up.

You see, um, I was a bit of a loner too, Lil, but a secret one, not an obvious one like her. She kind of celebrated her difference, but I guess, ha, that I was too chicken to.

The startling honesty, the flash of it. I hold the phone closer and try to still the loudness of my breathing, it's rattling too much. I loved the library, he says, but I couldn't tell anyone, it was my secret. Hey, I bet you don't remember any of this? No, I reply, baffled. We weren't supposed to like books in our town, Brother Sleet didn't encourage it, I thought I was the only library-haunter around, hadn't really noticed anyone else. But it was worse for boys to like books than girls, I remember that, it was easier for us to be word-wanting and weak.

Anyway, Lil, one day I was picked on in the playground, it was some stupid fight about being a policeman's son and a pansy or something and my library books were spilled from my bag and I was pushed to the ground and you know what? That girl I hardly knew marched right over and scrummed through that ring of boys and got them all quiet, she brushed me down and picked up my books and wiped my scraped legs and told the teacher despite my protests and the kids all hated her for that, they jeered her home. And I never forgot. She still didn't know my name. She never asked, I don't think she wanted to be tied to any of us too close.

I don't remember any of this, Dan.

And then after it all happened—

All what?

The fire, the school, all that. After that I saw you in church, every Christmas. And I sometimes saw you when you'd go for a walk at night – *what?* – and goosebumps are misting across my skin, I don't like this now and my hand's clamped across my forehead.

It wasn't just me, Lil, it was a whole group. All these young guys.

Dan, I'm not sure I want to know this—

It's OK, don't worry, it was just something to do, there wasn't much else. And over the years they all kind of drifted away but I stayed with you, I guess I became a bit obsessed with seeing the girl who stood up for me once. I just wanted to *know* you, what made you tick, because even locked away you still seemed so bloody possessed and I couldn't work it out. And the one gift I could give you was to get you out, to bring you back into the world. It just seemed so unfair, Lil, I couldn't concentrate on anything else. Sometimes for the hell of it I used to flick out a whole toilet roll into the wind, from our bathroom window, to try to give you some kind of crazy hope while I worked something out. Did you ever see it?

The white scribbles in the sky, of course.

You mad bugger. And all the time I was dreaming it was my knight in shining armour.

He chuckles. He tells me that one day he found out I was going to England and he even discovered the name of the place I'd be staying at. Ed, I ask, as it all starts softly clicking into place. Yeah, Ed, and another chuckle, I imagine the grin and he's telling me it was his one chance to get me out into the world, to get me free before I was meant to come back and there's silence and I'm clasping the phone so tight I can hear it creak in my hand and I'm flattered, bewildered, stumped. Why? I'm saying, I don't understand, all the effort. But he cannot explain, he's stumbling something about feeling sorry for me and I'd been kind to him once and then he's stopping, lame, and Why? I'm asking, why? but he cannot say. When can I see you? I'm asking, needing to touch his face, see the telling, read the truth in there somewhere but I don't know, he's saying, it's all complicated, they're not ready for you yet, I thought they would be but they're not. He didn't have the courage to tell me all this before I got to Sunshine because he was afraid I'd run and never come back and he couldn't bear that after he'd gotten so close, he needed me somewhere he knew while he sorted things out and safe at home seemed the obvious place.

I can't stay here much longer, Dan, I'm going stir-crazy.

I know, he says. There's a plan, he says, to break open the Sunshine church one midnight and steal its sanctity by candlelight. *What?* Ed can be the celebrant because she's a justice of the peace, he has it all worked out, it'll be easily done and what a magnificent thumbing at them all, imagine that. And then we'll be off. And I'm laughing at the ridiculousness of it, God, it'd never work but there's a melting there too, at the decisiveness in his words, his mad want, and there's a joy churning in my stomach that I cannot fight and it floods my groin for it all makes sense, suddenly, it's OK, the suspicion is wiped. There's my high of relief and I'm laughing and saying I'll have to see about this marriage thing and I'm slipping my fingers absently into my panties and forgiving him everything just to have the old Dan back and we're bantering softly, deep into that night, savouring the words *husband* and *wife* and feeling them on our tongues, poring over the map of our future and journeying its dreams.

I haven't said yes to you yet, mate. My teasing farewell and his joy-thrummed laugh.

But what a delicious thing this will be, Lil! Imagine it, our coming out . . .

My God, is he as driven as that? I think back to a hand clamp and a garden tug and a slammed door and a carrying home at two a.m. and an oyster slurp. Yes.

Dozing back to sleep with a vast settling and a calm blooming over me for I still have that ached-for possession, love requited, and I hold the gift of it tenderly in the palm of my hand. But waking several times over that night and imagining the young Dan Smith that I know so much more of now, slotting the jigsaw pieces into place. Seeing him with a motley group of other teenagers from the village sitting in a line on a hill of a neighbouring property, newly smoking their self-rolled cigarettes and jostling with ever-more spectacular kidnap plans that never amounted to much. For Dan told me that throughout the growing up they'd all paid secret homage one way or another and God I wish I could've seen it as they ignited lighter fuel on the palms of their hands and shoved spark plugs up exhaust pipes and drove with tails of flame and used lighters to blare fire from aerosol cans and raised stashed beers to the strange, stupid peer on the hill who'd once stopped the town still. But over the years they were all lured away by parties and bible studies and other girls, girls they could talk to and touch.

Except one. And what I'd have given to have seen him then, so intent and knowing and sure.

Watching as I pushed my legs through tall grass like a trout fisherman flighting the butt of a stream, he told me that, watching as I held my arms into the caress of the breeze, watching as my face flashed pale in the night. I can imagine the public shine of him back then for he was one of those intriguing ones rarely spotted, and straight backed, and girl-watched, a golden boy, Rebecca and Tiriel had said that. But there was a private restlessness there too, I know that now, a bristling at having to toe the line too much, it was all humming under his skin but it rarely snapped out. He was outwardly sky blue, respectable, clean, so shiningly normal, so loved. But with something secret all combusted within him, something reckless and burning and vividly non-Shiner that only to Ed could he speak of. He'd meticulously befriended her with an enthusiasm for library books and prompt returns and he told me that one Sunday afternoon in a sweet-smiling dope-stoning from her hidden stash he'd garbled his dream to her: to get me out, to watch me fly.

He barely knew what to expect. There were rumours that my speech had rusted up like a never-wound clock, they were fuelled by a local doctor called in to treat a wire-sliced hand who'd been unnerved by my silence. I vaguely remember the visit, I didn't want talk, didn't like him, the crude hunger to know me or the nervousness that stained sour his breath. There were rumours I was mad, a sexual deviant, warped, but Dan said he didn't believe any of it.

A new passion was stumbled upon: photography. He didn't talk about it to anyone but Ed for cameras were pansy, not a Shiner boy's thing and a policeman's son at that. But he'd decided on a photographer's life so much that he was prepared to deliberately fail his final exams that would elevate him into law. So in his late teens, instead of being ensconced in a college in the city he was filling in time in the local motorbike shop and experimenting with slow shutter speeds and wide apertures and shooting me in the distance, pedastalled, my flesh white, like cool stone. And as my freeing day galloped closer he longed to cup my face and still it between the brace of his hands for he was desperate to keep me in range, un-lost.

Waking late the next morning to the wind-scoured land and the scent of its dirt and inhaling its familiarity and wondering how many more days I'll be waking to it as I stretch my nakedness under the sheets. How we'll live, and where, beyond marriage. Not in Sunshine, I know that, because I'd never get a job in the community and like many women who've experienced the tonic of working for a living and then had it snatched from them I can feel boredom and a loss of esteem now yapping at my heels. I'm unused to not deciding every aspect of my own life, at being so accepting of the will of someone else, of not being in control.

Love, its wipe.

Late that morning a giant scribble is licked high on the breeze, it's tugged into curves and it flips and banners and I smile for it won't be long, I'll be seeing Dan soon and my stomach dips and the hours settle into their pregnant waiting, and the days, and my hands flutter often to my neck.

Having a child will settle you, you know.

Rebecca, at two a.m., leaning on the doorframe and examining me as I hang up the phone all chuckly with Dan's talk of his niece:

of her toddler eyes that go on for ever, of his explaining to her that her bottom will fall off if her bellybutton's unscrewed. I tell my mother hey, slow down, we have to get married first and Rebecca holds out her hands and pulls me from the floor and says it's good, so good to have me laughing again. And as I climb the old stairs to my room there's a smile in my heart, for who would ever have imagined marriage, to a golden boy from the town? And yet I also write out a wondering on that night: *Why can't I completely relax with happiness, just lie back in it and float and enjoy?* But Rebecca sees none of that, just the confidence and centredness of a woman loved, of a woman fat with content.

Vigorously I shake my head, no, *no*, but Rebecca mouths, Why, come *on*, girl.

I snatch up the phone and tell Richard I'm well and enjoying being back and I'm getting married, perhaps next week, and there's laughter in reply but a telling catch.

I am . . . well, I can't say I'm pleased.

And as I talk I imagine pushing his cheek from me with my hand, can feel his skin under my touch and my fingers connecting in a simple gesture of tenderness and playfulness and I imagine the startledness of memory in his face. I see him clearly now: a man disdainful of love and with no respect for it for he believes that it weakens anyone who succumbs. A man who can't love and has sought power instead and I don't hate him, I'm too fascinated for that, intrigued by someone so culled.

He asks if I've made the spectacular entrance into Bony Mountain society yet and I say no, they don't know I'm back and he wants to know where this fiancé of mine is and why he's not shouting his love from the rooftops.

You're too big for that place, girl.

My skin flushes into bumps for at his words I'm experiencing a tantalizing desire to crash calamity into my life, to cultivate rupture and bring about change just as I did, spectacularly, when I was thirteen and it's such a slitherly, dangerous, silky thing and I can feel a tug in my groin at the dare of it. Richard has a point, Dan *should* be shouting his love from the rooftops and proud with his catch for there's been too much now of this stewing wait.

And as I speak my shielded small talk I understand for the first time what Richard saw in me at the start of my journey and what he saw later on and why his interest has waned, for I've grown up through a big couple of years and Richard doesn't want women with that knowing that comes with age and there's a hackling distaste at that. Vivacity is surrender, I read that once and there's no surrender during that conversation with him, I'm curt, and held, and old. And thinking of a rooftop shout.

The first Sunday following the crash-landing.

Awoken by a sliver of light stealing like a cat through the curtains and smiling sleepily at its intrusiveness as it pushes me into grabbing the day. Tiriel's away for the weekend at a newspaper conference and I leave the house before Rebecca has stirred, the baseball cap low on my head and sunglasses firm. I walk bush taut with sound, feeling the crunch and dryness of it underfoot that's so unlike the soft, dark land that I've come from. This country's wet doesn't penetrate, sink in, unlike the spongy damp of my adopted land. And which do I want? Need?

I'm walking straight into Sunshine, lured like a child to a two-day fair. I wander anonymously those neat Sunday streets, absorbing the stillness and the contented quiet, absorbing the glances and giving nothing back. Pause by a driveway with its smell of a hose on hot concrete and it's plunging me back to my childhood and I continue on, walking the smells of my primary school past – a lawn sweetly mown, browning roses by a fence, a posse of kids wheeling bikes, a car's exhaust.

So many lives, not moving. The old man in the corner shop hardly changed, just more hair, oddly, and shorter and the lolly counter and drinks fridge in the same spot and city tabloids three days old and my father's paper still the same price. There's the morning straggle of kids and two growling, circling dogs and the sudden flurry of a fight pulled apart. I perch on the back of a park bench with my feet on the seat, sucking an icy pole, and overhear a woman on a nearby public phone telling someone too loudly that she loves her daughter but hates her, loves her as a daughter but hates her as a woman because she has all the worst traits of the relatives and as the speaker steps from the box I catch sight of an alert, intelligent face and recall several lines from an Elizabeth Riddell poem that Ed gave to me once, urging out.

> *Now all the dogs with folded paws*
> *stare at the lowering sky.*
> *This is the hour when women hear*
> *their lives go ticking by.*

It's not a novelty, being back.

And then the spire.

Walking up the path and the mildness of their glances, even a nod or two, even a smile. Stepping into that lovely lemony light, stepping into that familiar smell of swept wood and breathing it in deep. Daring a seat near the front, just near the seat that's always my own and settling into the chair and there's familiar stern back and rush seat, it'll never be forgot.

Smiling. Waiting. Confident now.

That's Lillie Bird, from somewhere behind me.

Brother Sleet ignores the triumphant voice.

It is, Brother, it is.

The indignation will not rest.

Of course the church is to be the journey's end, I'd known it as I spoke to Richard and as I set out even if there were moments of wavering as I walked through the town. But as I drew closer to the building it seemed so meek in its morning light and my courage was spined in those few, last steps.

Brother, stop the service, remove that hat.

It's the first sermon but he doesn't have to stop for I turn and face them all, netting the eyes and I take off the baseball cap

222

and can read the shock, the hair's shorn and the clothes are odd, of the city and there are no longer glasses but it's definitely that Lillie Bird, God help us she's back and all changed and an elderly man slams down his bible and walks out and then another does too and Brother Sleet's voice struggles gamely on as I catch all the eyes that are left, one by one, I skim that room with my new, adult smile and all confident with it and then I catch Dan, back corner, left-hand side, near where the indignant voice has been spat.

Dan.

He'd never been to church in London, he'd told me he didn't have any God in him. But there he is, eyes straight at me and holding tight a child, his niece perhaps and not coming to me and his eyes are telling me to back down, to stay put, not to spoil all the careful planning by doing something spectacular and ridiculous and rash. Is there a wink, I'm not sure, if it is it's not bold enough and next to him is a man who's stout backed and almost a carbon copy, it's the same body, the same lips and there's a woman there too, a whole family of them, oh God help me out of this.

Serene, floating, half-smiling, I'm turning back to the pulpit, crumbling, for he's here among it all and he's not coming to me, he's *mine* now not *theirs* and yet he doesn't acknowledge me in any way and the service resumes jaggedly and everyone's thrown. The pulpit swims and I hear nothing through the rest of the service, not one thing, and Brother Sleet is distracted the whole length of it, he's cutting it short and there's the final hymn and the scab of their curiosity and I will not lift my fingers to my face, I will not give them that and then the service is over and I'm sitting very still, not turning and not moving and there's no hand placing itself warm and firm and with ownership on my back.

The congregation begins its filing out but I'm still not turning, I'm waiting until I sense that I'm the last one left and only then am I rising, slowly and wound down with my hands straightening my face. Brother Sleet meets my eyes and the questions are all bunched in his brows and I bow my head to him and smile, remembering the word *grace* from a Christmas long ago and remembering all the optimism contained in a stream of light and I'm walking steadily in front of him, down that church aisle, and there's a knot of Sunshiners by the entrance and Dan, my Dan, my man is pale and unreadable among them at the back. All cloistered by his family, and this place.

You can feel my distress, it's deep in your hardening bones, you're churning with your fists and your feet as I write this.

What to do, what to do, and my skittering breath.

I could walk straight up to him and drink him long on those too-known lips, I could declare the entwining right there and then but you know all I can see are his eyes, impeached. You could almost lick the air between us on that Sunday morning, so weighted it was. And in the midst of it I'm struck by the placidness of the child, of how potent is the sight of a man holding a baby and I go over to them and the crowd parts in a sullen drawing back and the toddler holds a tiny, chubby palm to my cheek and quietly stares and the gesture is so tender and grave and curious that it's all I can do to stop a buckling right there in front of them all. Dan's still and pale and his eyes are telling me in a frozen face not to blow it all, *please*, there's a smell on him of fear and panic and it stains his body, it pushes through his skin like garlic and I recognize the intimacy of it for I've smelt it once before, during that night of fretful sleeping in Scotland when he'd first told me he had to go home. Now there's a phalanx of family around him, closing in and pushing me out and I've experienced that once before too, sandy and salty on the boulevard by the beach in veil-bordered, Muslim eyes: away with you, girl a world apart.

My hand fidgets to my neck, to the imaginary necklace that only last night had rested on it and that one day our daughters are to fight over.

He steps forward. Lillie, he says, a stranger to me and the crowd edges closer, Lillie, I have something to say and it's a public voice and it's ready to blurt something out and I look around, check-mated, willing myself not to flinch at the blow of whatever's to come and then a hand grips my elbow, it's firm and reassuring and it steers me away and I curve gratefully into it and Dan's voice is cut off and only then do I notice the rescuer – Brother Sleet. I look back to the crowd and all I can see is Dan's face, not coming to me and not explaining, staunched of all talk, one of them. The squall of my thinking.

The Brother's fingers dig deep as he hurries me to the rectory and I thank him once inside, for what, I'm not sure. Barely able to soften the suspicion for there've only ever been two types of people in my estimation, heart sinkers and heart lifters and he's always been one of the former. And yet I can't work him out on this topsy-turvy day, or Dan, or anyone, it's all upside down and I flutter that rectory entrance like a bird in a fresh cage.

Brother Sleet ushers me into a modest room of crisp neatness that shouts the individual, the man who insists upon calling cockroaches *roaches* and cockerels *roosters* because he can't bear to hear God's language stained by obscenities. And I'm refusing to give him any of my recent history or even my voice and the splintering is kept for the upstairs bathroom, on the toilet, my face rammed to a towel, for fifteen minutes or more.

Rebecca's car screeches around the church corner and pulls up by the front door and she strides inside and swallows my shaking in her arms and we drive home with the tyres furiously fanning the dirt road and the young Lillie back and the prospect ahead of the watch-ticked days beginning all over again, and Rebecca freshly old.

The phone pushes incessantly into that Sunday afternoon but I won't take Dan's calls and I forbid my mother from passing on any news but he won't stop and the phone rings again, and again. There's something he has to tell me, he's not going to let it go shouts Rebecca through the bannisters, he'll only say it to you, chick, but I won't speak, I'm resolute, he's shredded me enough, and there's an adrenalin flit in my heart and my chest is tightened, protesting, it feels heart-attack primed and I will not come down.

Brother Sleet has had his quiet word with Rebecca. The community's not willing to accept me back, it doesn't trust me, doesn't want me among them and for the first time – and there's the regretful inclination of the head at this – it feels a betrayal by Tiriel and Rebecca, the outsiders, of course. When Tiriel finally gets the message he's scratchy and breaking up but he shouts to lie low, he'll come home, he'll fly, but Rebecca says no, she can handle it, he's not to cut his conference short and he must take the car and drive carefully back.

And all through the knot of that long afternoon there's something physical there, something too strong: I want to hold Dan, smell him, taste him, want my torso wrapped in his and my head resting quietly on the pillow of his chest and I'm furious at the ferocity of my body's want. I open the windows wide, vividly wet for him and a jasmine smell rushes in at me as if every flower on every backyard fence in Bony Mountain is giving itself to the air on that day and I think of our little sprig on a sunny windowsill once and I'm taunted by the deep happiness of that for I've seen him among them now, and I've lost the soul quiet.

Trust me, he'd said once, and it's no longer enough.

Below me, Rebecca paces to the windows and staunches the shrill phone.

But there's Ed. She crashes into the bleakness late on that Sunday afternoon for she's heard of course, the whole village has, the news has skipped quick. She apologizes for not being with me that morning and tells me she can't endure going to church once a week and Poor bugger you, I softly laugh and tell her, hey, it's OK, everyone invents God for themselves, Dan had told me that once. I'd love to know *your* God, she responds, and tells me to come over, to get out of the house.

Rebecca's car roars to Ed's bungalow down the familiar dirt road and when it hits the bitumen I wordlessly fold my body onto the floor, just like old times, just like the girl under the blanket when I was fifteen but there's one difference this time, a town's awareness, and I peek up at eyes peering in, at palms slapped on the roof at stoplights, at someone daring a stone.

Rebecca's car bulls into Ed's ready garage and she's waiting, she slams the roller door shut and my mother steps slowly out as if she's just finished a marathon and is walking from the line and I follow her, unfolding myself awkwardly and my eyes rimmed with rubbing and hurt. Rebecca won't stay, can't, she's all jittery and tight. Ed offers to drive me home, asks if my mother needs anything, she's massaging *her* shoulders for the first time: no, she'll be fine, she just wants to get back. Ed walks me inside, her hand tight around my hip as if she's propping me up. I feel like I need a stiff Scotch and I don't even drink, I laugh, my eyes saucer-shiny and my lips rolled inward, bloodless and tight. Ed propels me into the kitchen and she tells me later that she does not regret what comes next.

Dan.
 Crumpling at the sight.
 He's coming across to us firm and pale, his arms spread. He's taking over from Ed and holding me and there's a trembling intensity shot through him and I'm weeping great perplexed sobs into him, my mouth webbed with wet, I'm hitting him on the shoulders and pummelling my hurt out. He's walking me to a kitchen chair and brushing away strands of tear-slimed hair from my cheeks and saying *hey* as tender and sorrowful as a mother to a child and with soft kisses he's soothing my gulping and drinking my salt and I'm stumbling into a sit, a ball of it, and he's untangling the mess of it and crouching before me, holding both hands and kneading them, rubbing and rubbing my fingers and not letting go.
 Hey, hey, it's OK and not letting go. I'm going to break open the church tomorrow night, and we'll be married at midnight, and there'll be candles, hundreds, and Ed, it'll all work out, shhh, shhhh. How about that?
 Nothing my response.
 We'll get away from all this, we'll start again.

Nothing my response.

At midnight, tomorrow, how about it? Lil? *Lil?*

No spark and then Dan takes a deep breath, stilling some resolve and OK, he says, OK, and he laughs, soft. There's something else. And at that, I'm looking up.

It was what I was trying to say this morning, outside the church, and it's what I should have said on the night we arrived, and in London, and at Evendon, and even, Christ, when I was ten. *Fuck,* Lil, I didn't want it to be like this.

My eyes right at him, my breath held and his cheeks are bright red, there's the vividness of a flush that's claiming his whole face and dropping down to his neck and I've never seen it before, didn't know it was in him.

It's what I'd been planning to sort out while I was here, with you all safely in London, it's why I didn't want you with me. I wanted to keep you away from the mess of it and then I'd come back and everything'd be fine and we'd just get on with our lives.

The mess of what?

Well, he says and laughs, and looks away, and then back, he looks right into my eyes, right down into them.

I was going to confess.

What about?

Everything.

Everything?

An awful clarity in that still, still room, my face composed and just my knuckles bone-white at my shoulders, my fingernails digging into my shoulders and trying to clamp down the trembling, to stop it with hurt.

It was *you?*

The nod, he can't speak. And it had always been immaterial to me who'd lit the fire, until now, I'd never wondered, I didn't care. It'd always been just a means to an end, a convenient excuse.

But this.

My eyes opened like curtains. *Of course, of course:* why else had the fascination been white with heat for so many years, when the

228

obsession of all the others had drained away with the growing up? Why had it consumed all his days? Why did he need to know, so much, my thinking, who I was and what made me tick?

Bewilderment, gratefulness, astonishment, guilt. *Of course.*

My knuckles, bone-white.

A reassessing of our whole past.

And how it all makes sense.

I cradle my forehead in my palms, and groan.

So there we are, deep into the early hours of that morning both moving to bayonets where we can smell each other's breath and Ed is all forgotten in it, I don't even know if she's there in that room, with our shout.

You can't confess. It'll ruin you. You'll never be able to come back.

Hey, give me more credit than that.

It's all in the past, Dan, let it go.

So weary with it, so tired but *he's* not now that it's out. I can't, Lil, I can't, he says over and over and I'm not able to bear seeing his life ripped apart, this golden boy with his lovely, lopsided grin, I'm not sure he's strong enough for it and I'm snapping in the thick of it that the truth isn't always clean, it doesn't always have to be known and for God's sake it's best this way, can't he see that? I'm trying to get it through to him that it'll keep him strong with his family and his community if we just let it go for he doesn't know what's ahead, he has no idea and he doesn't need a breaking, neither of us does.

Why did you do it in the first place, anyway? Grinding the heel of my hand into my temple, trying to fathom it out.

I don't know. A schoolboy prank, I guess.

Nodding, trying to fathom his stubborn unknowability, so tired, wanting it gone.

They *have* to know, Lil. For both our sakes, not for them, for *us.*

No.

I've been planning this for so long, how I'll say it, how it'll come out.

No.

And he drops close to me with his hand entwined in mine like a handkerchief at tears but the tears are his own. I stare at him, this man I hardly know. *Him* of all people, the policeman's son with the simmer underneath and there I was doubting his oddity once but of course he was always the game player, the risk taker, the prankster. And all I want now is for the fire to be buried, and a fresh start. And I was almost there. *Fuck.*

I look at him so close and think, perhaps, that I understand: he's believed all these years that I spoke up in the school assembly out of selflessness, that I'm someone so saintly, so shiningly good and he's been snared by the thought ever since.

But no, I was much more greedy than that. I didn't do it to save someone else, I did it to save myself. Our community taught me to lie, and simmer, and clam up and hate because its sense of right and wrong was too absolute for anything else. Can't he see that? How selfish I am?

He takes one photograph over that night, I have it with us now but it's not on my window spine, it's too intimate for that.

Early morning, curled on a kitchen chair with one leg propped and a cold mug of tea forgotten in my hand with the milk slurred on its surface like oil on a still pond. There's the blurred, slugged look of a sacrificial woman, it's a face I've never seen before, it's raw and vulnerable and open and there's something beautiful in it, it's the only time I've ever thought of myself as beautiful and of course Dan had always understood that beauty is at its most alluring as it begins to splinter and on that night he couldn't resist, just one shot. On the kitchen chair, alone, hardly able to bear seeing it all, stripped.

Thinking of ahead, trying, somehow, to work a way out.

Click.

His soft thanks and my nod in the stillness after the storm's blown itself out, it's around three a.m. and over and over there's my nod, yes, we'll get married, tonight, it'll all be sorted out, I love him still, I'm OK, shh. But as I pour the cold tea into the sink I tell him not the church, please, it's too weird and too hard and it'll never work, can't we just do it in the quiet of Ed's house and then properly, later, somewhere else?

Of course, of course.

Nodding, rubbing and rubbing my brow.

I was so afraid of telling you this, Lil. I could never find the right moment. I didn't want to lose you for good, didn't want you running off.

His love on that night as tough as mercury, magnificent and foolish and heroic and young.

And he's had it for most of his life.

Please don't bring it out into the open, Dan, *please*.

We must.

Ed drives me home.

Thunder comes into me, the tremor crawls under my skin and nudges me awake. From an early age I've swallowed the thunder that rolls across Bony Mountain and on that day I look up at the steel in the sky, late morning the light tells me and I rise from the bed and lie flat on my back on the floor and feel the murmuring in the boards, feel the sound somersault in my belly and whisper through my knees to the tops of my thighs. My wedding day, of sorts, and I grin at the ridiculousness and magnificence of Dan's original plan, the *youngness* of it, but the block of sullen light pushes me into preparation and there's bustle elsewhere in the house and I listen, the walls speak.

Of village women who are shocked and questioning and shrill and trying but not succeeding to erase the smiles that curl in the corners of their lips, I can hear a vanquishing closing in. And there's my mother, calm and tight in it all and there are more footsteps and the scrape of a chair and a rattle of a thin, crazed cup on a saucer, there's a glut of people poking and chattering and prying.

Hurriedly I dress, my hands a clot of fingers finding wrong buttons for the holes and trembling and veering wildly and snapping the lace from a shoe and I run down the stairs and the voices one by one drop away and I feel the strain of the listening and take a deep breath. Step into the lounge room. To eyes, to scrutiny, to fingers reaching to my shorn hair and a policeman crisp in his uniform, Dan's father, of course, the man in the church and to Brother Sleet stepping forward and holding a hand to me, his palm raised skyward as if to calm a wayward horse. A blush blooms on my neck and cheeks that I cannot control and I step back, my eyes flitting around the room that's steely with the presence of the town women, their expressions are saying I'm trouble and always have been and I've never trusted the harshness in their faces, the sharp, judging planes and the eyebrows pruned and plucked, the eyes all cold into me since that episode a lifetime ago when I was brimmed with a furious silence at the age of eight, and the hate is still fresh.

Swerving from Brother Sleet's fingers and like a child running from the house and not sure why, knowing it's stamping myself with some kind of guilt but still I'm running and running. Lillie, stop, wait, it's despairing and stern behind me, from Brother Sleet and from the women but I'm running and running, my legs instinctively flying me along the secret childhood paths and then Rebecca's voice is soaring above it, *Stop*, it's to the gathering not to me and the whip-crack in it silences them all abrupt and I keep running with my face splitting into a smiling for my mother's working with me, she's finding a new voice, she's shouting at them all like a cicada scrabbling from its shell and I'm smiling and smiling at that.

Soon out of sight of the house. No one's following and I slow to a walk and the hum of the wind whispers into my skin and the grass jumps as I move through it – there's the soft pfft pfft of small grasshoppers around my legs, the dry flick of them. A distant congregation of birds lifts like a cloud from a tree and I slow even further, stilling the rasp of my breathing and when I get to the top of the hill behind the house I climb a rock and put my hands above me and hold my palms flat to the breeze and feel like I'm nudging the roof of the sky and I grin in the pump of the sun's brightness. The girl obsessed by light: it was one of the things that'd lured me from the land where the sky nestles sullenly on rooftops too much.

And Dan.

My craving for him wrenches my belly as I stand tall on that rock. And I feel very calm, and very clear, for I've decided what has to be done. A great giggly smile comes over that day, a strange zooming high, for I know absolutely now something I've always suspected, that being bad is one way a woman has of declaring her strength. Dan's waiting in the village and I soften my belly for I have an opening now, a way out, and the tension of uncertainty that's been with me since I've been home is at last snapped, and decision is falling over me like soft rain.

Late that afternoon a steeliness colours the sky, a stillness drops down like a blanket, it's as if the world is holding its breath. It's an afternoon for dogs to be curling like commas in cold grass and sheep to be huddled and still. I can read that sky, I've had twenty-two years of practising and it's in my blood still and it tells me on that gaunt afternoon to watch and listen and wait.

My journal's open on my lap, my thighs the trestles for the bowed table of my long, Sunshine skirt. My fingers grip the shaft of the ink-pen in my pocket and my thumb worries at it, for freed from all those who are closest around me I can feel my true self unfolding and I know, absolutely, what has to be done. But do I have the courage for it?

Late into that evening there I am, contemplating the people made ragged by consuming love, whose lives are devoured by it, contemplating the people who step into star-smeared skies. A cup of Tiriel's red wine is dragging me into sleep but I turn back to my desk and take up my pen, the ink one, Dan's gift, and the letter to him is finally done.

This is the hardest thing I shall ever write, I think. Where to begin, Dan boy? It's so hard to explain how I feel on this night. I've read of a woman who crushed diamonds and drank them, I've read of a woman who rowed into a lake and dived deep into the water with an anchor around her neck. Imagine that, the bubbles closing over you or the fragments grinding in. But hey, that's all much too courageous for me and I've never owned a diamond in my life, never wanted to, mate. But I've come to a decision and God knows whether it's the right one or not. What I've decided is that I'm going to walk down the Tanner Road and just disappear from your life. Dan, it's easiest that way, it really is. Don't try to find me, and don't try to set the record straight. Promise me that, please, if nothing else.

My love, my sweet, lovely man. I can hardly bear this, you know.

My breath drying the ink is the last soft kiss.

Freeing us both, I hope.

The great calm of that going.

Putting on my coat and walking down the stairs and trying not to stir the tattle-tale floorboards. An unseasonable chill has seeped into the house, it's collected in the walls and slid under the sheets and nestled in the fibres of the towels and clotted in the tips of my fingers and I try to shake it out. I slip onto the verandah and drink in gulps of night air so cold that it punches at my throat, I stare at the spread of stars that blur and dance and at the lightning in the rainless sky flickering behind a cloud and there's God in the breadth of it and I smile at that. I step from the verandah in that new alone, vivid and aware, feeling close to the surface of my skin. I leave our farm in the darkness not of night but the strange day of a full, flooding moon for all the storm's rumbling has not been borne out and the sky has shunted mostly into clearness. I walk through fields of long, yellow grass that's fanned out and flattened like the hair on a shaggy pony's flank and somewhere I pause and scribble that down, the page lit by the sky, and I don't look back at the lights of the town or the house or the land and I hear a low, menacing grunt from somewhere in the trees and I feel fearfully alone but still I walk on.

Dan so vividly with me.

His voice saying yeah with a rising inflection, his hip under my hand, the softness of his belly to mine, the cup of my foot on his calf in sleep and the night of our haunting in a room with a trembling match and his fingers on a cat.

I hesitate at the mailbox. Push my forehead into its coldness like I'd pushed it, often, into Dan's chest. The letter's dropped inside, it's gone, it can't be got back and as it slips from my fingers I know that I'm never so strong or so in touch with what fuels me as when I'm alone. Within the thick of contentedness and coupledom I'd lost the sharp flint, I hadn't looked outward, I'd softened and stopped. Dan had offered me everything but control and in that walking away on that night from all that binds me I feel like I'm stretching a hand to some kind of destiny, that the bands are finally cracking that have been welded for so long around my heart. For I know now who's begun this journey, and ended it.

And I know now that there are two types of love: the shrill, unanchored, romantic love where all that's wanted is the other person, and the great calm of real love, where all that's wanted is the other person's good.

And my heart is utterly broke.

Three days later that young Lillie Bird is skimming above clouds that stretch to the horizon like an ocean of ice. She's on a plane to the rest of her life and Dan Smith is not told where and neither is the community-gaggle she's lived among, in clamped silence, for too many of her years. She's leaving for the last time the land where the light roars and the sea hurts.

And she's praying, so hard, for the courage of surrender.

–14–

Now

You push and jab with your fists and I can feel, sharply, the wanting out. You wriggle when I write for some reason, is it urging me on? Shhhhh, it's coming, not long now. I'm speeding, little one, and the overnight bag is packed. You're in position, head down with your spine obediently to the left, you're readying yourself for out.

I put my palm on my belly and you calm, as if you're listening to my skin.

But look at me.

Riding air like men, the travellers of old. Flying to so many places on my father's nest egg at first and ending up one day in that city called New York, a place so crammed that the car bumpers chattered to bumpers and all around them was an architecture of noise and I couldn't, anywhere, find a quiet. And the light, God, the glare of it, it stopped the stars. But I loved it, of course, I held my head high to it and gulped it all in.

And in that canyoned place, on my last day in it, there was a sudden, drenching late summer downpour and I pushed into the Jackie-O cathedral to escape it and a lunchtime mass was in progress and the priest was saying the words that Brother Paina had said so long ago, about that question at the end of our lives: *how well we have loved*, and Dan, of course, came hurtling back. There I was, sitting by myself in a pew at the back and willing him to me, trying to arrow his thoughts. For he drenched all my days, no matter how much I tried to travel him out.

It took me a long time to return to London, always afraid of what might be found. And in my new life back in it I rolled like a dog in memory, the hot stink of it, for in that city was the history of our love. Postman's Park, Ronnie Scott's, the Royal Albert Hall, the 73 bus, I couldn't escape all the memories that came hurtling back. Dan flooded my wakefulness deep in those early winter nights, night after night when I was harangued awake by the thinking: was success possible without betrayal and without being an outsider in some way and would I ever experience again the falling, the bloom of it?

Silence yelling between us and each day of fresh exile I wrote to him and each day of fresh exile balled my scrawl for I was determined to stick to the path I had set, there'd be no turning from that, no giving in, from a young age I'd perfected that.

I craved weather back in London for its rain was weak, there wasn't any weight in it, I wanted wind and push and bash and wet, I wanted rain like at home that vanished clothes in three seconds, I wanted wet that was soaking and triumphant and complete. But the new weather didn't reach the shy window of my bedsit at the bottom of a tall alley and I had to lean my body far out the window and twist my head until it hurt to catch the sky. The dampness pushed through the walls like yoghurt through muslin, it flowered its soft, insidious spores and foolishly I began counting days – fifteen since sun, fifteen since a shadow – for I craved the tall blue, stretched land, hurting light, craved breathing in sun like the desert with rain.

Craved Dan.

Like I craved sleep. He rustled through my blood, a feverish disease, relentlessly he called. And each night there was a wavering and each day a balling of my scrawl and gradually the writing stopped. But not the want.

*

A year or so later, more or less, I don't know for you're hiccoughing and yawing too much and I'm hurrying this tale on, can't even sit for too long in this seat now, and so tired, and the toilet too much, anyway one summer evening I'm walking up the alley to Mrs Green's flat for I'm back at the old room for a while, working at Jeremy's and gathering money for another trip and I'm laden with shopping bags from Tesco. And there he is.

Just like that.

Sitting on the doorstep.

Just the same.

Like we've never parted.

He stands.

He smiles his lopsided grin, one side up, one side down. He says just one word. *Lillie.* The downward fall of it, I will never forget. *Lillie.* The relief in it, and so much else. And careful not to touch.

He's been waiting for three hours. He still has a key but he doesn't want to use it, it doesn't seem right and I laugh at the politeness in that. I don't know who might be in there, he says, shy and grinning and asking but not. And I'm all stopped, just smile and tears and this great, spreading warmth. I step forward and am folded in his arms and nothing's changed, nothing, the feel or the smell or the intensity of it and my God, how long do we hold.

How did you know where to me find me, you bugger? I say as I hit him on the shoulders, for I know that Tiriel and Rebecca wouldn't have let on, they'd promised.

I had a hunch. I rang Mrs Green. Her number hasn't changed, of course.

Of course.

He's come straight from a plane from the other side of the world and we curl on the bed, in our jigsaw fit, and meander with talk and soon he's asleep. And I'm hungry but don't eat that night, I stay wrapped for I don't know how long this will last. It's the sleep of a man found and my arm wings him tight and I breathe in his dreaming until I sleep too. The questions can wait. He sleeps for fourteen hours, he drinks it up, it's the sleep of a man who's had none for several years.

We take a train to a strange stony beach an hour out of London and walk down the hill from the station and hold our heads high into the slap of the breeze. The waves are tight and demure, they fold too neat and the water is the colour of cold, milky tea. It's late summer and the skin of the people doesn't suit it, it's leaky and protesting and pale, wrong in the sun. There are boys with wetsuits on in the water, thermoses of tea, matchstick mats under towels on the stones and there are Sunday couples doing what Sunday couples do the world over and family groups and pensioners and I stare at it all with Dan by my side and we do not speak of a future together, we're careful not to do that.

But there's touch, there's more surety in that.

Never speaking of ahead, never giving him that. Not having the courage to tell him how much I want him, still smarting from his decade or more holding back.

He can't contain it for long.

He wants to photograph again. He's bitten the bullet and left Sunshine for good, he's gone to art college in the Big Smoke and is all jumpy with wanting to do it now, to make a living from it, to leap. He faces me square on and digs his fingers into my arms, We could move somewhere cheaper, how about it? he asks, he tells me to have a go at the dream, to try it for six months while we're still young and flexible and not tied down and his hands grip me tight.

You could write, Lil.

But what about, I laugh, for I've tried and it hasn't worked, it's harder than I ever expected. I haven't quite lived enough yet, I say.

You have a story. Something that only you and I know.

His grin, and from me a cushion or a chocolate thrown, I can't remember what, God, he still wants it out, will he never let it go.

Have you ever let on, Dan boy?

Nope. I was asked to keep a promise, once.

Faltering, not faltering, not wanting too quickly to succumb, not wanting to be womanly and weak. Not wanting it too easy for him, he needs a taste of my own holding back.

But there we are on another train to another piece of the country and my heart's lifting as London's vastness thins and drops away and Dan's knowing that this togetherness means something, or nothing, a brief nothing and he's grabbing it while he can. Daring to inspect a place to rent that he's read about in *The Times* and daring to take the plunge with photography, the dream, and daring to be with me at all. Just for a couple of months, but I'm not committing, I'm punishing him perhaps, he doesn't know. I'm not saying any more that I love him and he's not sure what to make of that but he tells me that when he wakes me in the early morning and I crumple my face in sleep and say Dan, only half awake but so tender and instinctive, he knows I'm still with him and he'll always have that close. He teases that I'm toying with him now, that I've learned retribution and games and debt, that I've perfected the holding back.

Mate, *you're* the master at that.

I'm just here for a look, Dan. Nothing else.

A tongue poked, and then slugged into my ear.

Ow! Get off, you!

We alight at a station by the coast and walk across a field of pebbles that look like winter snow, we walk to the soft brown, cantankerous, broiling sea and there are furious, spiteful little waves and a nuclear power plant in the distance and as we're pushed and knocked and whipped by the wind I feel on the brink, that my life's poised and could march off in several directions. Do I succumb? I don't know. It's all changed between us. And not.

Late that night back in London, by myself, on the way home from the supermarket, I run my fingers through hair that's still sticky and heavy from ocean-laden wind and the rain comes into me and I don't shy away from it for the earth softly spatters into my memory, the hint of a smell carried by the wet, the hint of rain flogging an attic window and scudding paper scribbles and the feeling of being tombed, once, in a faraway place and I'm remembering, vividly, all the waiting for my life to start and the feeling that it's slipping from me quick and I fever home for my mind is suddenly made up.

OK, let's give it a go.

A floral-spattered room in a bed and breakfast by the sea.

Sulky damp in low corners and hairs slicked on bathroom tiles and vinegar on breakfast eggs but we hardly notice any of that for I've slipped off my underwear and told him I don't care any more about waiting for a marriage, that life is too short for all that.

Well well, Miss Bird, I never would have thought. You constantly surprise me, you know.

You too, mate.

Not wanting our time running out, for I'm learning, at last, that I can't always tightly plan, can't always control what's ahead with a clenched fist.

We take a train to our newly rented cottage and I stare out the window at the fleeting countryside, so soft and fragile and tamed. We've got the house for three months, our savings will almost last the stretch and Jeremy's sighed and said all right, just.

I hope you know what you're doing, Miss Bird.

Nope.

It's coming into winter and darkness drops down early and out of the vast blanket of haze that's the sky a sunset peeps through like a rip in a curtain. When we step from the taxi the wind is muscular in the trees and there's fat rain. It's pitch black, so unlike the skyless and starless orange city-glow I've grown used to and deep in that first night the wind buffets the lopsided old cottage near the nuclear power plant by the sea, the rain spatters in gusts and then the thunder comes and the house murmurs with it and the channel is restless and wild nearby and the sound of the water agitates, it doesn't soothe, it teases and taunts the gypsy in me and the choice that I've made. Dan's body thuds into mine as if he's trying to draw the warmth from my flesh, he's demonstrative in slumber, his limbs and his torso cling to me and clamp me down but I let him do that on that night, my resistance gone, just to have it all back. To be held so tightly, to relax. But I don't tell him any of that.

I wake at seven twenty-five, it's still dark, it's as if the day and the light have slept in. At seven forty-five there's pink in the sky but the day's so reluctantly dragged from the night and then as brightness firms the winter light comes stealing in and I uncurl on the window seat and the beautiful sun repairs me. So, this is my choice: a man and an Aga, smug and fat in its corner. A settling, for the first time, and I stretch like a cat and wonder at it.

But I can't write. I try. It doesn't work. Not that story, my only one, there's just too much betrayal within it and I can't live with the cannibal's guilt. There is no other for nothing else will come, nothing else sings no matter how much I try. Each day I tinker and each day I ball my scrawl and each day something fresh is thrown out. What am I to do with my life? How am I to make it work? A poster shop is not my profession, Jeremy and I both know that.

But God's cruel gifts.

A Sunday night. Coming home from the movies, crossing to the car park, it's in the nearest big town and that's, what, two hours away. We've just bought bread and milk and chocolate, there's the pedestrian underpass and the roundabout above it, there's Dan yelling, Race ya, come on, you below, me above, and there's my laughing and pushing him, All right, all right! And he's off, for ever the little boy, always racing me across the road or pouring eggs over my head or falling asleep on my arm or burping his love.

I take my time, he doesn't know that already I'm beginning to feel the tiredness, I hide it too well and I'm smiling all the way through that long, long tunnel, I'm reading the ads for novels and I'm thinking of my man and the hot chocolate ahead of us on such a cold night. I'm climbing those stairs, he's not at the top, it's strange for him, I thought he'd be waiting, all puppy panting for his victory kiss. I'm climbing those stairs and it's oddly quiet, the traffic's still and I'm coming up into the night and searching, where is he, and then in a far corner it's all stopped.

The milk's dropped.

It's all right, I remember him saying that, rubbing his head and shaking the concussion out. Let's just get home, I want to rest, you drive, love, and waving on the shaken driver, saying, It's fine, really, I'm OK. No, I think we should take him to the hospital, the woman's saying, there's her fevered biting of her nails and her toddler mewly in a car seat but No, Lil, no, there's Dan's insistence, come on, let's get back. Not even bothering with a licence plate or an address, just wanting his hot chocolate and his nuggling and his home. And I'm saying that maybe we *should* go to the hospital, just for a check-up perhaps and he's rolling his eyes, I couldn't bear it, an eight-hour wait on a plastic chair, you know what they're like here, let's just go.

So, home.

Laying him by the hearth and covering him up with a crochet blanket that doesn't quite reach to his toes and there's the nag of that still. It's a night so uncharacteristically cold that the chill nestles deep inside a granite boulder behind the house and it freezes the rock and it snaps it, the cleave's clean down the middle but the two halves of the rock do not part for centuries of soil clench them firm, I notice that, God knows why, as I slip out for some air and it'll never be gone, the detail of that. He refuses any doctor's help, they're two hours away, he's barely uttering a word except for my name and there's a tattoo of a lily on his ankle, it's only a year old and my fingers worry at its faded ink, they worry at it like an archaeologist with a snippet at a dig.

And he sleeps.

And then, and then.

I cannot write much of this bit, in a daze, never properly out. And you've gone oddly still, as if you're listening.

There are some knocks that kill instantly, and some slowly, so slowly that you hardly know. I was told later that I should've kept him awake, kept him conscious or else he'd slip into that coma and never come out, a *subdural haematoma* I kept on being told and don't tell me how much I hate those two words for that *subdural haematoma* was already vining its dirty work, it was enlarging and gulping and neither of us had any idea on that night for we were too far from anything in our wild place and *no doctor* he kept on saying and I was happy with that. How could I have kept him from a hospital, how could I have driven him away from the town, there are so many questions and I've taunted myself ragged with them all night after night after night. And there are so many people back in Sunshine who were quick, so quick, to have the story all figured out for they knew exactly what that Lillie Bird had done, or hadn't done, more to the point.

But there's this, my defence, an alternative history of their place. Our truth, Dan's and mine.

There I am, crouching by the man who loved me so much and I didn't know for so long and screaming to the sky and bending down and with a soft whimper of a kiss washing Dan's ears of the last sounds that they've heard and brushing his lips of the last words that they've spoken and with my thumb-tips stroking his lids to a close, erasing the last sights he's seen from his eyes and kissing the hollow of his ankle with eyelashes webbed by hot wet and in doing all that there's an intensity of love that I've never felt before and it's through me again now, it hurts so much.

There I am, rifling through his wardrobe again and again and gutting his clothes and plunging my face deeply into them and keeping him in my pillow and then haranguing my forgetfulness when my mother visits and washes him away.

Why didn't I tell her? I ask myself.

Why didn't I tell him? That the more we were together, the more I loved him. Why was I punishing him so much?

I'm telling him now.

And unravelling my grief in a place no one sees.

And letting the Shiners know. For he wants them to know. I'm sure of that.

I can feel him with us now, little one, can feel him with you, his hand hovering quiet on my belly. I'm wearing his red jumper, I'm breathing him though my pores.

Dan had said flippantly once that he wanted to be buried hard up against the press of the earth, close to the sun and the air, in the graveyard of weathered sticks and rusted tin-can lids. I'm an outsider here, mate, and that's the only place for me, once they know the story they'll never want me back and there was his chuckle at that. They have to know, Lil, but it has to come from you. And somewhere in that long, cold night of cleaved stone I imagined a headstone – an enduring one that the caustic rain would never wipe with a full name and two dates and a line from Yeats:

What made us dream that he could comb grey hair.

Of course he was buried by the Sunshine church.

Of course I wasn't asked.

I wasn't there.

The community closed around him.

And hardly any of them believe this.

Forever the prankster, with his matches and his cigarettes and his grubby little secret, the policeman's son with the obsessive love for the prickly girl, the master liar, who'd stepped forward in his place all those years ago. For some reason she wouldn't be scraped from him, not a therapist or a new city or a new woman could do that, she'd burrowed under his skin when he was ten years old and she would never be softened from it. She'd stepped forward for him once and then she'd done it again and he was never free of that.

There are letters, cruel, attacking ones, vicious with judgement and prejudice and hate. But his parents hold me close and I wasn't ever expecting that. There's such a tenderness, a bewilderment, a need, they want to know so much about a son they barely knew. They're the only ones I worry about, writing this, but deep in these nights is my certainty that their son wants them to know.

I knew his happiness at the end. Surely those who cherish him want to know of that?

So, my little one, I have scoured your father's secret life like a forensic scientist but there are so many blanks and I can only find more of him by writing this out. I write what I know, but I also write *to* know. Some men choose football or *Star Trek* or vintage malt whisky or MGs. But Dan Smith, for some reason, chose me.

There is just one photo of him. It's always close.

Newly arrived in the sun-splashed city and his face and his hands admonishing the camera's gaze and a blustery blue ocean behind him and already he's wearing the light in his cheeks. The memory of his lips is so vivid under my fingertips and each morning, in the dead hours, I take the photo and place it beside the laptop and I stare at the fingers that stroked a cat into a thrumming once and the skin hoarding the sun and the eroticism of the hips, and I turn him into words, for it's all I have left.

*

246

And as I bash this keyboard like I've got boxing gloves on there's a strange joy in me too, for what Dan's given me is a texture to this life and a serenity floating through my smile, oh yes, that. The bag is packed, I'm ready now. A different woman, under a different sky, and I will never be going back. I'm here now, laughing and in love and with no need of any of them. I have that, and I have you, and I'm not afraid of us alone.